# DIRTY SECRET

BIANCA COLE

# CONTENTS

Book cover design by Deliciously Dark Designs

Photography by Wander Aguiar

# BLURB

**He's my dirty secret, one I don't think I can hide much longer.**

Killian Callaghan has haunted my fantasies for years. Ever since we attended the Syndicate Academy. He's sinfully gorgeous, covered in tattoos, and totally off limits. There's too much bad blood between the Callaghan family and ours.

Five years after our last encounter, he comes blazing back into my life. Killian turns up at my twenty-first birthday party. The chemistry between us had always been palpable, but now it sets an inferno alight in my soul. He tells me he's done staying away. Screw the consequences.

He's our natural enemy, but I don't know that I can resist his advances. A man we're at war with. A man totally and utterly off limits. And yet that doesn't keep him away.

Killian doesn't take no for an answer. His tastes are dark, dominant, and addictive. He wants my innocence. He wants to corrupt me in ways I never imagined.

Meanwhile, my father has just agreed my hand in marriage to another man. Once Killian finds out, he'll tear the world down to keep me. I know that our passion is dangerous, especially while we're at war. The question is, will we survive once our dirty secret is revealed?

# AUTHOR'S NOTE

*H*ello reader,
   This is a warning to let you know that while this isn't my darkest book, that it is a **dark** mafia romance much like many of my other books, which means there are some sensitive subject matters addressed, but it's definitley one of the milder one. If you have any triggers, it would be a good idea to proceed with caution.

As well as a possessive and dominant anti-hero who doesn't take no for an answer, this book addresses some sensitive subjects. A full list of these can be found here. As always, this book has a HEA and there's no cheating.

If you have any triggers, then it's best to read the warnings and not proceed if any could be triggering for you. However, if none of these are an issue for you, read on and enjoy!

## MIA

*F*ive years ago…

My heart pounds unevenly in my chest as I walk into the ballroom of the academy for the last event of the year. Every year, the academy holds a ball for the Sophomores, Juniors, and Seniors.

All the younger students get a fancy meal in the dining hall instead. This is my first time at the ball since I'm a sophomore, but that's not why I'm nervous. It's because it's the last time I'll see Killian Callaghan. Maybe ever, since his family is the natural enemy of mine.

Our friendship during my time here at the academy was surprising and confusing. Killian is the most attractive boy at this school and yet somehow he always makes time for me, although our families are enemies and I'm three years younger than him.

"Mia," I hear Freya call my name as she rushes into the ballroom. "I thought we were going to meet in the corridor and come together." Her brow furrows as she approaches me, looking a little out of breath. "What the hell?"

I swallow hard, realizing I've been so wrapped up in my own thoughts I completely forgot. "Shit, I'm sorry." I shake my head. "I don't know what's gotten into me."

She waves her hand dismissively. "I think I know exactly what's gotten into you." She smirks. "Not seen Killian yet?"

I narrow my eyes. "Don't be an ass, Freya."

She hooks her arm with mine. "I'm not being an ass, but it's your last chance to tell him the truth."

"And what truth is that?" I ask.

"That you've been in love with him for years."

I roll my eyes. "I'm three years younger than him, Freya. He's eighteen, for fuck's sake."

"What's your point?" Her brow raises. "We go to a school for criminals. I don't think that any of that really matters."

Freya is my single closest friend, even though she's Irish and I'm Italian. We hit it off the first day of the academy and have been practically inseparable ever since, but it sucks that she lives on the other side of the country from me in Miami.

I sigh. "Even if you were right, our family is enemies with his, so he's totally and utterly off limits. No matter how hot he is."

Freya's face falls and I only then realize she was nudging me in the ribs. "Hey Killian," she says, her voice tight.

I turn around to face the man I've had feelings for ever since we met. "Hey," I say, hating how squeaky my voice sounds.

He smirks cockily at me. "And who is it that's so off limits, Mia?" Those crystal green eyes are so bright as they hold my gaze intimidatingly. It's as if he can see right through me and into my soul.

I shake my head. "No one," I reply, possibly too quickly.

His brow arches, but he just shakes his head. "Would you like to dance?"

My throat dries as I stare at his outstretched hand, knowing that my heart might give out at any moment. It's racing too damn fast, pounding against my rib cage like a drum.

Freya nudges me in the ribs as I stare at him, dumbstruck.

"Sure," I reply, taking his hand.

My lips purse the moment his skin touches mine. It feels like hot coals, and I know it's not because he's warm. It's because ever since I was old enough to notice, the chemistry between us has been electric, at least on my end.

One touch from Killian is all it takes to steal my breath away.

Killian smirks, a faint hint of amusement in his gaze

as he watches me. His hand goes to my waist, making me tense. "Relax, baby girl," he murmurs, the tone of his voice setting my body on fire. "It's only a dance."

Only a dance.

It's easy for him to say, as this means nothing to him. To me, it's everything.

Killian Callaghan has haunted my dreams and fantasies for as long as I can remember.

As the music plays and he leads me to it, I realize just how much it's going to hurt not seeing him again.

Those beautiful green eyes and a charismatic smile that could turn even a confident woman into an incoherent idiot.

"Why would you want to dance with a sophomore?" I ask suddenly, trying to break the tension in the air.

He tilts his head. "Because, sophomore or not, you are the single most beautiful girl here, Mia."

My mouth dries and I do not know how to respond to that. "I don't think that's true," I mumble.

"It is true. You should stop being so hard on yourself." His grip moves lower on my back, sending tingles right down my spine as he leans closer. "If you were eighteen, I would have had you in my bed by now," he mutters, only loud enough for me to hear.

My eyes flicker shut at the pulse of need racing between my thighs. I should tell him he's being a cocky son of a bitch for thinking I'd even want to be in his bed, but I'd be blatantly lying.

I pull away from him as the music stops, knowing

that if I don't keep some distance between us, I might do something I regret. "Thanks for the dance," I say awkwardly, freeing myself from his grasp.

He nods and watches me with those intense eyes as I walk away, searching for Freya as my cheeks flame so hot.

Freya stands by the buffet table, stuffing food into her mouth. "How was it?" she asks when she notices me approaching, wiggling her brow suggestively.

"Awkward as hell."

She laughs, shaking her head. "It can't have been that bad."

"It's so hard to be around him when I want him so badly," I admit, pulling my lip between my teeth. "Do you know what he said?"

Freya shakes her head, leaning in to hear.

"He said if I was eighteen, I'd have been in his bed by now."

Freya's brows shoot upwards in surprise. "That's cocky, and hot," she says, giggling a little. "Who would have thought that Mia Morrone could bag herself the hottest senior at the academy?"

"It was hypothetical, meaning he wouldn't touch me because of my age."

She sighs. "Morals, smorals. He should have you, regardless of your age."

"Don't be ridiculous." I take a sandwich and shove it in my mouth, turning to gaze across the dancefloor.

My stomach dips when I see Killian dancing with

7

Kimberly Veitch, the hottest girl in school. She's eighteen and totally his type.

They've been on again, off again for years.

I hate the bile rising in my throat as I watch them, knowing that jealousy is never a good look. And yet I can't help it. Anytime I see them together, it feels like my heart is being ripped out of my chest, literally.

"You are way hotter than her," Freya says, shaking her head.

"Now you really are being ridiculous. Has someone spiked the punch?"

"Most likely," she says, shrugging. "I feel a little tipsy."

I force my eyes away from the couple and grab a glass of punch, hoping it has been spiked. If I'm going to make it through tonight without going insane, I need a stiff drink.

Freya chuckles next to me as if reading my mind. "You are hoping it's spiked, aren't you?"

Freya knows me so well that sometimes it's scary. "Yes, I need alcohol."

"Hey, nerds," Alejandro says, approaching us. "What are you two sniggering about all the way over in the corner?"

Alejandro De León is our friend, even if he's an asshole half of the time. I turn to glare at him. "What we're talking about is none of your business."

He raises a brow, reaching to snatch my glass out of my hand.

I read the move well ahead of time and shift my arm so he can't reach. "Get your own."

He chuckles, shaking his head. "You shouldn't drink that shit. Cas spiked it with vodka."

"Good," I reply.

His brow furrows. "Are you saying you want to get drunk?"

Freya sighs heavily. "Killian troubles."

I notice the way a muscle ticks in Alejandro's jaw. He hates that I've had a crush on Killian for years, as he's been trying to get me to agree to date him. "When are you going to get over that guy?"

"I don't know what you two are going on about." I feign ignorance.

He rolls his eyes. "Everyone in the God damn academy knows you have a thing for him, Mia. You'd have to be an idiot not to."

"Are you saying I'm obvious?" I ask, downing the rest of my drink.

Freya and Alejandro nod in unison. "Yeah, you're like a little lost puppy when you follow him around," he says.

"Fuck you," I say, punching him in the arm.

"Ouch," he says, glaring at me. "There's no need for violence, Morrone."

Someone clears their throat behind us, and we all turn around to find Killian standing there. "Can I steal Mia away for a moment?"

I swallow hard, as this is the second time tonight he's approached me.

Alejandro folds his arms over his chest. "What for, exactly?"

"I need to speak with her." His green eyes never leave mine as he talks, barely paying any attention to my friend, who is staring daggers at him.

"Sure," I say, walking past Alejandro.

I'm pretty sure he mutters 'lost puppy' as I walk past, but I ignore it.

Killian surprises me by leading me out of the ballroom.

"Where are we going?"

He glances over his shoulder at me, those green eyes alight with mischief. "Somewhere a little quieter."

My heart is racing so fast I'm pretty sure I'm going to go into cardiac arrest at any moment.

*Why the fuck would Killian need to speak to me somewhere quiet?*

He stops in front of a door and opens it, nodding toward the room. "Inside, baby girl."

My stomach tightens the moment he calls me that, and I walk into the library, wondering why he'd want to talk in here. The door slams closed, drawing my attention back to the man I've secretly, or perhaps not so secretly, if my friends are right, pinned over for years. "What did you want to talk about?"

"I can't believe it's my last night here," he murmurs, those piercing eyes fixed on me. "Can you?"

I shake my head, as I honestly can't believe I still have three years here without him. "No, it's going to be weird."

A smirk twists onto his lips as he moves closer to me. "Will you miss me, Mia?"

It feels like he's mocking me, and suddenly my friend's words echo in my mind.

*You're like a little lost puppy when you follow him around.*

I shake my head. "I'm sure I'll survive," I say, but it doesn't even sound convincing to my own ears.

His eyes flash, as if that wasn't the response he expected. "Well, I'm going to miss you." He edges ever closer to me, bridging the gap between us.

All I can do is watch and wait, wondering what he's going to do. My heart thuds more aggressively in my chest the closer he gets.

"We've been good friends, haven't we?"

"Yes, it will be strange when you're not here."

He tilts his head. "Strange?"

I nod in response. "Yeah. What did you want to talk about?" I ask, hating the way the tension swirls around the room, starving me of oxygen.

He's so close to me now I can smell the musky scent of his cologne and can see the flecks of hazel in his beautiful green eyes. "Did I say talk?" he murmurs, shaking his head. "I meant something quite different." His hands grab my hips rather forcefully, sending a shock wave right through my being. "Relax, baby girl," he breathes, pulling me toward him hard.

I can hardly gather my thoughts before his lips descend on mine. My heart flutters in my chest as I place my hands on his chest to brace myself, struggling to stop my knees from wobbling as his tongue swipes against my lips. They break apart for him like the waves breaking against the shore and I moan, instantly feeling embarrassed as I try to pull away.

Killian holds me tightly, not allowing me to move away. His grip on my hips tightens painfully as his tongue swipes incessantly around my mouth, as if he's trying to consume me from the inside out.

My inhibitions lower as I wrap my hands around the back of his neck, drawing him closer. And that's when I feel the hard press of his arousal between us, making my entire body burst into flame. I shudder, struggling to believe that after all this time of wishing he'd kiss me, he is. A soft, manly groan escapes his lips as he deepens the kiss, stoking the flames of desire deep within as I ache for him. I've never been kissed before, and this is no doubt the most perfect first kiss ever.

My fingers tangle in his hair as his hand dips lower, cupping my ass. I've never felt so desperate before in all my life. When he breaks the kiss, I'm panting and my heart is fluttering in my chest. And then I see his expression. It's predatory and hungry, and it scares me to my very core.

"Killian?" I murmur his name, taking a step back.

"I've wanted to do that for so damn long, Mia."

I shake my head. "You've got a girlfriend," I say,

realizing only then that he's kissing me only moments after dancing with Kimberley.

"No, I don't. We broke up."

I narrow my eyes, searching his for any sense that he's lying. "Why are you kissing me the last night of school?" I ask, hating the way my voice shakes. He could never understand how much I have longed for that kiss and yet it's too late. As of tomorrow, we'll never see each other again. My stomach churns as I stare at him, wondering why he would do this now, as it will only make it harder when he's not here.

He moves closer again, and I can feel a pain squeezing around my chest. "Because it's my last chance, Mia."

*Last chance.*

"Our family are enemies. And what exactly are you expecting of me?"

The twist of his lips turns almost cruel as he continues to move toward me, backing me into a bookshelf. "Everything." He tries to kiss me again, but I duck under his arm, knowing this will only lead to heartache.

"What's wrong?" he asks, looking at me like I'm mad.

"You kiss me on your last night at the academy and expect me to just give you everything?" I set my hands on my hips, shaking my head. "Do you really think I'm that easy?"

Killian's expression falters as those beautiful eyes remain entirely unreadable. "No, I just—"

"Save it," I snap, holding my hand up. "You just thought I had no self-respect. Well, I do. I may be younger than you, Killian, but I'm no idiot." And with that, I bolt out of the library like a coward. I don't want to hear his retort, because I fear if I stay in his presence much longer, I'll start crying like a fool.

He wanted me to give him *everything*, what exactly he meant by that I'm uncertain. If he wanted me, he should have done it before his last day at the academy, not as an afterthought, because it was his last chance. As of tomorrow, I'll never see Killian Callaghan again.

The thought is enough to rip my heart to pieces, let alone having the memory of his lips on mine. He's always been off limits, and that made my fantasy less attainable. Now he's given me a taste of what I'm missing and it makes it hurt more.

I slam into Freya, whose brow furrows. "Woah, slow down. What are you running from?" I take one look at my best friend and then burst into tears.

Freya's expression turns serious. "Hey, what's wrong? Shall we head back to the dorms?"

I nod in response as she places an arm around my back and steers me down the corridor toward the girl's dormitories. My heart feels broken, which is silly, but I can't help but feel used.

Perhaps some space away from the man who has

held my heart for years will do me some good. The Syndicate Academy may not be the same without him, but perhaps it will be easier.

## 2

## KILLIAN

*P*resent day...

Rourke paces up and down our father's study, or I guess I should call it his study now. It's hard to get used to the fact that Father is gone, and he's not coming back.

My brother has well and truly cemented himself as the leader of the clan, and to be honest, I don't give a shit anymore. He's dealing with a war that I wouldn't have the first clue how to navigate. He may only be four years older than me, but it's enough to give him the upper hand.

I'll support my brother one-hundred percent, but our scrap for the top spot is over. To be honest, I'm not sure it ever really began. Besides, I prefer being in the shadows and always have.

"I don't like it, but I'm going to reach out to the Italians to discuss what Torin learned about Adrik and the cartel." There are dark patches around his eyes and I can tell from just one look he's not sleeping well.

"Why not go straight to the Russians?" I suggest, since we have serious bad blood with the Italians, that goes back further than our disagreements with the Russians. The Russians killing of our father was the catalyst for the war, but deep down I'm not too sure that it was Spartak who was behind it. He's not the kind of man to deny something he was responsible for, which may mean we went to war for nothing.

"Because Spartak is a crazy son of a bitch, and I can't be sure he'd believe me." Rourke crosses his arms over his chest. "I know you hate the Italians, Killian. We all do, but this is about survival."

I hate the Italians except for one beautiful young woman. Mia Morrone has been the bane of my existence for so many years, as she's always been off limits. It meant my secret obsession with her has had to remain simply that. An obsession that I can't act on. The Irish and Italians are natural enemies and always have been. And then her father's men murdered my mother, even though they insist it was an accident, but I know the truth.

Rourke believes I don't know about his threat to Remy before our mother's murder, but he's wrong. It seemed an odd coincidence that they hit her a few hours after he issued it. Remy insists they hadn't intended to kill her, only send a message, which went horribly wrong. A part of the blame lies with my brother trying to take matters into his own hands. A guilt I'm certain he carries to this day.

Tonight, the Italians are throwing a party for Mia Morrone's twenty-first birthday. A woman who I've desperately tried to keep away from for five years, watching her from afar. She's never noticed my presence as I stalk her through the city. Some would say it borders on unhealthy, the obsession I have with a girl who can never be mine. And yet, there's a part of me that still hasn't accepted that reality. When I heard the rumors that Remy was trying to find her a husband, something inside of me snapped.

Mia Morrone has been mine since the academy, and I'll be damned if that son of a bitch marries her off to anyone. I have every intention of sneaking in and surprising her, even though we've not spoken to each other since my last night at The Syndicate Academy.

One thing that stood in my way with Mia was her age. She's only three years younger than me, which was an issue when I was eighteen and she was fifteen, even if I bent the rules and stole a kiss on my last night. Now, though, we're grown adults and I have a feeling breaking the rules might just be a hell of a lot of fun.

"I've got somewhere to be, if that's all?"

Rourke's jaw clenches. "Sure, I need you with me at the meeting, though."

"Just tell me when and where." I clap him on the shoulder.

"Thanks," he says, but his voice is strained. "I'm not sure it will be that easy to convince them to meet."

I can't deny that it's been difficult watching my brother change from the carefree man he had been to our father over night. He's short-tempered and difficult to be around unless he's with Viki. When Viki is around, he's a different man entirely. I'm thankful he found her, even if I wasn't too keen on him bringing a Russian into the family after what happened.

I walk out of the study and down the corridor, stopping in front of a mirror to check my appearance. The suit I'm wearing is tailored to perfection and my hair is in its usual messy style, which I like. The question is, will Mia like it?

My jaw clenches as I stare at myself, realizing I'm nervous about seeing Mia Morrone for the first time in five years. Although, it's not the first time I've seen her, but it's the first time she will have seen me. The last time we were together, I kissed her like my life depended on it and she ran away.

It was humiliating, but I wonder if my baby girl has changed much.

Hopefully, this time when I kiss her, she won't be able to escape. I'll corner her and force her to accept the reality. She's belonged to me since the day we met. Fuck the consequences, as there's no way I'm letting her marry another man.

*Let the games begin.*

\* \* \*

The guard at the front door eyes me warily as I hand over my invitation. An invitation I scored from a politician who needed a favor and couldn't attend. His eyes scan it and then he glances back up at me before moving to the side.

That was easier than I expected, but I don't think the guys they have on the door are a part of the mob. If anyone had recognized me, then I wouldn't have been let it. Although I had a backup plan to sneak through the back window of the mansion. Nothing is keeping me away from Mia Morrone tonight, not even this fucking war waging between our families.

I walk into the hallway and follow a couple through to the party. This place is far more pompous than I expected. Everything about the decor is extravagant, from the enormous crystal chandeliers to the expensive Amalfi marble running through the entire fucking place. It doesn't suit my image of Mia, who, despite having a ridiculous obsession with clothes shopping, isn't totally materialistic.

I guess I should have expected nothing less from bastards that profit from trafficking people. They're the lowest of the low in my book, excluding the woman I'm here to see. Whenever she used to talk of what her family did at the academy, it was clear she hated it.

Once I'm in the main ballroom, I turn to the right and keep myself against the wall, blending into the shadows. The last thing I want is to be spotted and then turfed out before I even get to approach her. I scan the room, searching for any sign of the woman who haunted my dreams for years.

She believes the last time I saw her was five years ago, but an obsession like I've always had with Mia doesn't go away that easily. I've watched her from afar, knowing how utterly off-limits she really is. A Morrone and a Callaghan can't work and yet it has to. I won't continue to watch her from afar while she walks down the aisle and pledges herself to another man.

My heart stills in my chest as I glimpse her beautiful, angelic face on the dancefloor. And my fists clench when I see who she's dancing with. Alejandro De León. The guy was her friend at the academy, but all he's ever wanted was to get into her pants. I feel rage coil through me like a living, breathing thing infecting my veins. "Motherfucker," I breathe.

His hand slips too low on her back, practically on her ass as he pulls her closer to him. I dig my nails into the skin of my palm, breaking the skin, as it's the only way to stop myself from marching right into the middle of the dancefloor and knocking him out for touching what is mine. I have to keep cool, somehow. Otherwise, I'll end up out on my ass before I can even say one word to her. This is the first time I've seen Alejandro with her in years.

I narrow my eyes, wondering if perhaps the man her father is intending to match her with is Alejandro. It would be a powerful partnership for the Morrone family, and Alejandro certainly wouldn't oppose it. My throat burns with acrid hate as I wonder what Mia would think.

*Would she be happy to marry Alejandro?*

The mere thought drives me insane and I wouldn't be certain that I'd be able to stop myself from killing him if he so much as kissed her in front of me. They stop dancing, thankfully, and move toward the edge of the room quite a distance from me.

I watch as they chat and then I notice Alejandro head toward the bar, which is packed. He'll be awhile and I know it's my chance to strike. She's alone and keeps glancing nervously around the ballroom, as if she can sense me watching her. Anytime I've followed her to the mall, she does it and it's adorable, especially since she never notices me. I can't deny that my obsession with Mia Morrone has turned into something toxic. I guess that's what happens, trying to stay away from a woman who so clearly belongs to me.

I'm careful to remain at the edge, drawing little attention to myself as I approach her. My pants tighten when I get closer, seeing how fucking gorgeous her curves look in the tight pale blue dress she's wearing. The curves of her ass make me want to grab her and throw her over my knee just so I can torment her, spanking her and teasing her until she can't take it any longer and is begging me to fuck her.

I shake my head, clearing the sex-crazed stupor from my mind as I stop a mere yard from her. My heart is hammering hard and fast against my rib cage. There's no stopping me now, not when I'm this close to her. I breathe in a deep breath, inhaling her sweet berry scent I know so fucking well. And then I take a last step toward her and grab her hips, groaning softly at the feel of her beneath my palms.

Her gasp tightens my pants across my already straining crotch as I lean toward her ear and murmur, "Relax, baby girl."

She turns rigid before me and I wonder what her reaction will be. It's been five years since she's seen me, even if I've watched her from afar. I can't wait to kiss her again, claim her, and make her mine for good this time. Now that I've got my hands on her, I won't let her run away again.

## 3

## MIA

*T*sit on the edge of my bed, staring at myself in the mirror opposite.

Twenty-one years old and no one to celebrate with, at least, not really. Imalia has abandoned us and Camila is at the academy, so it just leaves my brothers. As much as I love them, it's not the same as hanging out with my cousin or sister.

My father always has ulterior motives for throwing parties, which means he will expect me to have fun despite the guests being a bunch of strangers. Freya really wanted to be here for the party, but her father wouldn't allow her to travel to Chicago while there's a mafia war raging behind the scenes. It's been ages since I last saw her. The music from the party, which started half an hour ago, drifts up the stairs toward my room.

Warning me that if I don't get a move on, I'll be very late for my party. Not that anyone would notice.

A knock echoes against my door, forcing me to push off the bed and walk over to open it. My eyes widen when I see Alejandro on the other side. "What are you doing here?"

He smiles. "That's not the warm welcome I was expecting."

I shrug. "I'm just shocked, is all." Alejandro and I have remained friends ever since the academy, even if we don't see each other very often. He doesn't live as far as Freya, but he's still a good day's drive in Philadelphia.

"I'm here to make sure you have an amazing time and don't mope in your bedroom while the party is in full swing." His eyes narrow. "Why are you moping up here?"

I raise a brow. "Did Freya send you?"

He sighs. "No, but she told me her father wouldn't allow her to make the trip."

I nod in response. "Yeah, her dad's too uptight about the war. I'm surprised yours let you come."

He smirks.

"He doesn't know, does he?"

Alejandro shakes his head. "I'm a grown man, Mia. I don't need my father's permission to travel."

"Lucky son of a bitch," I mutter.

He laughs. "Women have the short end of the stick with liberty in our world, don't they?"

"Yeah, I guess so." An awkward silence pulses

between us as he looks at me the same way he always does. Alejandro still won't drop the fact that he thinks we'd make a perfect couple. He's broached the subject a few times, but I can't see him as anything other than a friend.

My father would probably agree with Alejandro. After all, he comes from a powerful Mexican family from Philly who would be prove the perfect ally.

I clear my throat. "Shall we head down to the party and get drunk?"

He smiles at that. "Sounds like a plan."

I lead him out of my room and shut the door, locking it as I go. It's a habit that I learned from having three irritating brothers growing up. Always lock your door if you don't want anyone to mess with your shit.

"How have you been?" I ask, as we walk toward the ballroom, which is no doubt packed with people.

As we descend the stairs, he sighs. "Same old, really. Philly is as fucking boring as always." He shoots me an odd look. "I couldn't wait to leave."

I raise a brow. "And walk right into a war zone?"

He chuckles. "A war zone beats boring."

I shake my head. "I have to disagree. A war zone *is* boring. I'm barely allowed to leave the house." We walk through the entrance hall and through the kitchen toward the ballroom. "Father has even restricted how often I can go shopping."

"Good," Alejandro says, an irritating smirk on his

lips. "It's about time someone put a limit on your insatiable desire to buy more stuff."

I narrow my eyes. "Are you here to help me celebrate or just irritate me?"

"Both," he replies as we walk into the ballroom, finding it already packed.

The dancefloor is full of people dancing and Alejandro's eyes light up. He's always loved dancing more than most guys I know.

"A salsa?" he asks, offering me his hand. "It is your birthday."

I laugh. "Alright, but only one."

His expression dips at the suggesting. "You have to dance at least twice on your birthday. It's the rules."

"And who exactly made these rules?"

He grabs my hand and drags me onto the dancefloor without an answer, his hands moving to my hips as he pulls me close. "No one made the rules. They're just universally acknowledged," he murmurs. And then he sweeps me into a fast dance, never once missing a step.

I can't help but laugh, feeling a lightness flood my chest. The past few months, I've felt caged in and unhappy, hoping that this war would end soon. Trust Alejandro to appear and make this night bearable for me. Freya may not have been able to make it, but at least I'm not entirely alone.

He spins me around, his hands dropping a little low on my back as we sway to the music. I'm not stupid. I know that even after all these years, Alejandro still holds out hope. Hope that I'll see him the way he sees me. Hope that somehow I'll come to my senses and want him like that, but I know deep down it will never happen.

I love him, but it's in the way I love my brothers. I've felt what it's like when I'm touched by a man I want or kissed by a man I want. Alejandro doesn't entice any of those feelings.

Killian Callaghan possibly broke me for all the other men on this planet, as I've yet to find anyone who affects me the way he did on his last night at the academy.

As the music ends and I try to catch my breath, I yank him off the dancefloor. "I need a drink. Can you get me one?"

He raises a brow. "Have I come all this way only to serve you?"

I pout. "It is my birthday."

He smiles. "What do you want?"

"Surprise me."

He nods. "Wait right here and don't move. I'll be back shortly."

I nod in response and lean against the table nearby, trying to catch my breath. I'll give Alejandro one thing. He sure as hell can dance.

A prickle of awareness skates lightly down my spine as I get the sense someone is watching me. I glance around the room, searching for the culprit, but find no eyes are on me. Clearly, all the talk of war and my father's incessant need to protect me has left me paranoid.

I let out a heavy sigh and glance toward the bar, where Alejandro is waiting in a ridiculously long queue. My birthday and I can't even get a drink quickly. I glance around the room again, searching for any sign of my father or brothers, but see neither. None of them have wished me a happy birthday yet, but to be honest, it's unsurprising considering how wrapped up in the war they've been. Father has seemed particularly pressured lately, as I fear the war is weighing a heavier burden on him than any of us realize.

A pair of hands land on my hips, making me gasp as I try to turn around. "Relax, baby girl."

The blood drains from my body as I freeze to the spot, wondering if I've finally lost the plot at the sound of *that* voice. A voice that has haunted my dreams and fantasies for years. I draw in a deep breath, inhaling that intoxicating scent of him that somehow smells even more masculine than I remember.

"Killian?" I murmur his name.

I feel his breath against the back of my neck, and he moves his lips so close they brush against my skin. "Have you missed me?"

I've missed him every fucking day of the five years since I ran away from him in the library, too scared to give him anything more. At fifteen years old, I wasn't ready, not to mention he was eighteen and about to leave for good.

My heart hammers erratically against my rib cage as I try to gain control over my emotions. I draw in a deep breath and then break away from his grasp, spinning around to set eyes on the man who has haunted my dreams for five years.

I feel my mouth unhinge, as he's even more beautiful than I remember. His body is bulkier and more muscular, but hidden well under a tailored gray suit that frames his muscles like a second skin. Beneath the jacket, he's wearing a white shirt buttoned only three-quarters of the way up, revealing ink scrolling across his chest. At the academy, he had some tattoos, but not as many as he has now.

If I thought the man I knew at the academy was the most beautiful man I've ever seen, Killian, all grown up, is utterly breathtaking. Since I last saw him, the tension between our families has only heightened. My father killed his Mom barely three years ago now and I hardly know what to say to him. I hate what our families do to each other and I hate the world my father and brothers operate in, believing it's fine to exploit people for their own gain.

"Surprised to see me?" he asks, snapping me out of the stupor I'd fallen into.

I shake my head. "Yes, why the fuck are you here?" I place my hands on my hips. "If my brothers found out, they'd—"

He moves forward and grabs me again, his touch sending a shot of liquid fire right through my veins. "What would they do, baby girl?" He slips his hand into mine and yanks me away from the party, through a door into the small study just off the ballroom and shutting the door quickly. "I had to see you, Mia."

My brow arches. "You suddenly had to see me after five years?" I ask.

His eyes narrow, and he yanks me toward him. "Yes, because no matter how hard I try, I can't get you out of my mind." His grasp is so tight it's almost painful. "And this time, I have no intention of letting you run away."

I stare at him in shock, wondering if I'm just having a very realistic dream right now. "Why now?" I murmur.

A muscle in his jaw contracts. "Because you are twenty-one years old, and if I wait much longer, someone else will take you." His nostrils flare. "And you belong to me, Mia."

My eyes widen at the half-growl of his voice as his fingers tighten on my hips. "I'm done messing about. It's time for me to take what I want."

My breath hitches as his lips get even closer to mine and it feels like I'm right back in that library at the academy, cornered by him. "And what do you want?"

"You," he breathes, before his lips descend on mine.

As if I'm that fifteen-year-old girl again in the academy's library, I let him kiss me. My fingers wrapping around the back of his neck and into the soft curls of golden hair, pulling him closer. My lips part and his tongue delves inside of my mouth, stoking a hot and heavy need pulsing between my thighs.

For this blissful moment, the fact that this man belongs to a crime family who is at war with my own doesn't register. It's just me and Killian. The rest of the world and all the bullshit that comes with it melts away as I drown in him. Killian's lips move away from mine and he kisses my neck, making me moan. I clamp my eyes shut, struggling to believe that he's here, and he's touching me.

"Killian," I breathe his name.

"Yes, baby girl?" he asks, before continuing to kiss me as his lips skate over my collarbone.

"We shouldn't be doing this."

I feel his lips curve against my skin into a smile. "Do you think I care?"

"Why now?" I ask again, suspicious why after five years he picks my twenty-first birthday party to come blazing back into my life like a chariot of fire. All that emotion and desire tugging at my insides, driving me insane. If he's here just to torment me and then leave, I won't survive it.

"I told you I can't keep away." He moves his lips from my skin and those piercing green eyes find mine. "I should have claimed you years ago."

"Claimed me?" I ask, raising a brow. "What do you think I am? Lottery winnings?"

He chuckles at that. "No, you are far more precious."

I hate the way my insides flutter at his words. It's as if I'm that teenage girl again, hanging on his every word.

"Go on a date with me."

I stare at him for a few moments, wondering if I heard him right. "A date?"

"Yes, I want to do this right."

My brow furrows. "Are you insane?" I ask, shaking my head. "Our families are at war with each other. Not to mention…" I swallow hard, pain clawing at my throat.

"Not to mention what?" he presses, eyes narrowing.

"The famiglia killed your mother."

A flash of hurt enters his eyes, but it's gone quickly. "Yes, but I don't hold it against you, Mia." His jaw clenches as he shrugs. "My grandfather shot your mother when you were only young. There's blood on both sides, but I don't care about any of that."

I raise a brow. "Other people will. My family and yours."

"Screw them," he growls, moving forward. His hands grab my hips firmly. "I want you, Mia. And I'm not taking no for an answer."

My jaw clenches and I glare into his eyes, knowing that despite how badly I want him, I won't let him push me around. We can't be together, no matter what he says. Our family is at war with each other and we've been enemies for years. "No," I say.

His eyes blaze with such rage it sends a tremor right through my core as his nostrils flare. I fear I'm going to see a side of Killian Callaghan that I don't like tonight. Happy fucking birthday to me.

## 4

## KILLIAN

"*N*o?" I repeat, searching her stunning chestnut brown eyes.

"That's what I said." She takes a step back, knocking into the wall behind.

An inferno of possessive rage bubbles beneath the surface of my skin, like an active volcano preparing to erupt. "You belong to me, Mia, and have done since the day we fucking met," I growl, struggling to contain that rage.

Her face pales as she tries to sidestep away from me, but I block her with my body. "Killian, I—"

"Don't speak," I say, my voice low but dangerous even to my own ears. Mia Morrone is rejecting me. I won't stand by it as I know she wants me. Her eyes are full of desire even now as she fears my rage. She wants me. No girl kisses like that and doesn't want the man she's kissing.

Our situation may be complicated and our families may be at war, but I don't give a shit. "I don't care if our families are mortal fucking enemies, baby girl. You are mine." I press my fingertips harder into her hips, pulling her against me. "You drive me so fucking insane I can't think of anyone else." I let my lips tease her ear. "Anytime I even kiss another woman since the last night at the academy, I can't help but think of you."

She stiffens against me. "Lovely," she says, her voice irritated.

I pull back and search her eyes. "What's wrong?"

"Nothing, I just don't like you telling me about you being with other women."

I smirk. "Why? Are you jealous, Mia?"

Her nostrils flare, and I see a flash of irritation in her eyes. "No."

"Do you think of me when you kiss other men?" he asks, his lips teasing down my neck. "Or when you fuck them?"

Her jaw clenches. "I'm a virgin, Killian."

*Virgin.*

My pants get tighter across my crotch, and I find it almost impossible to believe that Mia Morrone went through the last years of the academy not getting fucked. "Good," I murmur, my voice sounding strained with desire. "Because I'm going to be your first and last." I nip her earlobe and she gasps, the sound making me even harder.

She writhes against me, gasping for air as I kiss her

neck and along her shoulder. "Killian."

I can't work out if she's saying my name just because or if she wants me to stop, but there's no reasoning with me. I've waited and watched her for too fucking long. Now that she's this close, I'm lost in my desire and obsession with her.

She pushes at my chest, trying to break away. "We can't do this."

"We can and we will," I murmur, looking into her fiery eyes. "What's stopping us?"

Her mouth falls open. "The war, for one thing."

"It doesn't concern us personally. So my brother and your father are coming to blows. Screw em."

Her lip wobbles slightly as she searches my eyes. "You are insane."

I smirk. "I'm fed up with staying away. Now tell me you will at least agree to a date."

Her eyes narrow. "And what happens when someone spots me meeting you and accuses one of us of betrayal?"

I shrug. "There's no fun in life without a little danger. I'll protect you, no matter what."

Her throat bobs as she swallows. "Killian, this is crazy. Where are we going to go on a date?"

"Give me your cell phone," I demand.

She looks at me warily for a few beats before nodding and pulling it out of the cup of her bra, drawing my eyes to her beautiful breasts.

I tighten my grasp on her hips. "You should have

told me where it was and I would have gladly retrieved it myself."

Her eyes flash with desire as I take the cell phone out of her hand.

I key my number in to her contacts and add it under the name Kill. And then I tap on it and ring myself, so I have her number too. "Now we have each other's numbers. I'll send you the details of our date."

"I haven't agreed yet," she points out.

I chuckle. "Believe me, baby girl, you will."

"I don't remember you being this cocky at the academy." She pulls away from me and takes a step backward, placing some distance between us.

"I think your memory must be hazy then, lass."

She raises a brow. "What makes you so confident that I even want to go on a date with you?"

Mia is different. She's less of a puppy dog and more of a wolf now. Her dark eyes hold suspicion and she will not fall into my arms as easily as I'd hoped.

"The way you kissed me. No one kisses like that unless they want the man they're kissing."

Her cheeks flush a deep red as she shakes her head. "I don't know what you're—"

I close the gap between us again and place my hand gently around her throat, enjoying the way my tattooed hand looks around her neck. "Don't lie to me, Mia. You've wanted me since we were kids, and now." I shake my head. "Now, you want me even fucking more."

A muscle in her jaw flexes as she blows out an irritated breath. "I need to get back to the party."

"Back to Alejandro?" I ask, tightening my grasp around her neck. "What is going on between you two?"

Her brow furrows. "Alejandro is my friend and has been since the academy."

"He had his hands all over you while you danced. I think he wants more than friendship, Mia."

"You were watching us?" she asks, her eyes widening.

"I'm always watching, baby girl."

She shudders, shaking her head. "That's creepy, Killian."

"I don't give a shit what you think it is," I growl.

Her eyes flash with fear, but I can't control my possessive rage with Mia Morrone.

"You belong to me, not Alejandro or any other man. Do you understand?"

Mia tries to pull away from me. "I don't know who you think you are, but no."

"Mia," I say her name in warning and she stops struggling, meeting my gaze. "Stop fighting the inevitable."

"And what exactly is that, Killian?" she asks, glaring at me with such a fiery look in her eyes it makes my cock harder than stone.

"Me and you were always meant to be."

Her lips part slightly as she considers my declaration. "It's a fantasy and nothing more."

She tries to twist away from me, but I don't let her. Instead, I kiss her again. Somehow, I have to get through to her that this can be real. The alternative isn't even an option. I will not watch her walk down the aisle and marry another man.

I don't know how we're going to navigate the insane dynamic of our feuding families, but I don't care anymore. All my life, they have taught me that the single most important thing is my allegiance to my family, but Mia is more important to me than anything. It goes against the grain and it will piss off my siblings and uncles, but none of that matters. Not when she's standing so close to me, her intoxicating scent driving me wild with the need to claim her.

Mia moans into my mouth as I draw her closer, pressing her body to mine so she can feel the strength of my arousal. I'm hard for her and so fucking ready to claim the Italian princess that has haunted my dreams for years.

Her hands tighten on the back of my neck as she tries to draw me closer, as if she never wants this to end. I never want this to end, because once it does, she'll go back to telling me how we can't do this. Mia has always been stubborn.

I lift her off the ground, making her gasp in surprise. Her back hits the wall as she wraps her legs instinctively around my waist. Despite fearing her speaking the moment I remove my lips from hers, I can't help myself as I kiss her neck and collarbone, grazing my teeth over her perfect, tanned skin.

"Killian," she moans my name, her voice breathless.

I ignore her and continue to move lower, my heart hammering hard against my rib cage as I kiss her exposed cleavage, forcing a shocked gasp from her lips.

"What are you doing?" She tenses as I slip my finger into the cup of her bra and pull it down, groaning at the sight of her nipple so hard and her perfect breast bare to me.

"No questions, baby girl," I answer, before sucking it into my mouth.

Mia's back arches as she claws her fingers through my hair. "We shouldn't," she breathes, her voice so full of desire it drives me crazy.

I bite into her collarbone, which makes her yelp in surprise. "What the hell was—"

I silence her with my lips, kissing her again with all the pent up frustration of five fucking years. When we break apart, I murmur, "Agree to go on a date with me, Mia."

It's as if those words break the spell I'd cast over her with the kiss, as she shakes her head and pushes me so hard I have no choice but to let her down. "I already told you no, Killian." Once she's on her feet, she manages to move around me and put a few paces between us. "Don't you know the meaning of the word?"

"Not exactly." I tilt my head slightly. "Your mouth may say no, but your body sure as hell wasn't a moment ago." My eyes dip down to her exposed breast, in turn, drawing her attention to it.

"Oh my God." She pulls her dress and bra up to cover herself and shakes her head. "You are crazy. Certifiably insane to think that you can come in here and crash a Morrone party and force me to agree to a date with you."

I raise a brow. "Force you?"

"Yes, I said no, and no means no." She backs up a few steps, and she looks like a deer ready to bolt. I've seen that look in her eyes before. "You should stay away from me for both our sakes and our families."

I shake my head, as she can't comprehend that I've tried staying away and I'm done with it.

"Okay?" Mia asks, searching my eyes.

There's no world in which I'll agree to staying away from her. I wish I knew what was going on it that pretty head of hers. I see the warning signs before it happens. Her bravado is slipping as she's losing her strength, so she turns around and bolts for the door without a word and disappears through it, leaving me standing in the little study alone, just like my last night at the academy.

I smile at the spot where she stood, shaking my head. I've got my work cut out if I'm going to break down my baby girl's walls. And I'm more than willing to work for it, as Mia is worth it.

# 5

## MIA

It feels like déjà vu as I flee across the dancefloor, running away from the man who has haunted my fantasies for years. Only this time I know Freya won't be here to save me from my cowardice.

Killian has lost the plot. How could he believe we can ever truly date like normal people or be together for that matter?

Our families are mortal enemies and have been for as long as I can remember.

His grandfather killed my mom, for fuck's sake, before I even got to know her. Pain claws at my throat as I realize by association Killian has a responsibility for me or Camilla never knowing our mother.

It makes his belief that he can just march in here and demand that I date him even more absurd.

I'm so flustered that I slam straight into someone. "Shit, sorry," I say, smoothing the front of my dress down. "I didn't see you there." And that's when I glance up to see I just ran straight into my eldest brother, Massimo.

His brow furrows as he eyes me warily. "Hey, little sis. Are you enjoying the party?" he asks, searching my face.

I feel heat pulsing through my entire body, warning me I'm probably blushing. "Yeah, it's great. Thanks." I instinctively glance over my shoulder, wondering if Killian is following me or not.

"Is everything alright, Mia?" Massimo asks.

I return my gaze back to him and nod. "Yeah, everything is fine. I need to go to the bathroom." I clock the makeshift signs at the other end of the room and dodge around him, rushing through the crowd. My heart is pounding so hard it makes me feel sick.

Alejandro appears in front of me just before I make it to the ladies' room. "There you are! I've been looking for you everywhere." His brow furrows. "Where were you?"

I know I can't tell him about Killian, as he'd probably hunt him down before he escaped this party. "Sorry, I got sidetracked chatting to an old friend."

His brow creases. "Oh, what friend?"

I wave my hand dismissively. "No one important."

"I got your drink," he says, holding two glasses of champagne up. "Shall we?"

"In one moment, I just need to use the bathroom." I flash him a smile, but it feels forced. "See you in a minute." I dodge around him and head down the corridor toward the bathroom. My heart is in my mouth as I head past the bathroom and then through a door at the back into the kitchen, needing to be alone. No one is allowed back here, not during an event like this.

I slump onto the stool at the kitchen island and hold my head in my hands.

"Something wrong, Mia?" Luca asks, making my entire body tense at the sound of his voice.

*So much for being alone.*

I shake my head and turn to face him. "No, I just hate these parties."

His right brow moves upward as if he doesn't believe me. "You should be happy. I hear Alejandro came to visit." There's a strange look in his eye.

"How did you know he was visiting?"

His lips purse together in a way that tells me that he's not supposed to mention something, but it's killing him to keep quiet. Out of all of my siblings, Luca is the easiest to read and the biggest gossip. "I really shouldn't say."

"But it's my birthday, Luca." I stand and walk toward him, grabbing hold of his arm. "You know you want to."

He sighs heavily, the way he always does when I know he's going to crack. "Fine, but——" He holds a finger up almost comically. "You didn't hear it from me."

I mime zipping up my mouth, locking it and throwing away the key.

He chuckles. "Father is considering him as your fiancé. I overheard him speaking on the phone to Alejandro's father, convincing him to send his son to the party tonight."

It feels like all the air from my lungs escapes as I stare at Luca, dumbfounded because Father is actually considering forcing me into an arranged marriage with Alejandro. He's far better than a lot of men I could be shackled to, but I don't want an arranged marriage. My stomach sinks as I know exactly what I want. The one person who I can't have, no matter what delusions he may hold.

*Killian Callaghan.*

"Are you serious?"

He gives me a sad smile. "Yeah, I mean, it's not the worst possible match when you think of it. I can think of worse things than being married to a friend, can't you?"

"Yes, but…" I shake my head. "I always thought I had longer. It's alright for you." I nod my head toward him. "Guys don't have to be forced into marriage."

"That's what you think, Mia." He gives me a pointed look. "We may get a choice, but have you seen the ridiculous list Father gave Massimo a few weeks ago?"

"What list?" I ask, answering the question with another.

He rubs a hand across the back of his neck. "A list of suitable mafia princesses for him to select a bride from."

My eyes widen as I had heard nothing of it, but Massimo shelters me almost too much. He sees me as this sweet, innocent little girl he remembers when I was little and he had to step up after Killian's grandfather killed our mom. "Really?"

"Yeah, Leo and I are worried he'll start trying to force us to marry soon." He laughs. "Although I doubt it, since Massimo is in line to inherit everything, that's why it matters so much to Father. Thank God."

I shake my head. "True, but marriage would do Leo some good. He's obsessed with that damn strip club."

Luca smirks. "I know, Massimo and I joked about holding an intervention."

"You should do it just to see the look on his face."

The smirk on my brother's face widens. "I'll consider it. So, are you going to stop mopping in the kitchen and get back to your party?"

I sigh and nod. "Yeah, but now you've told me Father wants me to marry Alejandro, I don't think I can face him right now." My brow furrows. "He lied to me and told me his father does not know he's here."

Luca claps me on the shoulder. "How about we stick together for the night?"

I smile and stand up. "Sounds good."

"Besides, I haven't given you your birthday present yet."

I raise a brow. "We don't do birthday presents anymore."

He shakes his head. "You didn't think I wouldn't get my little sister a present on her twenty-first birthday, did you?"

We walk out of the kitchen and back toward the party. "What is it then?"

"You'll have to wait and see." He walks ahead of me slightly as we enter the ballroom. My heart sinks in my chest when I spot Alejandro deep in conversation with my father.

"Great," I murmur, drawing Luca's attention to them as well.

He puts a supportive arm around my shoulders and squeezes. "Ignore both of them. It's your birthday and nothing is going to bring you down. Come on, your gift is this way." He leads me out of the ballroom, thankfully, as I don't want to see Alejandro or my father right now.

"Where are you taking me?"

Luca just grins like an idiot over his shoulder. "Wait and see."

I shake my head and follow him left into the garage. "What are we—" I stop in my tracks when I see my dream car parked next to his Ferrari.

"Happy birthday, Mia." He signals to the white

Mercedes Benz Sl convertible and I can't help but squeal.

"Are you serious?"

He nods. "Yeah, Massimo and Leo chipped in for it."

I cross my arms over my chest. "Does Father know?"

His expression sours slightly. "Of course not, he'd never of let us buy you a car."

I run up to my brother and wrap my arms around his waist. "Thank you. You're the best."

He wraps his arms around me and hugs me tightly. Despite his tough guy exterior, Luca has always been the softest of my three brothers, and the most fun.

Someone clears their throat behind us. "I'm going to pretend I didn't hear that since I also chipped in," Leo says.

I turn to face him. "You're the best too," I say, walking toward him and giving him a hug.

Leo shakes his head. "And what about Massimo? Is he also the best?" He glances at Luca. "This one has no loyalty."

I chuckle, but I can't help the twisting sensation in my stomach at the comment. He really would believe that if he knew I'd been wrapped in the arms of a Callaghan barely twenty minutes ago. "It's an expression." I shove his shoulder playfully. "You can be a real ass, you know?"

"I know," Leo says, holding his hands up as if admitting his guilt. "And I don't care." He glances at the car and then at me. "How much have you had to drink?"

I shake my head. "Would you believe me if I said nothing?"

Both he and Luca laugh. "Only you could be at your own twenty-first birthday party and not had a drink by." Luca glances at his watch. "Nine thirty at night."

I shrug. "Why do you ask?"

His smirk widens. "It means you can take it for a spin." Luca holds up the keys and I rush toward him, about to take them from his hands. "I call shotgun, though."

Leo sighs. "I should probably get back to the party and pretend I have no idea where you two are."

I smile at him as he turns away. "Thank you, Leo. This is the best present ever."

He glances over his shoulder, smiling. "You deserve it, little sis." And then he leaves me with Luca.

"Okay, enough talking and more driving." He chucks me the keys, which I only just manage to catch. "Get your ass in the driver's seat now."

I unlock the car and slide into the driver's seat, hardly able to believe this is mine. It will give me a freedom I've never had before, but I fear father will soon put a stop to it once he realizes. "Where's the ignition?"

Luca shakes his head. "It's push start. Just press that button there."

I push the button and the engine roars to life like magic. "Nice."

"Where shall we go?" I ask, glancing at my brother as he presses the button on the garage door remote.

"Anywhere you want. How about we go get some ice cream at Bella's?"

I smile and nod. "That sounds good." I rev the engine, perhaps a little too much, as I pull out of the garage and drive down the long, winding driveway toward the gates.

Luca salutes at the guys standing watch as they open the gate for us and I head out onto the open road. "Take the freeway so you can test out the acceleration on this thing." He nods to the exit and I take it, putting my foot down the moment we're on the vast open roads.

He cheers as he puts his hands up in the air, the wind rushing past our faces. I can't help but smile. Luca always knows how to cheer me up and somehow this is exactly what I needed right now. To escape from that stuffy party and the man that my father is trying to match me with, as well as the man I want and can never have. No doubt Killian has already snuck out of the party, but I can hardly believe he was there, telling me he wants me after all these years.

My biggest fear is that he only wants to use me to get ahead in this shit show of a war. The thought is enough to tear my heart in two, just like his last night at the academy. Right now, all I want to do is forget about Killian and Alejandro and all my problems and have fun with my brother.

## 6

## KILLIAN

*I* pace my brother's study, wondering what the hell he's thinking. In one hour, we're going to sit down with the Morrone family and tell them about the threat Adrik poses to all of us. The question is, will they believe us?

Mia has returned none of my calls or texts since her twenty-first birthday party, which is also driving me crazy.

"Would you stop pacing up and down?" Rourke says, his voice unnaturally calm, considering. "You are making me nervous."

I stop pacing and glare at him. "Good, you should be fucking nervous." I shake my head. "Remy could kill us."

Rourke folds his arms over his chest and leans back further in his leather desk chair. "He's not that stupid. This is a peaceful meeting."

"Aye, but didn't you hear what happened when Spartak went to a peaceful meeting with those crazy Italians?"

A muscle in Rourke's temple flexes. "Yes, but Spartak also stole a shipment from them at the same time." He shrugs. "The Morrone family had every right to retaliate."

I blow out a deep breath and continue to pace up and down. "Father wouldn't have agreed to sit down with them." I don't look at Rourke, but it's the truth. He never could have forgiven the Italians for taking his wife's life.

But then he never knew about the threat Rourke issued to the Italians behind his back.

"He may not have, but there's no other way out of this war."

I glance at my brother, whose voice sounds tight. There's a change in him since he took over. Gone is the carefree man I once knew, replaced with a man who carries the weight of the world on his shoulders.

"I know," I reply, moving to sit in the chair opposite him. "Where is the meeting?"

"The old inn that closed down a few years ago on porter street. It's neutral ground."

I nod in response as a heavy silence falls between us. "Have you considered the fact that if we get the Italians on our side, it won't be enough?"

A muscle flexes in Rourke's jaw. "Yes."

"And you can work with Spartak if it comes to it?"

The man who was behind our father's death and also tried to kill Rourke's wife and his own fucking daughter, Viki. Spartak isn't right in the head and he's not the kind of man anyone can trust, even if my father had a deal with him before he died.

"If it is the only way, then yes."

I grit my teeth together. "I fear it will be. Does he still deny his involvement in Father's death?"

Rourke nods in response. "Yes."

For a while know I've wondered if there is more to the story surrounding our father's death than any of us know. Spartak isn't a man who would deny categorically his involvement in someone's murder if he was behind it. He's too unhinged and proud of any violence he commits, that it made no sense. Our rage drove us to strike, but now that time has moved on and I've been able to think about it in more depth, I fear that the war broke out because someone wanted it to.

"I wonder if Adrik was behind it," I mutter, almost to myself.

Rourke's eyes flash. "I've wondered the same thing."

"If that's the case, we started a war for nothing." I shake my head. "We orchestrated our own fucking demise."

My brother nods. "Possibly, but at least we have time to stop it."

It makes me wonder how on earth Adrik got coined as the black sheep of his family? The rumors suggest he's the stupid and irresponsible one, and yet he's gone behind all of our backs and orchestrated one of the most sophisticated attacks we've ever seen.

"Torin couldn't find out when he plans to strike?" I confirm.

He shakes his head. "No, he can't push too hard or Adrik might know we're on to him."

Someone clears their throat at the doorway, drawing our attention. Kieran stands there, arms crossed over his chest. "Are we leaving yet?"

I glance at my watch, noticing that it's quarter past four already, which means if we want to be there before the Italians, we need to leave. "We should do."

Rourke nods. "Yes, let's go. We want to be there before Remy and Massimo arrive."

I stand and follow my brothers out of the study, a heaviness settling on my chest at the thought of facing Mia's family. My cell phone dings and I dig it out of my pocket.

Mia has sent me the first text since the party and it's simply one sentence.

**Be careful today.**

I smirk at her rookie mistake, feeling an odd sensation fluttering in my gut. If she wanted me to believe she wasn't interested, then telling me to be careful meeting her family wasn't very smart. I don't reply, as I want to make her sweat. After all, she's ignored enough texts and calls from me these past two weeks.

It may take some patience on my part, but I will

force her to give in, and once she does, I'll make her wish she did years ago.

"What are you smirking at?" Kieran asks, raising a brow.

I stow my cell phone back in my pocket. "Nothing, mind your own business."

Kieran clicks his tongue. "Not very nice to your little brother, are you?"

"Fuck off, Kier."

He smirks, satisfied he got a rise out of me. "You need to chill out, lad. We are about to go into a pretty tense fucking situation."

"I know." My jaw clenches as I think of Mia's warning.

Be careful today.

She's worried that things are going to go south between her father and Rourke. It's a possibility, one that we'll all have to be prepared for if we want to survive.

"Let's get this over with," I say, as I slip into the back of the town car next to Rourke.

"Aye, and get pissed up once it is over." Rourke rubs a hand across the back of his neck. "I'm going to need about a gallon of whiskey if we survive this."

I laugh. "And a few pints of Guinness to chase it down." I nudge him. "We're going to be fine. Remy may be ruthless, but he's not crazy like Spartak." I glance at Kieran, who doesn't look so convinced. "He wouldn't break a truce unless we gave him a reason."

"Right," Rourke says, nodding. "So let's not give him one. Let me do all the talking unless they speak to you."

"Fine by me," I say, holding up my hands.

Kieran, on the other hand, just crosses his arms over his chest and glares out of the window of the car as the buildings rush past.

Father's death affected him the most out of all of us and he's changed since it happened. Kieran was always the easy-going one of us three brothers, but he's harboring rage over the loss.

"What time are they supposed to arrive?" he asks, still staring out of the window.

"Five o'clock, so we should be there well before them," Rourke answers.

I sit back in the leather seat of the town car and shut my eyes, clenching my jaw when my beautiful baby girl's face appears in my mind.

It doesn't matter how hard I try to forget about Mia Morrone; she has a way of being everywhere and anywhere.

Today, we may pave a path toward a makeshift alliance with her family, which would, in theory, make our relationship less impossible. Not that I'm naïve enough to believe her family would accept us as a match.

All I can do is hope that today goes well. If it doesn't, then it means Mia might be right, even if I've not accepted it yet. Mia believes we're too star-crossed to bridge that gap and break down the barriers in our way. I say to hell with it all and let's burn the barriers to the ground.

---

I STAND at the back of the room, leaning against the wall with my arms crossed. Kier is next to me as Rourke watches Remy carefully since he's just announced the details of Adrik's ridiculous plans.

"Impossible." That is the first word out of Remy's mouth as he shakes his head. "There's no way in hell anyone could oust us all."

My brother tilts his head, but there's a tension in his movements. "I have evidence. Have you heard of Adrik Volkov?"

Remy's brow furrows. "Of course, he's Spartak's nephew and a waste of space."

"Perhaps not so much of a waste of space after all." Rourke moves the photo of him meeting with the Estrada Cartel at their mansion over to them. "He's pulling strings behind his uncle's back. Rumor has it they've only been having discussions with all of us to buy time."

"Motherfuckers," Massimo growls. "It makes sense why they haven't yet taken sides, but how did they expect to take all of us down?"

At least they believe us as I observe some of the tension ease from Rourke as he smirks. "The bastard is crazy. He's got some pretty hefty artillery." He pushes another photo over to them of the short-range and long-range missiles Torin managed to find evidence of.

"What the fuck?" Remy says.

Rourke keeps his gaze fixed on him. "He intends to blow us out of Chicago and then pick up the pieces with the Estrada Cartel behind him."

"And his family?" Massimo asks.

Rourke shrugs. "He hates his family, so I'd assume he intends to blow them away as well."

"Maledetto figlio di puttana," Massimo mutters expletives in Italian.

There's a short but tense silence as Rourke eyes the two men sitting opposite him. "Unfortunately for us, it means we need to work together to stop him."

Remy's back straightens. "How can we be sure this isn't some elaborate ploy?"

My brother sighs heavily, combing his fingers through his hair. "You can't be sure, but you can do your own research." He nods at Gael, who walks forward. "Gael will instruct your spies when and where to dig, and you can find the evidence for yourself if you don't trust ours."

Remy glances at Massimo. "What do you think, Massimo?"

I can sense everyone in the room practically holding their breath, waiting to hear the heir's opinion. "I think that partnering with the Callaghans would be suicide." Massimo looks at Rourke. "But if what he's saying is true, it may be better than complete anni-hilation."

Remy's right-hand man, Lorenzo, nods in response. "I can get our guys onto verifying the information."

Remy stands abruptly, causing people to move for their guns. "Thank you for reaching out to us, Rourke. We will discuss it with your man and get back to you."

My brother stands also and offers him his hand across the table. "Of course."

I watch carefully as Remy stares at it for a few painful seconds before finally shaking his hand. It feels like everyone in the room breathes again properly for the first time since they entered, as the Italians turn away and walk out of the abandoned old inn together.

I push off the wall and walk over to the table, setting my hands down on it as I look my brother in the eye. "Well, that could have gone a hell of a lot worse."

Rourke releases a shaky breath and nods. "Aye, it could have done."

"You didn't mention Spartak." I tilt my head slightly. "Why not?"

Kier sits down next to Rourke, glancing at him. "Yeah, why not?"

Rourke shakes his head. "I'd rather not put them off before they agree to work with us. If we get the Italians to agree, then Spartak will fall in line."

"You sound so confident talking about a man who is so unpredictable he shot his own daughter," Kier says, rolling his eyes.

I stand up straight and cross my arms over my chest. "Spartak is crazy, but he'll listen once he realizes that one of his own family is plotting against him."

Rourke looks thankful for my agreement. "Exactly, first let's worry about getting Remy and Massimo to agree, and then we can think about the Russians."

I swallow hard as Rourke stands, looking tired. "I think I'm going to head on back to the house." He eyes me and then Kieran. "What are you two up to tonight?"

I shrug. "No plans." I glance at my youngest brother. "Want to hit the bar tonight?" I know it does him some good when I get him out of that house, as he can be a bit of a recluse.

He smiles and nods. "Sounds good." He glances at Rourke. "You sure you don't want to tag along?"

Rourke sighs. "I'd best not. Viki will wonder where I am."

Kier smirks. "Whipped much?"

His eyes narrow. "She's pregnant, Kier, and believe it or not, I enjoy spending my time with her."

"Yeah, I'll never get that."

I don't say a word, but I can understand it. Kieran is young and immature and he doesn't know what it's like to be entirely consumed by another person. Mia Morrone is the woman who consumes my thoughts, and if she were at home waiting for me, I'd be damned sure heading straight home and not out to some seedy bar.

"Right, have fun." I wink at Rourke. "Let's get

going, little bro." I place my arm across his shoulders and we head out of the old rundown inn. "Where do you want to go?"

"Where do you think?"

I shake my head. "The Shamrock?"

"Is there really anywhere else I'd go?"

I clench my jaw and don't comment, as every time we go to The Shamrock, it dredges up painful memories of our father. Clearly, it's different for Kieran, as he always wants to be there.

"Aye, let's go." I unlock the door to my Porsche and slide into the driver's seat, satisfied when the engine roars to life beneath me. "Hold on."

Kier rolls his eyes but doesn't say a word as I floor it away from the inn and onto the street toward our late father's favorite pub. All the while, I know I won't be able to unwind. Ever since Mia's twenty-first birthday party, I've been on edge and one thing could tip me over it.

I haven't given up on my stubborn Italian princess, but I have to rethink my tactics if I'm going to secure her as mine and stop any plans her father has to marry her to another man.

## 7

## MIA

*P*aisley spins me around, laughing. "I must admit I haven't had this much fun in…" She pauses, thinking. "Ever."

I laugh, feeling the room spin a little as I wanna dance with somebody by Whitney Houston plays on the jukebox. "I love this song." I pull Paisley toward me and we both dance, laughing and tripping over each other. Earlier today, Killian was at a meeting with my brother and father. Thankfully, no one got hurt.

"You are such a great dancer," Paisley says as she spins me around again.

I roll my eyes. "You are only saying that because you're drunk."

She laughs, but I can tell she's not as drunk as I am. My head is spinning and my heart pounding in my ears as we continue to dance. It was the only way to forget about the man who came blazing back into my life a little over two weeks ago. I can't get Paisley's comment out of my mind about me saying I can't date him.

*Why the fuck not?*

She sounded like the man himself.

The music stops and we both laugh, hugging each other. I must admit, despite her reluctance to marry my brother, I'm thankful she's here. Having Paisley around gives me some much needed female company while Camilla is at the academy.

"Are you having fun, ladies?" Massimo's voice cuts through the silence.

I notice the way Paisley's eyes narrow as she stares at him. "Until you walked in here, we were having a great time."

Mia laughs. "Chill, Paisley." I rush up to my brother and wrap my arms around him tightly. "He's just a big teddy bear, really. Did you enjoy your night at the strip club?" I frown at him. "You're home earlier than I expected."

"It was shit. I didn't want to be there, so I got an Uber home." Massimo says, his attention on his fiancé. "The only woman that can get me going is right here."

I take a step back at the disgusting comment. "Gross."

He laughs. "You realize I'm getting married to her tomorrow, right?"

I shake my head. "It's gross to think of you with any woman. You're my brother." As I take a step back, I stumble over my own feet. "I need to go to bed, as the room is spinning."

"Make sure she gets to her room in one piece," Massimo says to Sandro, who approaches and guides me out of the room. I laugh as Sandro's hand lands on my hip, as I'm terribly ticklish when drunk.

Sandro doesn't say a word, as usual, and silently escorts me to my room, where he opens the door. "Can you handle it from here?" he asks.

I nod. "Yeah, I think I've got it unless you want to tuck me in?"

His jaw clenches at my sarcastic comment and he walks back the way we came, leaving me standing at the threshold of my room. I walk inside and shut the door behind me, resting my head against the solid wood and sighing.

Reaching into my clutch bag, I grab my cell phone and check for a text. Still radio silence from Killian. Perhaps I've blown it with him or perhaps a one sentence text doesn't exactly warrant a response.

Perhaps it's because I'm drunk that I pull up my contacts list and hit his name, my heart pounding hard and fast in my ears as the dial tone sounds.

He picks up on the third tone, but doesn't say a word. I can hear music and laughing in the background and I wonder who he's with.

"Killian?" I say his name, unsure what else to say.

There's a few beats of silence before he says, "Hey, baby girl. It's about time you returned my calls."

I swallow hard, realizing I've got no idea why I'm calling him. "Are you busy?"

I can hear him moving and then everything goes silent around him. "No, what's up?"

I walk over to my bed and sit down on the edge, trying to piece together the crazy, muddled thoughts running through my head at a hundred miles an hour. "Why the fuck not?" I say, repeating Paisley's comment about me dating Killian. I know how crazy this is, because he might have an ulterior motive for wanting to date me.

He chuckles, and it's a deep, rich sound that makes my stomach churn. "Am I supposed to know what you are talking about?"

"To the date. That's my answer." I'm insane, agreeing to a date with him when I'm drunk. I'll probably regret it in the morning.

"You are drunk," he says, not as a question but as a statement.

"Yeah, what's your point?" I ask.

"My point is, will you remember you've agreed to go on a date with me when you wake up in the morning?"

I clench my jaw. "I'm not that drunk."

"Hmm," he sounds unconvinced. "Text me now, so I have it in writing."

"Are you serious?"

"Deadly."

I swallow hard at the way he says that and put him

on loudspeaker, typing a text and confirming I want to go on this date. "There, happy?"

"Not yet, Mia." I hear him tapping something on the other end of the phone. "There is the address to meet me." My phone dings and an address comes through in central Chicago. "When do you want to go on this date?"

Probably never when I wake up tomorrow morning. "Not tomorrow."

There's a few moments of silence. "Why not tomorrow?"

"I've got a wedding to go to." I lie down on my back and stare at the ceiling. "The day after is fine."

"Who's wedding?" he asks.

A sinking sensation ensues in my gut as I realize that telling him about Massimo's wedding would almost be like betraying my family. The man on the other end of this phone is one of our enemies. "Couldn't say."

He chuckles. "Always so secretive, Mia. What are you doing right now?"

"Lying on my bed, staring at the ceiling."

There's a soft, manly rumble on the other end of the line. "And what are you wearing?"

Heat coils through my body as I realize where he's going with this. I glance down at the elegant cream dress I put on for Paisley's makeshift bachelorette party. "Just a dress."

"Have you been out tonight?" he asks.

"No, I've been drinking with family here at home," I

71

lie, as I can't mention Paisley. It's not common knowledge to those outside of the famiglia that Massimo is getting married, and I won't be the one to leak that information.

"Take off the dress," he orders.

I swallow hard, wondering if I should follow his orders or put the phone down. Right now, his voice alone is enough to turn me into a pool of liquid in the middle of my bed.

"And don't you dare put the phone down on me."

My nipples harden against the fabric of my bra at the tone of his voice. It's so dominant and demanding. "Why do you want me to take my dress off?" I ask, pretending to be oblivious to his intentions.

"Take. Off. The. Dress."

I sigh heavily. "Always were so bossy."

He chuckles as I set the phone down on the bed and then unfasten the zip on the side and slide my dress off, leaving it on the floor. I'm too drunk to make the trip to my closet and back. "There, it's off. Happy now?"

"What underwear are you wearing? Describe them to me."

I swallow hard as I look down at the match pair of lacy black underwear I'm wearing. It's sexy and sophisticated, but I've got no idea how to describe it to him. I'm too inexperienced. "It's black," I murmur nervously, twisting my fingers in the comforter beneath me.

"I'm going to need a bit more information to visualize, Mia."

I swallow hard. "It's just underwear."

"Take it off for me."

I do as he says, freeing the clasp on my bra and chucking it on top of my dress, followed by my panties. "Done."

"Now, I want you to touch yourself for me. Can you do that?"

My breath catches in my throat as a need so intense pulses to life between my thighs. I dip my hand between them, moaning the moment my finger bumps over my throbbing clit.

"Good girl," Killian purrs. "Now, dip those fingers inside your virgin pussy."

"Killian, what—"

"No questions. I want you to fuck yourself for me."

I moan, shocked at how dirty he's being. I slip my fingers inside of myself, groaning at how sensitive I am. "Killian," I breathe his name, unable to hold myself back.

"That's it, baby. Fuck yourself nice and deep and imagine it's my cock."

His words make me beyond horny as I thrust my fingers wantonly in and out of my soaking wet pussy, moaning as my nipples get so hard they hurt. "Please, Killian," I moan, unsure of what I'm begging him for.

"Are you begging me for my cock, baby?" He asks, making me gush more.

I swallow hard, unsure what I'm begging for. "Perhaps," I mutter, my inhibitions returning slightly.

"Good, because I'm stroking myself right now and I'm so fucking hard for you."

I bite my lip, struggling to believe what I'm about to say. "Show me."

"What?" Killian says.

"Send me a picture."

He chuckles, and it's a deep rumble that sends fire racing through my veins. "So needy, baby girl, but since you asked." I hear him fumbling on the other end of the phone as he takes a picture and then my phone dings.

My heart is in my mouth as I pull up the multi-media message and moan so loud when I see it. Killian is sitting in an office chair with his cock jutting out of his suit pants, and his hand firmly wrapped around the base. To say it looks huge is an under-statement.

"Like what you see?" He murmurs, sounding so self-assured considering he just sent me that picture.

"Yes," I rasp out.

"Do you wish you were here right now riding it?" There's a few moments of silence as I struggle to speak. "I sure as hell do."

I can't believe how turned on I am at the prospect. No man has ever got my heart racing or my pussy drip-ping like Killian, and I've wanted him for so damn long it just makes the ache almost unbearable. "Yes," I say, so softly I'm not sure he'll hear it.

"Good girl," he purrs. "Now it's your turn. Take a

picture of your pretty little cunt with your fingers in it for me."

I swallow hard at the thought, as no man has ever seen me that bare. Not in a picture or in person. "But—"

"Now, baby girl. Fair is fair."

He has a point, as I was the one that started this.

"One moment," I say, moving the phone away and pulling up the camera app. And then I position it between my legs and spread them wider, my fingers still wedged inside. I snap the photo and then check it, wincing at the sight. However, he can't see my face, which is a bonus. I then send the picture and hold my breath.

The sound Killian makes is arousing as he groans down the phone. "Fuck, I need to be inside you." I hear his breathing become more labored. "Keep fucking yourself for me, imagining I'm inside of you, fucking that pretty little cunt."

I gasp at the use of that word, as it's so damn dirty. And yet it turns me to liquid for him. My body shudders as I feel myself nearing an explosive climax as his heavy breathing rattles through the phone.

"Tell me how good it feels, Mia."

I lick my too dry lips. "It feels so good," I moan, thrusting my fingers in and out of myself harder and faster.

"Fuck, you are soaked. I can hear you fucking your-self, baby girl."

I cry out as my orgasm hits me with such intensity that my hips rise off the bed. My mind feels like it shatters into a thousand shards of glass as I try to catch my breath.

"Mia," Killian groans my name, a soft manly grunting sound following as he no doubt comes apart, too. "Fuck," he growls.

I can't believe I just had phone sex with Killian Callaghan. As the effects of my orgasm wear off, I feel mortified. I reach for the phone as he doesn't say another word, and cancel the call. It's too embarrassing to say anything as I get off the bed and head for the bathroom to wash up. My heart is still pounding long after I lie back down on the bed, and then my cell phone dings.

I pick it up and it's just a simple message from Killian

**Sweet dreams, baby girl. See you on Sunday night.**

I swallow hard and place my cell on the wireless charger on my nightstand, sighing heavily. He will not like it, but there's no way I can face him after what we just did. I'll call it off tomorrow and tell him I changed my mind. It's best for everyone that way.

## 8

## KILLIAN

*A*xel won't know what hit him.

Supposedly, he's agreed on a fucking deal for product from the Italians over two weeks ago, despite having a contract with us.

Spartak has fucked us over so badly in the past few months we've hardly been able to supply him, but that's not the point. The weasel went behind our backs to our enemy none the less, and we can't let that lie.

I crack my knuckles as Gael and I get out of the town car and walk toward the bar. It's quiet at this time of day, but Axel is here as I spot his bike parked out front.

"Let me do the talking," I say, glaring at Gael, who has a tendency to overstep the mark. He may be my brother-in-law, but he's not family, at least not blood. I've never liked the guy, and Maeve marrying him hasn't changed that.

Gael holds his hands out in surrender. "Sure thing, boss."

I grunt and walk through the front entrance of the dive of a bar, wrinkling my nose at the strong scent of piss, whiskey and rotten food. "This place makes me sick."

"Tell me about it," Gael says, also grimacing.

A girl is standing behind the bar, twiddling her thumbs. She looks surprised as she notices us. "Can I help you?"

"We're looking for your boss, lass. Where's Axel?"

She worries her lip between her teeth. "He's busy at the moment, I'm afraid."

I smirk and lean over the bar, glaring at her. "He won't be too busy for us. Tell him Killian Callaghan is here to see him and if he doesn't get his ass out here in one minute, I'll burn the place to the fucking ground."

Her face pales and she nods as she scurries away from the bar and into the back room.

Raised voices come from the back room, but after perhaps two minutes, Axel finally makes an appearance. "Killian, to what do I owe this pleasure?" He walks behind the bar and leans against the far cabinet, crossing his arms over his chest. If he thinks the bar between us will save him, he's mistaken.

"You have a contract with the Callaghan Clan for supply." I point at him. "So why the fuck have you signed one with the Morrone family?"

He maintains an air of cockiness, but just shrugs.

"You couldn't deliver, so I had to find supply elsewhere. What did you expect me to do?"

I clench my fist on top of the bar. "I expect you to come to us with your problems, rather than fuck us over and go running to our enemy."

Axel tilts his head. "And if I'd come to you again, what would you do?"

"Again?" I ask.

He nods. "Yeah, that little brother of yours has been a real asshole about it."

"Kieran?" I confirm.

Axel pushes off the back cabinet of the bar and walks closer. "Do you have another little brother? I've had meetings with him countless times, but he told me there was nothing you guys could do."

I clench my fists, knowing that once I get my hands on Kieran, I'll wring his bloody neck. Kieran was tasked with dealing with the bikers, but he never mentioned he'd had any meetings with Axel.

"What is it going to take to get back the contract?"

Axel shakes his head. "There's nothing I can do for you."

I reach for the collar of his jacket and yank him forward over the bar. "You listen to me, you son of a bitch. Break off the agreement with the Morrone family, or I'll make sure your life is a living hell."

Axel just smirks. "What makes you think you have that power?"

I release him and glare at the president of the

motorcycle club, wondering when he got so cocky. "What do you mean?"

"Massimo offered me protection in exchange for my help, too. You shouldn't even be here, as you are trespassing in their territory." He drums his fingers on the bar. "In fact, I called him the moment Claire here came back and gave me your pathetic threat. He's sending his men over now."

Gael steps to my side and murmurs in my ear. "We need to get out of here. He might not be bluffing."

I nod in response. "Our contract was ironclad."

"If you met your end on the deal, yes." He crosses his arms over his chest. "I'm afraid you broke the terms by not supplying me." I can't deny that Axel seems to be very confident that Massimo will back him in the event of a disagreement. "The contract I agreed with the Morrone family is unbreakable. Massimo even wanted one of my best bartenders as part of the deal."

"Bartender?" I ask, frowning at him. "What the fuck for?"

Axel chuckles. "I believe he's marrying her as we speak."

The wedding Mia was talking about is her brother's wedding. Now it makes sense why she was so coy about it. If she told me about the wedding, she felt like she would be betraying her family.

I flex my fingers, desperate to let Axel feel the full wrath of my rage.

Gael leans closer again. "Seriously, if we want to avoid a standoff, we need to go."

I clench my jaw. "This isn't over, Axel." I point at him. "You fuck with us and join the Morrone family, then you can expect to be embroiled in the war."

His eyes narrow, but that's the only sign he's rattled by the idea. "Bring it on."

I turn around and lead Gael out into the parking lot. "That son of a bitch needs putting in his place."

"Aye, but not right now. If we want the Morrone family to consider working against Adrik and the Cartel with us, then we need to lie low."

As always, Gael is the voice of the reason. The guy has such a level-head it's irritating at times. "You're right, as always."

My cell phone dings and I dig it out of my jacket, smirking when I see Mia's name on the front. Although, it's quickly eradicated when I read her text.

**Forget last night, as I was drunk. The date is off.**

I clench my fists by my side, knowing nothing could piss me off more right now than Mia backing out of our agreement. "You go on ahead to the house. I've got something to deal with," I say to Gael.

He nods. "Sure, no worries."

I open the app on my cell phone and book an Uber to take me over to the Morrone residence. Mia has clearly underestimated the kind of man I am. If she believes I'll be tormented like that and then drop it entirely, she has to think again.

No more playing nice. It's time to make her realize she belongs to me and nothing she can say will ever change that.

———

THE WEDDING RECEPTION is in full swing as I easily slip past the guards, who appear to be enjoying themselves a bit too much, drinking and chatting, rather than monitoring security.

You'd think during the middle of war, they'd be a little more switched on.

Mia shouldn't have mentioned this wedding, as it gave me the perfect chance to see her again. Big events like these are the easiest to go by unseen, and once I find my target, I intend to make sure she doesn't back out of the date. In fact, I intend to make her realize just how much of a mistake it is to tease me.

I walk into the ballroom where I'd been a few weeks earlier, scanning the room for any sign of Mia. There's no sign of her initially, although I spot her brothers, Luca and Leo.

My jaw clenches as I keep my head down and stay close to the edge of the room, ensuring I don't draw attention to myself. If those idiots notice me, then it's game over. "Where are you, baby girl?"

I pull my cell phone out and ring her number. The dial tone sounds, but it quickly cuts to messaging.

I type a text to her.

**I'm here at the wedding reception. Lovely affair. It would be a shame to ruin it. Tell me where you are, or I'll make a scene.**

It's a desperate move, but the longer I linger in the shadows, the more chance I have of getting caught.

**What the fuck? I'm in my room**.

I smirk at her irritated response and head out of the ballroom and back toward the main entryway. Mia's room must be upstairs, but the question is, which one is it? As I ascend the stairs, thankful to get away from the crowds, I type a one word text.

**Directions.**

She sends me an angry emoji in response.

**Don't push me, Mia.**

The bubbles on my phone ignite, proving she's writing back to me.

**Up the stairs, the first door on your left.**

I smirk as her bedroom is the perfect place for the punishment I have planned for her. I crack my neck and walk toward the door, resting my hand on the doorhandle. When I turn it, I find it's locked from the inside.

**Unlock the door, baby girl.**

"What are you even doing here?" Her voice sounds on the other side of the door.

I tap my foot impatiently on the hardwood floor.

"I'm here to discuss the ridiculous text you just sent me half an hour ago."

"It's not ridiculous. I wasn't in my right mind."

"Bullshit," I reply, tightening my grasp on the doorhandle and shaking it forcefully. "Open. The. Door."

"Or what?"

I grind my teeth, as Mia can be a real brat. It's not something I had anticipated, perhaps foolishly. "Or I'll go back to the party and ruin your brother's wedding reception."

There's a long, over-exaggerated sigh on the other side of the door as the lock clicks and she opens it. "What do you want?"

I walk forward and push her inside, making her eyes widen. "I want you right fucking now."

Her throat bobs as I slam the door behind me and turn the lock, glancing back at her.

"Do you think you can play games with me?"

She shakes her head, backing up a few steps as I advance forward. "Killian, you're scaring me."

"Good," I growl, hardly recognizing my voice. "Because you tempted the beast to come out to play, and here I am, baby girl."

Her nostrils flare. "What are you talking about?"

I grind my teeth. "Last night, you fucking come for me on the phone, and then tonight you send me that text. What the fuck are you playing at?"

Her cheeks turn a dark pink as she continues to

back up until the back of her knees knock into her bed. "I was too embarrassed to face you after that."

"Embarrassed?" I question, shaking my head. "You should never be embarrassed to face me, as I want all of you, baby girl." My eyes move down slowly, admiring the cute little night gown she's wearing and I groan, adjusting my hardening cock in my pants. "I want that tight little virgin cunt wrapped around my cock, and I want it right fucking now."

She gasps, looking scandalized as if she's the pinnacle of innocence. I can hear her raspy voice now, begging me over the phone when she asked me for a picture of my cock. The dirty little virgin will get everything she wants and more tonight, no matter how much she denies she wants it.

I'm done messing around. It's time for me to claim what has always belonged to me.

## 9

## MIA

*I* feel dumbstruck as I stare at Killian, knowing I've never seen him like this before. He's angry and determined, and it scares me more than I'd like to admit.

"What about the date?" I mutter, sounding foolish since he's here because I called it off.

He moves forward. "I tried to do this the right way, Mia, but you left me with no choice."

I have nowhere to go as he comes toward me, my legs pressed against the edge of my bed. "What are you going to do?"

My breath catches in my throat as Killian wraps a firm palm around my throat, squeezing in warning. I've never seen this side of him. Dark and dangerous. There's rage swirling in those beautiful green depths of his and suddenly I realize calling off our date was a mistake.

The mere idea of facing him after our phone sex made me sick to my stomach, and yet he's standing before me, growling like a possessed animal because I told him the date was off.

"I'm going to make you realize what you've been missing." His fingers flex around my throat as he lowers me to the bed. "Relax, baby."

It's almost impossible to relax while Killian is acting like this.

My heart skips a beat as he pushes the nightgown I'm wearing up to my hips, groaning when he sees my thong.

"Fuck, Mia," his voice sounds different, as I glance down at him. "I need to taste you."

I swallow hard at the thought, wriggling in an attempt to break away from him.

"Hold still," he growls, as his fingers hook into the strings of my thong and he pulls them down, exposing me to him.

I've never been this bare in front of a man, and it feels like someone lit a match and set my face on fire.

A soft rumble comes from his chest and then I feel his mouth close over my clit, making my body jolt in pleasure.

"Killian," I squeak his name, unable to get my thoughts straight as he drags his tongue right through my center.

"So fucking delicious," he murmurs, before continuing.

I glance down at him and it feels like I'm in a dream, as he works his tongue in and out of me, eyes fixed on my face.

He nips at my clit and it feels like I'm on the edge of exploding. "Good girl, I want you to watch me eat your virgin pussy."

I swallow hard, realizing I've been transported into my own filthy fantasy, only I never could have imagined how good his dirty talk could be.

"Killian," I moan his name, back arching as he continues to feast on me like an animal. My thoughts are all muddled up as he drives me crazy with need.

Suddenly, he grabs my hips and flips me over on all fours. It feels like time stands still as he parts my ass cheeks and then licks me there.

I tense, trying to fight away from him. "What are you——"

He spanks my ass cheek hard and the pain along with the forbidden pleasure makes me gush.

I swallow hard, struggling to come to terms with all the sensations this man is giving me.

Who could have known that any of this could feel so fucking good?

His hands roughly claw at my ass cheeks and the pain only heightens the pleasure.

"Oh God," I cry, realizing that at any moment, he's going to make me come.

"I want you to come for me, baby," he breathes, his

tongue probing at my asshole. "I want you to make that pretty virgin cunt come for me."

My nipples are so fucking hard they hurt as my legs quiver.

It feels like I might black out from the pleasure at any moment. And then stars burst behind my shut eyelids as his fingers dip into my pussy, driving me right over the edge.

I can hardly breathe as I come apart, my thighs getting wet with my arousal.

"You come so fucking well," he breathes, continuing to pump his fingers in and out of my wet entrance. "Look at me," he orders.

I glance over my shoulder at him and he pulls his fingers out of me, sucking my arousal off of each one slowly. I moan, unable to stop myself at it's such an erotic sight.

"You taste like heaven, baby girl."

I swallow hard, struggling to believe that this man wants me the way I've wanted him for years. "Killian," I moan his name.

"Yes, baby?"

I shake my head. "What are we doing?"

"Accepting the truth that we've spent too long ignoring."

He grabs my hips and forces me over onto my back, covering my body with his. "You belong to me, Mia."

I feel the press of his heavy erection between my thighs as he lets his weight rest on me, pinning me to the bed. A wicked smirk twists onto his lips. "Now, it's your turn to taste me."

Every inch of my skin blazes with heat at the thought. "I don't know what to do," I murmur.

His eyes flash. "Are you telling me that not only is this beautiful cunt completely untouched?" He slides a finger inside of me, making me gasp. "But also, your mouth has never had a cock in it?"

I nod in response. "I've never done anything with anyone." I shrug. "Except for kiss."

He growls softly. "And you will never do anything with anyone else again." His lips press against mine urgently as he teases my mouth open for him. And then he kisses me as if his life depends on it.

As if he's trying to infect me with him and ensure that his claim on me lasts forever. "You belong to me, Mia," he says, his lips moving to my neck as he kisses me there. "Forever."

I swallow hard as he moves off of me and unfastens the zip of his pants, my heart racing hard and fast. It's one thing seeing it in a photo, but actually being here in front of him is surreal.

And I can't believe how badly I want it. Even though he just made me come, I've got an ache deep inside of me. He releases the length of his cock through his the zipper of his pants.

I gasp, my jaw aching at the sheer thought of fitting it in my mouth.

"Come here, baby," he says, signaling for me to approach.

I sit up as if mesmerized and crawl toward him, which earns me a loud groan.

"That's it, on all fours for me," he encourages.

I stop when the tip of his cock is merely an inch away, gazing up at his beautiful green eyes, which are filled with such manic desire.

"Now, wrap your fingers around the base and put it in your mouth," he says, his voice strained.

I groan as precum drips from his cock onto the bed, before I take the thick shaft of his cock in my hand and open my mouth.

Moving forward, I suck on the head, which earns me a sharp hiss of pleasure.

He tastes of pure masculinity and I feel myself getting wetter than I've ever been between my thighs.

My nipples are so hard and I can't believe how arousing it is having his cock in my mouth.

I watch his face as he stares down at me, looking almost pained, as I lick and suck at the tip of his cock.

"Fuck, Mia." His fists clench. "I don't know that I can stop myself."

My brow furrows as I wonder what he's talking about, continuing to work his shaft with my mouth.

And then, as if he snaps, his hand grabs hold of a fistful of my hair and he forces the entire length into the back of my throat.

I gag, shocked by the sudden change in tempo.

His cock thrusts in and out with frantic, jerky movements as I struggle to breathe.

My heart pounds so hard in my chest it feels like it's trying to break out. His nostrils flare as he glares down at me like an angry god, taking what he needs without a care in the world.

It's dark and dominant and I can feel my desire heightening.

This violent assault should turn me off, but it feels so primal and desperate that it makes the ache between my thighs increase.

He goes so deep my gag reflex is almost impossible to control and I feel so much saliva spill out of my mouth, dripping down my chin and onto the bed.

"Fuck, you are so damn sexy, baby girl," he growls, his hips pumping in at an unrelenting speed as he fucks my throat. "I want to come down your throat and I want you to swallow every fucking drop. Do you understand?"

I can't speak with his cock wedged down my throat and I'm in too much of an unnatural position to nod.

He doesn't seem to expect a reply though as his cock swells in my mouth and he roars like an animal, his release coming in thick ropes. I try to keep up and swallow it all, but it's impossible. There's too much cum and a lot of it spills out of my mouth.

He continues to fuck my throat jerkily, and it's only at that moment I realize how much my jaw and throat aches from the assault. I continue to swallow as he pulls his still hard cock from my mouth, eyes ablaze with such purpose it makes me ache more between my thighs.

"That was so fucking good," he murmurs, leaning down and kissing me.

I moan into his mouth, feeling so damn horny. "Killian, please."

He pulls away and smirks at me, tilting his head slightly. "Please, what?"

"I need you," I gasp, the ache between my thighs becomes more desperate by the minute.

He shakes his head. "No, baby girl. I think we should go on that date first."

My eyes widen as I realize he's being serious.

Killian is torturing me, and I know why. It's his way of punishing me for trying to call the date off in the first place.

"After all, it's only twenty-four hours." He pushes his semi-hard cock back into his pants and zips them up. "Surely, you can wait that long." Moving away from the bed and staring at me with a cocky and irritating smirk on his lips.

I narrow my eyes at him and pull my nightgown down so I'm not so naked. "Who says I'll even want to?"

He chuckles, and it grates on my nerves. "Considering you were just begging me for my cock, something tells me you'll still want it tomorrow night."

"Tomorrow night?" I ask.

"Our date, you better be there, baby. Or I'll come and find you."

A shudder travels down my spine at the tone of his voice. "Why does that sound like a threat?"

His jaw clenches and he steps toward the bed again, green eyes darker than I've ever seen them. "Because it is, Mia. I'm done playing nice. It's time for you to get to know the real Killian Callaghan."

I get off the bed and move away from him. "And what if I don't like the real Killian Callaghan?"

A soft rumble comes from his chest. "I don't care. You belong to me and once I'm through with you, you'll want me whether you like it or not." His voice is deep and dark and it makes me realize just how dangerous he is.

After all, he is a mobster. A mobster who belongs to a family we've been enemies with since before I was born, and before he was born. The feud between the Morrone family and the Callaghan family is historic, and yet these kinds of feuds have a way of repeating over and over throughout time. I mean, look what happened to my mom and Killian's mom. Our families slaughter each other, and somehow Killian believes we can be together, despite all of that.

Killian moves closer, green eyes flashing with such desire and purpose. "Sweet dreams, baby girl," he murmurs, before kissing me with an aching softness. His tongue delves into my mouth, caressing my own with soft, fire stoking strokes. I moan into his mouth as the need increases between my thighs, and just as fast as he kissed me, he breaks it.

His lips twist into a cocky smirk and he holds my gaze for one heartbeat before turning and leaving my room, shutting the door behind him.

I stare at the shut door, wondering what the hell his plan is. There is no world in which a Callaghan and a Morrone can be together without causing a catastrophic rift in one or both of our families. The problem is, my family means the world to me, and yet so does Killian. How the hell am I supposed to choose one or the other?

## KILLIAN

*R*ourke is sitting behind our father's old desk as I knock on the door, which is open. He glances up. "Alright?"

"Yeah, I'm heading out for the night." I feel a flood of guilt kick me in the chest. If he knew who I was about to meet with, he would strangle me with his bare hands. I'm not stupid. I know messing with Mia could jeopardize everything if the Morrone family think I'm trying to steal her from under their noses. "I just wanted to check if you need anything before I go."

He shakes his head, loosening the tie around his neck. "No, I'm good." His blue eyes are so tired it strikes me hard, and I realize how much the burden of the clan is weighing on him. Normal times would be a breeze, but this war is costing us too heavily, and it needs to end quickly. His brow furrows. "Any luck with Axel?"

I clench my jaw at the reminder of the meeting with that piece of shit. I'd practically forgotten about it after my visit to the Morrone residence. After I indulged in the woman I've been obsessed with for years. Ever since, I've struggled to get my mind off of her and the way she looked with my cock deep in her throat and my cum spilling down her chin.

Damn it. I need to get a handle on my urges.

"I went to see him yesterday evening." I shake my head. "It didn't go well."

Rourke nods. "He won't back out of the deal with Massimo."

"No, he says it's ironclad, and that we broke the contract by not supplying him." I wince. "Unfortunately, he has a point."

"It was worth a shot." He shuffles some papers on his desk. "We just need an end to this war."

"If we can convince everyone to work against Adrik, it may come quicker than we think." I clench my fists by my side. "Did you know Massimo got married last night?"

Rourke's brow hitches upward. "Married to who?"

"Axel's bartender, apparently."

He sighs heavily. "Why the fuck would he marry a bartender?"

"Fuck knows." I shrug. "Axel said Massimo demanded her as part of his deal with them."

A crease forms between his eyebrows. "That's weird.

I was sure Remy would want a politically advantageous match for his son."

I can't deny that it is weird, but I was too wrapped up in Mia to remember to ask her about it. Perhaps I'll be able to get some answers from her tonight, as long as I don't push it too hard. The last thing I want is for her to think I'm merely dating her to get intel on her family.

"It's odd." I rub a hand across the back of my neck. "I'd heard rumors he was always intended for Senator Federico Russo's daughter, Caterina."

"Aye, so had I. Remy and Federico are close, so I'm surprised it didn't happen." His brow furrows. "I'll see if Torin can find out more."

"Leave it to me," I say, instantly regretting it.

Rourke's brow furrows. "Why?"

I shrug. "I think I can find out more from the bikers."

He waves his hand dismissively. "Fair enough. See what you can find out."

"Will do. I'll see you later." I pause when he doesn't look up from whatever paperwork he's pawing over. "Don't work too hard, lad."

He shakes his head. "You sound like, Viki. Someone has to keep a track of the accounts and money, or we'll end up in ever deeper shit."

"Employ a fucking accountant then."

A muscle flexes in the side of his temple. "It's too

risky while we're at war. I can't trust someone we've never worked with."

I nod, as he has a point. "True." I run a hand across the back of my neck. "Do you want me to help sometime?" I suggest, shrugging. "I've never been great with numbers, but—"

"No, it's fine." He nods toward the door. "Now go on and get out of here."

I shake my head, laughing humorlessly. "You sound just like Dad." He never wanted any help either.

His eyes flash with an undetectable emotion as he sighs. "I miss him."

"Aye, so do I." It's all that passes between us. A solemn acknowledgement of the fact that we miss our father. We've rarely spoke of him since his death, but that's because me and Rourke are the same. We keep everything bottled up on the inside. "Don't work too hard, bro." I turn and head out of his study and down the corridor, knowing that I can't be distracted by grief or anything else right now.

I've got a princess to win over, and I'll be damned if I'm late.

---

THE BAR I told Mia to meet me at is in the city center and not a place where we should bump into anyone either of us knows. It's a little rundown and cheap for either of our families. I search the crowd, looking for her, but she's nowhere to be seen.

It's five minutes to eight, so I guess I'm a little early.

There's a quiet booth near the back of the bar that's free, so I head over to it and sit down, drumming my fingers impatiently on the hardwood table. I pull out my cell phone to make sure she hasn't sent me another text, telling me she's not coming.

It's crazy how angry I was when I saw that text the night before—angry enough to risk everything. I had no plan if I got caught crashing Massimo Morrone's wedding, but I guess I was lucky.

My eyes remain fixed on the entrance to the bar, waiting impatiently for Mia to arrive. I'm on edge, anticipating another attempt from her to get out of this date, even after she practically begged me for my cock last night.

It feels like time slows down as I recognize her instantly. She walks through those doors in a beautiful powder blue dress, glancing nervously around the room. Initially, she doesn't spot me tucked away in a dark corner, and I kind of enjoy just watching her from afar. I guess old habits die hard.

I stand and move out of the shadows so she can see me and give her a nod. Her eyes are unreadable the moment she spots me and she bows her head, walking over to meet me. "Hey, Killian."

"Hey, baby girl." I grab her hand and yank her against me. "You are late."

Her eyes widen. "Hardly." She glances at her watch. "It's only two minutes past."

"Hmm, perhaps I should punish you for being tardy."

She sucks on her bottom lip, driving me crazy with need. "Are you being serious?"

"It all depends how well you behave tonight."

Her nostrils flare, and she pushes away from me. "I don't remember you being this much of an ass at the academy."

I sit down and smirk at her. "Strike one."

She rolls her eyes. "I thought this was supposed to be a date."

"It is, but I expect you to be on your best behavior if you want me to fuck you."

Her mouth drops open and she just shakes her head. "You are being an asshole."

I chuckle as I love seeing how flustered she gets. "Relax, Mia. I'm messing with you."

Her eyes narrow, as if she doesn't quite believe me.

A waiter approaches and clears his throat. "What can I get you?"

"I'll have a scotch on the rocks." I glance at Mia. "What do you want, baby girl?"

Her cheeks flush a deep pink at me using that nickname in front of the waiter, and she gives a little shake of her head in disapproval. "I'll have a mojito, please. And a side of fries."

I smirk. "Make that two sides of fries."

The waiter nods. "Coming right up."

Mia releases an irritated sigh the moment he's out of earshot. "Don't call me that in front of people."

I raise a brow. "I'll call you what I want."

Her jaw clenches and she looks away from me, glancing around the dimly lit bar. "Why did you pick this place?"

"I know it's not exactly the luxury you're used to, but it means people you know are unlikely to spot you here."

Her beautiful brown eyes snap back to mine. "Are you suggesting that I'm spoiled?"

I shake my head. "No, merely that you are used to a certain level of luxury."

"That's bullshit. I don't only go to expensive places."

I raise a brow, but can't exactly tell her I know she's lying through her teeth. After all, stalking is a rather creepy thing to do. And, for the past couple of years, my constant following of Mia Morrone has grown more frequent. I know the restaurants and places she goes to normally with her family and friends are far more elegant than this dive.

She huffs at my unconvinced look and then crosses her arms over her chest. "I liked you more at the academy."

"I'm not sure that's true, Mia." I watch her, searching her flawless face. "I think you liked me far more last night when you come with my face buried against your cunt."

She gasps, eyes widening as she glances around, checking if someone heard me. "Do you have to be so crude all the time?"

"Sorry, did I offend your innocent sensibilities?" I ask.

Her eyes flash with fire at that comment, but she doesn't say a word. The waiter returns with our drinks and fries. "Is there anything else I can get you?"

I shake my head. "No, that's all, thanks, lad."

He walks away and leaves us alone again as Mia picks up her drink and takes a long sip, glaring at me over the rim.

"Good mojito?" I ask.

She sets the drink down and nods. "Yes, thanks."

I watch her as she grabs a fry and stuffs it in her mouth, still glaring at me. It makes me chuckle. "You really are in a bad mood, baby girl."

Her nostrils flare. "Perhaps that's because you put me in one."

I tilt my head, reading her comment as a challenge. "Is that right?"

She nods in response.

I stand and move to her side of the booth, slipping in next to her. "Perhaps I can make amends for that."

She turns as still as stone next to me, inching away on the bench. "Killian." Her voice sounds a mix between scolding and begging, which is enough to make me harder than stone.

I grab her thigh hard to stop her moving away and lean toward her, pressing my lips to the side of her neck and kissing her softly. "I haven't been able to think of anything but you naked since last night."

A soft gasp whooshes past her lips as I lick a path up from her shoulder to just below her ear.

"Does that feel good?" I ask.

It's so fucking hot how shy and innocent she is acting right now, considering she was practically begging me to fuck her last night. Her cheeks flush a deep red and she won't even look at me as she nods her head slightly.

"Look at me, Mia." Her eyes meet mine and there's an inferno of passion swirling in those beautiful brown eyes. "We're safe here. Let go," I murmur, before kissing her lips.

The tension melts, and she becomes limp in my arms, submitting to me in the most delicious way. Her mouth opens, drawing me inside as I thrust my tongue in and out of it. Mia moans and I feel the sound vibrate through me, tightening my already uncomfortable pants across my crotch.

I groan, pulling away enough to murmur. "You are going to be the death of me." I grab her hand and press it to the hard length of my cock, forcing her to squeeze. "You make me so fucking hard."

Mia's eyes dilate as she squeezes my cock again, clenching her thighs together. "This is crazy."

"Crazy in a good way, though, right?"

She nods, capturing her bottom lip between her teeth. "Yeah."

I smile, as it looks like I'm finally getting somewhere. "I think I'd better return to my side of the booth before I end up feasting on you instead of my fries." I give her a wink and stand, returning to the opposite side.

Mia's cheeks are flushed a beautiful pink color as she watches me and sips her drink, the rage no longer present in her eyes. She's looking at me like a woman who can't wait to be fucked, and she has no idea what I have in store for her.

## 11

## MIA

*K*illian is being infuriatingly cocky and yet I can't seem to stop my mind running wild with erotic fantasies just looking at him.

What we did last night in my bedroom was earth-shattering and I fear if I go there again tonight, then there will be no stopping this. Killian may have an ulterior motive, but my heart, body, and soul don't want to believe it. All I want to believe is that he's seriously interested in me and nothing else.

"So, what next?" he asks, as he throws dollar bills down onto the table. "Shall we head over to the Waldorf and get a room?"

I swallow hard at the prospect of booking into a hotel with Killian. It's not like it's safe for him to sneak back to my place or vice versa, so a hotel is really the only choice. "We could get spotted."

Killian shakes his head. "No, I'll go in and grab us a

room. Once I've got the number and I'm in the room, I'll text you." He shrugs. "After five minutes, you can enter the hotel and go to that room. So, we won't be seen together."

My head spins as I wonder if I'm really going to sleep with Killian Callaghan. A man who is so totally off limits, but who I've wanted for too damn long. I'm too scared that if I speak, I'll break the spell, so I just nod in response.

"Good," he murmurs, yanking me into his hard, muscled body. "Because I can't wait to fuck that beautiful cunt over and over until you've come so many times you can't even walk."

"Killian," I breathe his name, partially from shock at his dirty words and partially from the arousal that pools between my thighs.

"You like the sound of that, don't you?" he whispers, his lips brushing against my earlobe. He doesn't wait for a response, merely tightens his grasp on me as I whimper softly. "Good, because I'm going to do so many dirty fucking things to you tonight."

"This is crazy," I breathe.

Killian kisses me hard, his lips possessing mine as he pulls me tighter against him. "There's nothing crazy about it. In fact, it's the most sane thing I've done in years." He bends down and grabs a briefcase from the side of the table and then laces his fingers in mine, pulling me toward the exit of the bar.

"Mia?"

I freeze at the sound of the familiar voice calling my name, instantly dropping Killian's hand. Sal is standing there, glancing suspiciously at the two of us. "What are you doing here?" he asks.

I swallow hard. "I just came to meet a friend for drinks," I say, feeling my face blaze with heat.

His eyes narrow. "Who is your friend?"

Sal isn't exactly part of the mob world, but is almost a part of the famiglia. I can't be sure if he knows who Killian is.

"A friend from the academy. He's in town, so we're catching up." I hope beyond hope that he buys it.

"Okay, be safe. I'm surprised your father let you into the city at the moment." He shakes his head. "It's dangerous for the Morrone family."

I clear my throat, hoping he won't notice that tonight I escaped the house without Sandro. He believes I'm fast asleep in bed. "I will be." I give him a wave, which probably looks seriously awkward. "See you later, Sal."

He nods and gives me a weak smile, his eyes darting to Killian, who he glares at. "Take care of her."

Killian doesn't speak, merely nods in response. Perhaps he's worried the moment he opens his mouth, Sal will realize he's Irish.

I turn away and give him a look to tell him to get the hell out fast, and we both make a quick escape away from danger. Once we're out of earshot, I lean toward

Killian. "So much for no one we know coming here," I hiss.

Killian shrugs. "It's Chicago and we both know too many people, it would seem." He flags down a cab the moment we're on the street and I slide into it, nervously fidgeting with my fingers in my lap.

Once he's in and told the driver to take us to the Waldorf, I turn to him. "Are you sure this is a good idea?"

He sighs heavily and grabs my hands in his, squeezing. "Quit worrying, Mia. You know this is what you want, deep down."

I lick my too dry lips and nod. "It is. I've wanted it for as long as I can remember," I admit, regretting it immediately as he smirks at me.

"Good girl," he murmurs into my ear, his hand slipping onto my knee and then higher onto my thigh beneath my skirt. "That's exactly what I wanted to hear."

I stiffen and move away from him, swatting at his hand. "But I can't help but reconsider when you are so fucking cocky."

His chuckle is deep and rich, and it's hard to stay mad at him when he looks at me the way he is right now. "And I can't help but want you more every time you look at me like you want to stab me."

My brow furrows. "I don't look at you like that."

"You do more frequently than you realize." He tilts

his head slightly as the cab comes to a stop and he smirks. "We're here."

My stomach churns as he leans toward the front of the cab. "Hey, here's the fare and thirty dollars extra to remain here for ten minutes with this girl inside."

The cab driver's brow furrows, but he nods. "Sure thing, thanks." He takes the cash and counts it as Killian turns to me. "I'll text you in a bit. Don't go getting cold feet on me." He kisses me and then slips out of the back of the cab before I can say a word.

The cab driver looks in the rearview mirror. "Married?" he asks.

My brow furrows. "What?"

He chuckles. "Only people married to other people need to go into a hotel separately."

I shake my head. "No, I'm not married."

"But he is," he says, nodding his head. "Don't worry, I see this shit all the time."

I shake my head and just look out of the window, ignoring him. It's not like I can tell him the truth. That Killian is actually a mobster from an opposing family, and that's why we can't be seen together. Married is simpler, even if it's not the truth.

I dig my cell phone out of my purse and watch the minutes counting by. Finally, after what feels like an eternity, a text comes through.

**Room 5421**

"Thanks," I say awkwardly, before slipping out of

the cab and heading toward the front of the Waldorf Hotel.

I've been here for political events before, but never stayed in the rooms. It probably costs a fortune, but I guess neither me nor Killian have to worry about money. Tapping my foot on the marble floor, I wait for the elevator to arrive. When it does, I slip inside and press level five on the call buttons. I let out a shaky sigh the moment the door shuts and I'm alone, safe in the elevator.

What we're doing is insane and yet I'm tingling all over with excitement because my fantasy is about to become reality. Killian Callaghan wants me as badly as I want him. The question is, what does it mean to him? He may say the right things, but for me I've always known I loved him, deep down. I can't believe that he feels the same way. I sense this is more of a sexual connection for him, and the fear of having him break my heart makes me question my sanity.

The elevator arrives at the fifth floor and I step into the empty corridor, heading toward room 5421. Once I get to the door, I'm sure my heart is racing so fast that it feels like I'm going into cardiac arrest. I lift my hand up and knock on the door.

Killian answers within seconds, smirking when he sees me. "Come on in."

I can't understand why his invitation to enter feels like a warning, almost. Even so, I fight against my ingrained instinct to run and step past him into the vast, lavish bedroom. The click of the door shutting sounds so final, and then I feel his hands on my hips. "I've been waiting for this for too long, Mia." I feel his cock hard and heavy against my lower back. "I'm going to make you wish you never ran from me the last night at the academy. I'm going to make you wish you'd been fucking me every single day since."

I shudder as his lips tease against the base of my ear.

"Do you know what BDSM is?"

I tense at the question, wondering why he'd ask it. "Of course, I've seen the fifty shades of gray movies."

He chuckles. "That was child's play, Mia."

"Why do you ask?"

"Because I enjoy it and I'm hoping you will too."

I swallow hard at the thought. "And what aspects do you enjoy?"

His tongue darts out against my neck as he licks a path right down it. "I'm a bit of a sadist. I like restraining my submissive and inflicting pain. Do you want to try it?"

My nipples harden at the prospect, and yet I can't quite imagine what he means. Why would he want to inflict pain on me? "What kind of pain?" I ask, hating how squeaky my voice sounds.

"A good kind." He spins me around and looks into my eyes. "You would have a safe word. If it gets too much for you, all you have to do is say it and we stop."

I bite my lip, contemplating the idea. "What is the safe word?"

"Red," he says, shrugging. "It's classic, but effective."

I can't believe I'm even considering this, and yet I have this deeply buried need to please him. It's confusing as well as exciting. "Okay," I say, hardly able to believe I just agreed. "I'll give it a go."

He smiles, and it's not his usual cocky smirk, but a genuine smile that makes my heart flutter in my chest. "Good girl," he purrs, his hands moving to my buttocks as he pulls me closer. "Now strip for me." His voice turns darker and demanding.

I swallow hard and take a step back, holding his fiery green gaze. "Okay."

"Yes, sir," he instructs.

I swallow hard. "Yes, sir."

"Good girl," he praises as I unzip the side zip on my dress and slip it down my body slowly, holding his gaze. I feel so damn vulnerable, and yet the way Killian is looking at me gives me the courage to continue. He's looking at me as if I'm the only other thing on this planet that matters and it gives me hope. Hope that perhaps he feels as deeply as I do for him.

I drop the dress to the floor and step out of it, wearing only a matching see-through bra and thong I purchased specifically for tonight from Bordelle. It was expensive and is way more revealing than anything I've ever worn before. I reach around my back to undo my bra——.

"Stop," he growls, shaking his head. "I want you like this for now."

I swallow hard as I move my hand away from the clasp of my bra and watch him, waiting for his next move.

He grabs the briefcase which he had in the restaurant and opens it, pulling out some rope. "It's time for me to tie you up, Mia."

I swallow hard, wondering what the fuck I've gotten myself into as Killian moves toward me. Deep down, I know he'd do nothing to hurt me. The problem is, I'm not sure I know the man standing before me the way I knew the boy I attended the Syndicate Academy with. Killian harbors darkness and I can see it swirling in the depths of his eyes as he stalks toward me like a tiger stalking its prey.

## 12

---

## KILLIAN

*I* watch her as she writhes in the middle of the bed, wearing only her delicate see-through bra and thong with blue lace detail. Her body has been expertly restrained and I can't deny seeing her tied up for me makes me so fucking hard.

Her eyes are wide as she tries to pull out of the bindings, but she can't break them. No one could. I've always been good at shibari knots and seeing Mia Morrone at my mercy like this does something to me. It drives me wild with a primal and instinctive need to breed with her over and over like a fucking rabid animal.

"Killian," she breathes my name in protest again, begging me with my eyes. "What are you doing?"

"I thought you said you wanted to try it?"

Her throat bobs as she swallows. "Yes, but…" she trails off, shaking her head. "I'm scared."

My cock aches in my boxer briefs, which is so fucking wrong. I've always got a kick from fear, but I know that I have to be more gentle with Mia. She's a virgin, for fuck's sake. "You have a safe word. The moment you say it, I stop."

She sinks her teeth into her bottom lip, as if trying to decide whether she wants to stop this or not. "Okay," she says, nodding. "Carry on."

I chuckle at Mia's attempt to be so commanding, even when she has no control. Other than the fact that she can stop this at any moment. I may be driven by dark desires, but I follow the rules and always have a safe word.

I raise a brow. "What do you want me to do?"

That irritation flashes into her eyes again. "I don't know." She blows out a frustrated breath and then says, "I feel a little underdressed." Her eyes dip to my pants, which are bulging with my arousal. "Why don't you take some clothes off?" There's a bit of a challenge in her eyes, as she probably senses I don't normally take instruction.

I smile and walk closer to the bed. "Perhaps I will." I run a hand across the back of my neck. "After I've had some fun with you, Mia." I trace my fingers lightly over her inner thighs and her body quivers. "I'm going to blow your mind."

She moans softly; the sound spurring me on as I get onto the bed and kneel between her spread thighs.

"You are going to be so wound up, you'll beg me for my cock."

"Cocky much?" she asks, her cheeks flushing as she tries not to let me see how much my words affect her.

I arch a brow. "Yes, and for good reason."

Her nostrils flare as she shakes her head, but that irritation soon disappears the moment I flick my finger against her soaking wet core. "Killian," she murmurs my name, her dark brown eyes holding my gaze.

"Yes, baby girl?"

She shakes her head. "Stop messing with me."

I lick my lips and then grab hold of the fabric covering her virgin pussy, tearing it apart.

Mia gasps. "Killian! Those cost well over a hundred dollars."

I smirk. "Don't worry, I'll buy you more." I slide a finger inside of her and her face turns blank from pleasure as she writhes against the rope.

"Oh God," she mutters, eyes flickering shut.

I savor the image of her like this, memorizing it as it's the most beautiful thing I've ever seen. Her tanned cheeks are flushed a beautiful shade of pink and her chestnut brown hair is splayed across the white pillow. The bra she's wearing leaves nothing to the imagination, as I can make out the outline of her stiff nipples. And the way the rope looks crossing over her delicate, tanned skin makes me crazy.

Mia is right. Even though I hope to find a way around the obstacles in our way, I can't be sure that we can have this forever. No matter how badly either of us wants it.

Mia's mouth opens, and she moans as I thrust my finger in and out of her increasingly wet pussy. "Fuck," she curses.

I add two more fingers and she practically levitates off the bed. "You are so fucking sensitive when tied up like this, baby," I groan, burying my head between her thighs and lavishing my attention on her swollen clit. She tastes like pure fucking heaven as I move between her clit and her soaking wet entrance, tasting her.

Her hips buck more wildly toward me, forcing me to grab hold of them forcefully. "Stay still, baby girl."

There's a flash of something in her eyes as she licks her bottom lip. "Sorry, sir," she breathes, her voice almost breaking with desire.

It's crazy how naturally submissive she can be, considering she's as stubborn as a mule most of the time.

Mia isn't able to speak as she pants for air, watching me as I drive her wild. This is different from last night, as she's far more sensitive. I pull my fingers out of her and move my tongue through her soaking wet center, teasing her.

"Oh fuck, yes," she cries.

It figures she'd love being tied up since we're destined for one another and have been for years.

"Please," she begs, her eyes rolling back in her head. "Oh God, please."

I smirk at her begging and continue to push her higher and higher until I feel her muscles start to spasm around my fingers. That's when I stop, knowing I need to be deep inside of her before I let her come apart.

Her mouth falls open and she grunts. "What the hell?"

"No coming until I'm inside of you, baby girl."

The frustration melts and there's a little fear in her eyes. "Is it going to hurt?"

"Maybe at first, but if you like pain as much as you like being restrained, it won't matter." I get off the bed and stand at the foot of it, unbuttoning my shirt first.

Mia watches my every move, her lips slightly parted and her chest rising and falling with frantic breaths.

I drop my shirt onto her dress and then move to my pants, unbuttoning them slowly.

Mia visibly shivers as I drop my pants to the floor, revealing my tight black briefs framing my cock, which is as hard as stone.

"Do you like what you see?" I ask, tilting my head to the side.

Her mouth opens, and then shuts as if trying to find the words, and then she just nods.

I drop my briefs to the floor and my cock bobs forward, making Mia moan.

"How is it possible that it looks even bigger right now?" Mia asks.

I shake my head. "It's not." I get onto the bed and

position myself over her, my cock nudging at her soaking wet entrance.

Mia is shaking beneath me. "Killian."

"What, baby girl?"

"I need you so badly, it hurts."

I kiss her lips softly and then trail them lower, sucking on her nipples through the fabric of her bra. "You are so fucking beautiful," I breathe as I move to the other nipple and she whimpers.

"Please, sir," she says, begging me for my cock.

"What do you want, Mia?"

"I want your cock." She writhes against the restraints and the weight of my body pinning her to the bed. "Please, give me your cock."

"Such a filthy virgin begging to be fucked." I return to the position I was in before, allowing my cock to settle at the entrance of her cunt. I can feel the control slipping as the need to fulfill both our desires becomes almost unbearable. "I'm in control, baby girl."

She grunts in frustration as I hold her gaze.

"You belong to me, Mia, and after I've fucked that pretty little pussy, there will be no going back." I increase the pressure slightly, coating myself in her leaking arousal. "Do you understand?"

Her entire body shakes violently as she holds my gaze in anticipation, those beautiful brown eyes full of a mix of desire and fear. "Answer me, Mia."

"Yes, sir," she cries, her eyes clamping shut as she tries to move to find friction, but I hold her.

"Look into my eyes while I claim you."

Her eyes flicker open and I know I can't hold it any longer. I thrust my cock hard into her virgin cunt, stretching it open for the first time.

She cries out in a mix of pain and pleasure, her eyes going wide as I fill her to the hilt. Her muscles grip me so damn tight I have to grind my jaw just to stop myself from exploding instantly. Five fucking years I've waited for this. Five years to claim what always belonged to me.

"Fuck, Killian," she cries.

I don't know how to go slow, even though she's a virgin. I'm too far gone as I fuck her with fast, forceful strokes. All control I had is gone as I take everything I've wanted. My mouth covers hers as I swallow her cries of pain and pleasure, caressing my tongue against hers in a passionate kiss.

Mia's body becomes more relaxed beneath me as we kiss and I move my lips from hers lower, biting her collarbone enough to hurt. Her moans turning from cries of pain to cries of pleasure. All the while, she holds my gaze like a good little submissive.

"Fuck," she hisses, eyes going wide.

"I have wanted this too fucking long, Mia." My hips move in and out with jerkier, more frantic movements. I grab her throat, groaning at the sight of her with my hand around her throat like a collar. "You look fucking perfect being choked and tied up, baby."

She doesn't seem deterred by my roughness as I

tighten my grasp, cutting off her airways slightly. Her cunt starts to tighten around my shaft and it takes all my restraint not to come apart along with her, as I've barely even got started yet. "That's it, baby girl. Come for me." My balls slap against her skin, filling the room with the sound of our fucking.

Mia screams as her body comes apart, her eyes clamping shut as the pleasure overwhelms her. "Oh, fuck. Oh, yes," she cries over and over as her pussy squirts around my cock, making me growl.

I hold myself still inside of her, waiting for her to come down from the pleasure.

Once she's recovered, I release her throat. "I want to have you on all fours." I slide my cock out of her, which results in a cry of protest. "I want to spank that pretty ass while I fuck you." Mia can't move because of the ropes, so I lift her with them and position her how I want. "Just like that," I murmur.

She glances over her shoulder at me. "Killian, I don't know if I can take anymore."

I grab the back of her neck and thrust my cock deep inside of her. "You can and you will, Mia." I spank her ass hard and she groans. "I've hardly started yet. By the time I'm through with you, you won't be able to walk straight."

"Oh God," she moans as I use the rope to pull her harder into me, fucking her so deep which each and every thrust.

I part her ass cheeks and press my finger to her

forbidden back hole. "One day, I'm going to fuck this pretty little asshole, too."

Mia gasps and tries to move away, which makes me tighten my grasp on the ropes.

"I bet you'd love it, baby girl."

She shakes her head. "It's too big. It would hurt too much."

I spank her ass and groan when I see the red mark it leaves on her skin. "No, I'll get you nice and stretched using toys first and by the time I'm ready to fuck it, you'll beg me for it."

Her head falls back, and she moans as I increase the tempo of my strokes, fucking her harder and faster. My body losing control as I take what I've wanted for too long. Mia Morrone was always meant for me and right now, that statement has never felt more true.

We fit together as if we were made for each other, and that's what I've always believed since the academy. Mia is mine and I'm hers and the rest of the world can fuck off.

## 13

## MIA

*I*t feels like I'm floating above my body, watching as Killian drives me higher and higher toward the edge of no return. He's not gentle and I'm surprised how much I enjoy the raw passion as he loses himself in me.

Even though he's behind me, fucking me roughly, I have never felt more cherished or worshiped before. It makes little sense, especially since I'm bound in a way that robs me of all control.

Killian spanks me again with such force it should be painful, but it merely heightens the pleasure. I can hardly believe that the man I've longed for is taking my virginity.

"Killian," I moan his name.

His hand tightens around the back of my neck and he leans over my back, his breath teasing my ear lobe.

"You are such a good girl, taking my dick in that pretty little pussy so well."

My eyes clamp shut as I feel a rush of pleasure building beneath the surface of my skin. Killian's dirty talking is beyond arousing and the way he's bound me only increases the pleasure in ways I never knew possible. I love being at his mercy. It's a freeing sensation, being out of the driver's seat. Submitting all the control to another person and allowing him to have his way with me.

His cock is so deep inside of me, and each impale is harder and faster. I never imagined Killian would be particularly gentle, but my fantasies of this moment were so different. He's corrupting me in ways I couldn't have believed possible before tonight. The man fucking me is an animal.

"Do you like it rough, Mia?" he asks.

I groan, arching my back. "Yes, sir. It feels so good." My muscles quiver around his thick shaft and I know before long I won't be able to hold back. My nipples are so hard as the rope grazes against them, making my clit throb with more need. "I think I'm going to come," I moan, wishing I could use my hand to rub myself.

Killian thrusts all the way inside of me and then holds completely still, leaning down. "You only get to come when I say so, baby girl."

I shudder as the pleasure becomes almost unbearable as I long for more. "Please, Killian."

He spanks my ass three times on each cheek and it

only heightens my awareness of the excruciating pleasure waiting to erupt between my thighs. And then he
grabs my ass cheeks and parts them, spitting on my
asshole.

I tense as he teases a finger inside, sending a
completely new and filthy pleasure right through me.
"Oh," I murmur, conflicted over how I feel and what
he's doing to me. It shouldn't feel so good.

"Do you like that, Mia?" he asks, thrusting his finger
in deeper.

I groan. "Yes, sir."

He grunts and then adds another finger, stretching
my hole. "Such a dirty girl, enjoying my fingers in your
ass. I bet you'd love a butt plug in there while I fucked
your cunt."

I swallow hard, unsure what he's talking about.

Killian's hips move again as he starts to fuck me,
keeping his fingers lodged in my ass. "For now, you'll
have to come on my cock with my fingers in your ass."

"Fuck," I breathe, as my nipples stiffen and Killian
pushes me right toward the edge again.

"I want to watch while your virgin cunt comes apart
on my cock," he growls, his voice becoming deeper and
move gravelly.

Every nerve ending in my body feels alive and raw
as he pushes me over the edge, his cock thrusting into
me with so much force it's like he's trying to tear me in
half. "Fuck, Killian," I scream, unable to stop myself.
My body shakes with the force of my orgasm and I'm

sure for a moment that I may have stopped breathing as my brain short circuits.

"Oh, fuck, Mia. Your pussy is so fucking tight, squeezing me like a vise," Killian growls, sinking his fingertips so hard into my hips it feels like he's going to bruise them. "Take every drop of my cum in that tight little cunt."

I feel a flood of liquid shoot deep inside of me as he thrusts over and over again, draining every drop. We're not using protection, and that only hits me the moment he stops thrusting, and it's too late. It's crazy, especially given our situation. The last thing we need is an accidental pregnancy.

Killian's breathing is frantic behind me as silence falls across the room.

I swallow hard, heat blazing across every inch of my skin.

"That was so fucking hot," he murmurs, pulling his cock out of me and quickly undoing the knots on the rope binding me.

I glance down, noticing the angry red marks that are left across my entire body. As the pleasure begins to ease, pain takes over, and it's only then I realize it's burned my skin.

"Lie down," he instructs, but the hardness in his voice is no longer present.

I lie down on my back and Killian moves next to me, wrapping an arm around me and pulling me against his chest.

"Do these hurt?" he asks, running a gentle finger across one of the burn marks.

I nod. "A little."

His jaw clenches and then his eyes flash with something undetectable. "Perhaps I was a little rough."

I don't say a word as what does it say about me that I liked it so rough? Even now, as the full ache of the burns becomes more apparent, I can't regret a single moment of what we did. It was the most perfect first time, and I know I'm going to want to do it over and over again, perhaps for the rest of my life. My chest aches as I know that's never going to happen. Killian Callaghan can't be mine, no matter how much he insists he can be.

A Callaghan and a Morrone can't be together and that's just the painful reality of the world we live in.

---

"WHERE WERE YOU LAST NIGHT?"

Luca's voice makes me jump out of my skin as I push the front door shut. I turn to face him, knowing that I've got no idea what to say.

"A-At a friend's house."

His brow furrows, and he crosses his arms over his chest. "And what friend is that?"

*Shit.*

I don't have any friends in Chicago, at least not ones I'd stay with. I shake my head. "You don't know her."

His eyes narrow. "Mia, where were you?" The tone of voice he uses is deep and commanding and not like my youngest brother at all.

"I told you, with a friend."

He holds my gaze and I know if he questions me anymore, I might crack. I've never been good at lying. He sighs heavily and holds his hands up. "Fine, keep your secrets."

Thank fuck for that.

I shake my head. "Why are you lurking in the entrance hall, anyway?"

He raises a brow. "I was waiting for you. Father has been looking for you since last night." His lips pinch together. "I made an excuse and told him you were sick."

I want to kiss my brother for covering for me, as Father wouldn't have been so easy to lie to. And then I feel my stomach sink a little as Father never wants to speak with me. "What does he want?"

Luca's eyes flood with pity. "I think he's made a match for you."

It feels like all the blood drains from my body as I stare at my brother, feeling numb. I just spent last night with Killian, and it was the best night of my life. Now, my brother is telling me that my father has pledged my hand to another man. "Who is it?" I ask, hating how squeaky my voice sounds.

"Alejandro, I believe."

Even worse, it's a man who has wanted me for

years. A man who I can't marry, even if Father insists on it, not now I've had a taste of true bliss with the man I've been secretly in love with for so damn long.

I shake my head. "I can't."

Luca gives me a pitying smile. "I'm not sure you have a choice, piccola."

I grind my teeth as I hate when he calls me little one in Italian. "When did you tell him I'd see him?"

"I suggested you'd visit his office in the morning if you felt better." He raises a brow. "You've always been good at playing sick."

I narrow my eyes. "That's not true."

"It is. Remember when you didn't go to the academy for a month because you pretended you had glandular fever?"

I cross my arms over my chest. "I did have it."

"Bullshit," he says, smirking. "Get dressed and make sure you look like you've been unwell when you see him."

I shake my head. "You can be so annoying."

His smirk widens. "You know you love me, really."

As I walk past him, I stop. "Of course, but it doesn't make you any less annoying." With that, I walk up the stairs quickly and head for my bedroom, feeling numb at the prospect of being told today that I'm to marry Alejandro De León. It doesn't help that he's a friend, as my refusal is only going to be more hurtful. All I know is I can't marry him. And I have a feeling the moment

Killian finds out, he'll move heaven and earth to ensure that I don't.

I rush into my room and shut the door, resting my back against it. The only issue with that is that this war we're in could get even more dangerous the moment Killian tries to stop my arranged marriage. It would cause carnage and put the man I love in danger.

My heart gallops at one hundred miles an hour as I rush into the closet and change out of the dress I'd worn to meet Killian last night. I grab a sweatshirt and a pair of sweatpants, tossing them on before heading to the bathroom. My face is a mess since I didn't have any makeup to put on, so that should help with the appearance that I'm sick.

I wash my face and tie my hair up into a messy bun before heading out of the bedroom.

Father is far more intimidating than Luca, and I fear that he will see right through me. Once he tells me I'm to marry Alejandro, I'm going to tell him I can't. The only issue is, I can't tell him why I can't. At least, not the true reason. My steps falter as I get closer to his study, my heart in my throat.

I knock on the door and wait.

"Who is it?"

"It's me, Mia. Luca says you want to see me."

"Come in," he booms from the other side of the door.

I swallow hard, drawing a deep breath before

twisting the doorknob and opening it. "Sorry I couldn't come down last night. I wasn't feeling very well."

Father tilts his head slightly, observing me. "Do you feel better now?"

"A little," I reply, despite the fact my stomach is churning and making me feel sick.

"Good, take a seat." He gestures to the seat opposite his desk. "I have some important news concerning you."

I don't say a word, as I already know the news. The question is, how will my father react when I say no?

"I've found you a husband."

"A husband?" I murmur, twisting my fingers together in my lap.

He nods. "Yes, you knew this day would come. I've selected Alejandro De León for you to marry." He smiles as if he's giving me good news. "I know you were good friends at the academy and he will treat you well, amore mio."

I shake my head. "Father, I can't marry Alejandro."

His brow furrows. "Can't?" he asks. There's a lethal edge to his tone.

"It would be like marrying a brother." That is the only argument I have, and I know it's not a very strong one.

"Don't be so ridiculous, Mia." He cracks his knuckles. "Alejandro is a perfectly fine match. I selected him because I knew he would never hurt you. Many girls in your situation are married to men who…" He looks like he's searching for the right word, but he just shakes his head. "Very bad men."

I appreciate that he thinks he's doing me a favor, marrying me to a man who was a friend at the academy. He's right that I could have done a lot worse, but it's too painful to consider. Last night I had a taste of what my life could be with the man I love, and now my father is trying to rip it all away from me before it even starts.

"It just doesn't feel right, Father."

He shakes his head. "I don't care if it feels right or not. It is done."

I swallow hard, realizing I will get nowhere with him by arguing. "When is it to take place?"

"Two months' time here in Chicago." He gives me a wistful smile. "You will obviously live with him in Philadelphia."

*Two months.*

It's longer than I expected, which gives me the only thing I can hope for. Time to be with Killian and find out if he feels the same way I do. Time to figure out how to get out of this wedding. I hope it's enough time, because after last night, I no longer want to run from the man I've secretly loved. I want to hold on to him and never let go.

## 14

## KILLIAN

Three days after my date with Mia, and I'm desperate to see her again. The problem is, she won't answer my calls or texts. I had to wait until she left the house and now I'm following her and her sister in a cab to downtown Chicago.

Camilla is in town, so I assume she's going shopping with her sister.

Normally, I'd follow her and watch from afar, but I'm done with that shit. Mia needs to be punished for ignoring me, and I can't wait to dole out that punishment. If Mia thinks she's witnessed how dark I can get with a bit of bondage and a light spanking, she's in for a surprise.

Her town car comes to a halt out the front of Bloomingdale's, and I lean forward. "Pull over here, lad."

The taxi driver's eyes narrow at my lack of notice, but he pulls over despite the heavy traffic.

"How much do I owe you?" I ask.

"Twenty bucks." I pull out a fifty and pass it to him. "Keep the change," I say, as I slip out of the cab, monitoring Mia as she disappears into the building with her little sister following just behind.

This should be interesting, trying to speak with Mia while she's with one of her family members. Not to mention, Sandro, her bodyguard, is with her, but if any of the other trips to the mall I've watched her on are a sign of what to expect, he'll end up in the cafe stuffing donuts and drinking coffee while the girls shop. It should give me a chance to sneak into Mia's changing room and make sure she doesn't ignore any of my texts ever again.

My jaw clenches as I can't believe how crazy this girl is making me. I walk into the department store and call the elevator, knowing exactly which floor Mia and Camilla will head to. The third level is where she shops normally, so I push the button and ride up to that floor.

The elevator opens and I slip out, keeping my head down as I search for my target. As always, they've already got arms full of dresses and clothes to try on as I spot them over the far side of the store. Now, all I can do is wait and try to slip into the dressing room unnoticed to speak to Mia.

It doesn't take long for them to gather too many clothes to carry and head back toward the dressing room. Thankfully, it's quiet and there's no one monitoring the entrance to the dressing rooms, which means I can slip in easily.

I glance under the cabin to ensure I get the right one, instantly recognizing Mia's favorite black pumps. The same pumps she wore when I fucked her in that hotel room. I try the door, which is locked, but then pull a picklock out of my pocket and quickly unlock the changing room door.

Mia has her back to me as she pulls off her top and tosses it to one side.

My cock hardens instantly and suddenly I forget why I'm even here. All I want is to fuck her against the wall and make her come on my cock right here in the changing rooms with her sister nearby. It's crazy and insane and yet it's all I can think of.

"Hey, baby girl," I murmur softly.

Mia yells slightly as she turns around, eyes wide.

"Everything okay, Mia?" Camilla calls.

Her eyes dart from side to side as if she's trying to work out how to escape. "Yes, fine." She steps toward me, brow furrows. "What are you doing in here?" She hisses.

"You left me no choice, baby girl."

Her nostrils flare. "Everything has changed."

I arch a brow. "Everything has changed in three days?"

Mia's eyes flood with what I can only deduce as pain. "Everything changed the moment I stepped back into my home," she whispers, shaking her head. "I'm engaged."

Red hot fury slams into me as I move toward her quickly and grab her hips, pinning her against the back wall of the changing room. "What?"

Mia winces. "Keep your voice down."

I can't even consider keeping my voice down when a rage so fucking intense is flooding me at being told the woman who belongs to me is engaged to someone else. "Who is it?" I hiss.

She searches my eyes, unshed tears glistening in them. "Killian, we knew this-"

I wrap my hand around her throat and squeeze, making her eyes widen. "Tell me," I demand.

"Alejandro," she rasps out.

I release her throat and pace the small changing room, wishing that I'd acted quicker. "When?"

"Two months' time," she replies and when I glance back at her, she's rubbing her throat where I'd grabbed her.

Guilt hits me as I realize I was taking my rage out on her, even though none of this is her fault. "I'm sorry." I walk toward her, clenching my jaw. "I just can't let the wedding go ahead."

She tilts her head. "We always knew this would happen."

I shake my head. "No, I always intended to claim you before it happened." I step toward her, drawn in like a magnet, unable to resist the pull. "It doesn't mean you have to ignore my calls and texts."

She shrugs. "I thought it would be easier."

I pin her against the wall and press my body against hers. "Easier for who, baby?"

Her throat bobs as she searches my eyes. "It hurts too much teasing ourselves with this fantasy."

My chest aches at the heartbreak in her voice. I've always suspected that Mia felt the same way as I do, but I've never been sure. "It's worth it, Mia." I kiss her softly, pouring everything I feel for her into it. "You belong to me, and I'll tear the fucking world down to ensure that the wedding doesn't go ahead. Do you understand?"

"Killian," she breathes my name.

"Tell me you understand," I order, my voice raspy as my desire heightens.

She nods. "I understand."

I lift her off the floor and kiss her neck, knowing that I can't leave this changing room without fucking her. I don't care that her sister is just down the hall in another cubicle. All I care about is claiming the woman I love.

"Not here," she murmurs, trying to push me away from her.

"Yes," I growl back, biting her collarbone. "I need you right now."

Her eyes grow wide. "My sister will hear."

"Not if you are quiet." I kiss lower, moving toward her firm breasts.

She gasps as I pull down the cup of her bra and suck on her pert nipples, her fingers gently tugging through my hair as she loses herself to the sensation. I unclasp the bra from behind and then suck on her other nipple, enjoying the way her body responds to every caress.

"Killian," she murmurs my name, desire clear in her tone.

I drag my tongue down her abdomen and sink to my knees in front of her, groaning when I see how wet her panties are already. "So wet for me, baby girl," I whisper before yanking them to the side and thrusting a finger inside of her.

She claps a hand over her mouth to stifle the moan that escapes her lips.

I suck on her clit and she groans louder than she should, her back arching as she presses her needy cunt harder into my mouth. I grab her hips and force them hard against the wall, controlling her the way that my dark side craves.

There may not be any rope here, but there are other ways to restrain a submissive. "Don't move," I hiss.

Mia stills at my order and I thrust a second finger inside her, continuing to use my tongue to drive her wild.

Her thighs begin to quiver, warning me she's already close to coming apart, so I stop.

Which earns me a frustrated grunt as she glares down at me. "What are you doing?" she asks in hushed tones.

I stand and unzip my pants, freeing my throbbing cock. "Not until my dick is buried in that sweet little cunt, baby girl," I murmur, kissing her lips.

She moans softly into my mouth as my tongue thrusts in and out.

I grab hold of her hips and lift her, forcing her to wrap her legs around my waist. The head of my cock settles at the entrance of her dripping wet pussy and I break the kiss, holding her gaze.

"Be quiet, Mia." And then I thrust into her, burying every inch deep inside of her.

She yelps at the sudden invasion and I swallow the sound with my mouth, kissing her to stop her from giving us both away.

"Are you alright, Mia?" Camilla calls from the other stall.

I stop kissing her, remaining still inside of her to allow Mia to reply.

"Yes, I'm fine!" she calls back, and then there's silence as Mia shakes her head. "This is insane," she whispers.

"Don't deny you love the thrill of it, baby." I tighten my grasp on her hips and then begin to lift her up and down my shaft.

"Oh God," she murmurs, eyes rolling back in her head.

Her pussy is so wet that her arousal is dripping down my balls.

I move my lips to her ear. "You are so fucking wet, Mia. I can't wait to feel you come with my cock buried deep in that pussy, while your sister is mere yards away. Completely unaware that you're fucking a Callaghan, while you are engaged to another man."

She moans softly, her eyes flickering shut as I drive myself into her harder and faster.

"But, no matter what bullshit deal your father has made, it means nothing," I hiss, the possessive rage I'd felt earlier returning as I rut into the woman I own. "Because you are mine," I growl, trying to keep my voice down but struggling. "Do you understand?"

"Yes, sir," she mutters, her back arching against the wall as I drive her higher and higher.

"Good girl," I purr, before licking a path from her ear right to her collarbone and then biting hard.

She yelps softly and then I kiss her, silencing anymore sounds she might make that will give us away.

I know getting caught isn't an option, not until I figure out to how to break her engagement and have her for myself.

Her muscles begin to flutter around my shaft, warning me she's approaching the brink of no return.

"Fuck, baby girl, your pussy is gripping me like a vise," I breathe, thrusting into her even harder.

Her moans are quiet and breathy, but still too loud.

I kiss her again and then murmur against her lips. "I want you to come for me."

Her breathing becomes more labored and her eyes search mine as I drive her closer.

"I want you to come on my cock right here in the middle of this department store dressing room like the dirty girl you are."

"Killian," she moans.

I kiss her then, knowing that's she about to explode.

Her body shudders against mine as she comes apart and a flood a liquid squirts from her pussy all down my black pants.

I'm too lost in her to care about the mess we've made as I bite her lip hard and pump my hips two more times before spilling deep inside of her.

I grunt and groan, unable to contain the animal sounds as I fill her with my cum.

We're both so wrapped up in each other, we clearly don't hear anything outside the room.

Until Camilla bangs on the door and we both become statues pinned to the wall. "Are you sure you are okay in there?" she calls.

"Yes, I'm fine. Just trying the last few things."

Camilla grumbles something to herself and then shouts, "Fine, I'm going to keep searching for the perfect dress. None of these I like."

The tension eases the moment we hear her walk away, and then Mia surprises me by laughing the most beautiful laugh.

"What's so funny, baby girl?"

She shakes her head. "I can't believe we just did that."

I arch a brow. "You enjoyed it, though, didn't you?"

She sinks her teeth into her bottom lip and nods. "It was so hot," she says, her eyes darkening with desire again.

I slip my cock out of her and pull her panties back into place. "Now you have to spend all day with my cum dripping into your panties."

She moans softly, holding my gaze. "Good."

I clench my jaw as my desire begins to grow again and I know if I don't get out of here soon, I'll end up fucking her again. "Don't ignore me again." I grab her hips and pull her close. "We will figure it out, okay?"

She nods, her throat bobbing slightly. "Okay."

I kiss her once more and then take a step away.

Mia gasps softly when she notices the wet patch on my jeans. "I think I made a mess."

I smirk. "Yes, and I love it." With that, I turn away and reach for the door. "I'll see you soon, baby girl."

And then I slip out of the dressing room and away from the woman that drives me insane with need. Camilla is too caught up in looking at dresses to notice as I breeze past her and straight into the elevator.

It's clear my obsession with Mia is becoming more dangerous. If I keep on like this, we'll end up caught.

The question is, how am I going to break this fucking engagement and secure her for myself?

## 15

## MIA

*I*t feels like time stands still as the car races toward Mercy hospital.

*Cancer.*

Massimo's announcement came as a huge shock, but what upset me the most is that all three of my brothers already knew about his cancer. Why is it that us girls are always the last to know everything, even something as huge as this?

Perhaps foolishly, I always thought Father was invincible. It's the way he acts and yet he's been brought down and forced into a coma all by a disease.

Camilla is crying and clutching my hand and I feel like I need to be strong for her, but it's tearing me up inside. We lost our mom was too young, and our father has been the only parent we've known.

"Is this real?" Camilla asks.

I pull her toward me and hug her. "It's going to be okay, Camilla."

She sobs harder and I wonder if anything I could have said would have helped right now.

When the car stops at Mercy, we're both quick to get out and follow Massimo, who got here first to the ward where they've admitted him.

"How long have you known?" I ask as we walk toward the reception.

Massimo's jaw clenches. "Two days. He wanted to wait until he got his test results."

"The results were obviously bad, considering he's in here?"

"Yes." It's all Massimo says as he marches up to the reception and demands to see Father.

When he returns, he shakes his head. "Only three visitors at a time." He pauses, glancing between us all. "Shall us guys go in first and then you and Camilla after?"

"Sure," I say, squeezing Camilla's hand and leading her toward the seating area where Paisley follows. Paisley hasn't said a word.

"I can't believe this," Camilla says as she stares at the floor.

I shake my head. "Me neither."

As always, they left the women out of the loop, even if it was only for two days. "Did you know?" I ask, glancing at Paisley.

She sinks her teeth into her lip. "Only about an

hour before dinner. Massimo told me for some reason."

I sigh heavily, and a tense silence falls between us as we wait for the men to return. After what feels like forever, they finally return.

All three of them look grave, and I stand and approach Massimo. "How is he?"

He shakes his head. "They've got him in an induced coma. Prepare yourselves."

Camilla looks terrified as Massimo wraps his arm around Paisley. "We'll head home. Take as long as you need. I've got Sandro on his way with a car."

I nod in reply and steer my sister through the double doors to the ward where our father is. My heart thuds erratically as we get closer to the room where he is, and I can't help but gasp when I see him through the glass in the door.

"He looks so frail," I murmur, pushing open the door. "How did I not know he was sick?"

Camilla squeezes my hand. "Because he hid it well, I guess?"

I swallow hard and sink into one of the chairs next to his bed. "He can make it, though. You know how tough he is."

Camila smiles, but it doesn't reach her eyes as she sighs heavily. "They say his odds are bad."

"Fuck the odds," I reply.

Camilla shakes her head. "How is it you've always been such a positive person?"

I shrug. "I don't know. Would you rather I be negative?"

"Of course not. I just find it hard to be positive when something so awful has happened." She rubs her face in her hands. "It's hard to think that Father might not be around long."

I grit my teeth as I stare at the man who has always cared for us, even if sometimes his heart is in the wrong place. "He told me last week that I am to be married."

Camilla's eyes widen and she looks at me, tears still streaming down her face. "No, it's too soon."

"He said two months' time I'm to marry Alejandro."

She looks pensive. "Oh, it's far better than I expected. At least you know him and he will—"

"No, I can't marry him."

Camilla's brow creases as she regards me. "Why not?"

"I love someone else." I can't keep it from Camilla, no matter how fucked up the situation is. She's my sister and I tell her everything.

"Who?" she asks, her lips pursing a little.

I wince as I glance at my father's lifeless body in the bed. "You don't think he can hear us, do you?"

Camilla glances at her and then stands, nodding to the doorway.

We walk out into the corridor and she sets her hands on her hips. "Spill, Mia."

"It's Killian Callaghan."

Camilla gasps and then her face pales. "That's a problem," she murmurs.

"Tell me about it." I slump into a chair outside in the corridor and rest my head back against the wall. "I don't know what to do."

"Did it have to be a Callaghan of all the people in the world?"

I shut my eyes and contemplate the question, but I know it's a stupid one. You can't help who you fall for. Killian is right that we've been drawn to each other since the academy. Even if I haven't seen him for five years, the moment I set eyes on him again, it was like my world stood still. Fireworks ignited, and I knew I couldn't ignore it this time, no matter how much easier it was. "Unfortunately, it seems so."

Camilla seems stunned into silence as she sits down next to me, shaking her head. "You know, I think we're both going to be in a lot of trouble."

I raise a brow. "Why's that?"

She bites her bottom lip. "I've fallen for someone, too."

"At the academy?"

She nods. "And he's kind of off limits and also totally fucking crazy."

I laugh. "You've fallen for someone totally crazy?" I shake my head. "Who is he?"

"Oh God, I don't think I can tell you."

I nudge her in the ribs. "Oh, come on, it can't be worse than a Callaghan."

Her cheeks flush a dark pink and she looks like she's about to combust. "It's Gavril Nitkin."

I turn numb at the mention of the most sadistic professor at the academy, struggling to process what Camilla just told me. The man is renowned for being cold, calculated, and practically in love with torturing people. "Are you insane?"

I see the hurt in her eyes at the question and immediately regret it.

"No, it just happened." She shrugs. "He's not as bad as everyone thinks."

I scoff at that. "Do you know in fifth grade he took me down to a basement and strung me up by my wrists for an entire day just because I was chewing gum?" I shake my head. "He's not right, Camilla."

"Maybe I like how he is," she mutters, looking down at her hands in her lap.

I don't ask what she means by that, partially because I'm afraid to learn the answer. Camilla is only eighteen years old and Gavril has to be more than twice her age. I'm no prude and I understand that people can't help who they fall for. In fact, I know it better than most, but a professor seems a stretch too far. Especially that professor.

"Does he feel the same about you?" I ask.

She shrugs. "I'm not sure."

"How long have you been with him?" I ask.

"About two months."

I clench my jaw, realizing that I'm being a jerk for

criticizing her choice, especially after I just told her that I'm in love with a Callaghan. "Sorry for being a dick," I say.

She looks at me. "You are right. He's different." Her throat bobs as she swallows hard. "But, I think I am too."

"Different how?" I ask.

Her cheeks turn a deep red and I realize she's talking about sexually different. "It's embarrassing."

I nod in response. "You know you can tell me anything. I won't judge you."

"I think I'm a masochist," she murmurs, shaking her head. "It's weird, I know."

I draw in a deep breath, as it's exactly what I'd expected her to say. Professor Nitkin has always been a sadist, so only a masochist could fit his sick and twisted desire. It was rumored while I attended that they had caught him cutting one of his assistants as he fucked her in the basement, tied up. A shudder races through my body.

I can't quite believe that my sweet, innocent little sister would really be into that kind of treatment. "It's not weird. Everyone is different when it comes to sex." It's hard to believe Camilla isn't a virgin anymore. Only a short while ago, I lost my virginity, but that's not because I didn't have the opportunity. I think deep down I was always holding out for the man who stole my first kiss when I was fifteen years old.

I recall the way it felt when Killian tied me up the

way he did and the spankings he gave me. It was intoxicating and arousing.

"Do you think we'll be okay?" Camilla asks.

My brow furrows as I look at her. "What do you mean?"

She sighs heavily. "If you break your engagement to Alejandro for Killian, will it break up our famiglia?"

I swallow hard, as it's something that's been weighing heavily on my mind. "I'm not sure. You saw what happened to Imalia."

"And they won't like it if I want to be with Gavril." Camilla twists her fingers in her lap. "He's Russian and won't bring the famiglia any advantage."

It's true, but it probably isn't as bad as my match. No matter how much I try to tell myself that somehow it will all work out in the end, I can't help but feel that if I want to be with Killian, then I have to sacrifice my family. "Whatever happens, we'll always have each other, right?" I ask.

She meets my gaze and smiles weakly. "Of course. Nothing would stop me from seeing you."

I draw in a deep breath. "And nothing could stop me from seeing you. I just fear our brothers won't be so open to the idea." I glance up through the window at our father, who is completely lifeless. "Or Father."

Camilla clears her throat. "What will be will be." She tilts her head slightly. "Paisley seems nice. Do you like her?"

I smile at the sudden change of subject. "Yes, she

suits Massimo well. He's just lucky he's a man and can choose who he marries."

Camilla taps her finger against her chin. "I'm not sure that's totally true. If he'd chose a Callaghan, there would have been an uproar."

She's right. Even if deep down I don't want to admit it. Killian and I have been playing make believe if either of us really think we'll ever end up together. Our world is cruel and ruthless and feuds like the one that exists between my famiglia and his can't be over-come, not even by a love as passionate and true as ours.

"I hate to admit it, but I think you are right." I rub my face in my hands. "What the hell am I going to do?"

Camilla gives me a pitying smile. "If you are meant to be together, then you have to find a way."

I raise my brow. "Since when did you become so romantic?"

She smiles. "I've always been a romantic, deep down."

I nod. "I always tried not to be, as I knew marrying for love was never really in the cards for me."

"It's unfair, isn't it?" Camilla asks.

"This world that we've been born into is unfair." I grimace. "I mean, look at what our family profits from. Trafficking women no different from me or you. I hate it."

"So do I," Camilla says, nodding. "Maybe we'd be better off without the famiglia."

I grit my teeth, as forsaking our famiglia would solve a lot of problems, but at the same time, it seems too hard.

The idea of never seeing my brothers or Father again hurts, no matter what they put me through. "It would be difficult."

"At least we'd be free," Camilla murmur, as a tense silence falls between us.

She's right, but I never even considered forsaking them all so I could be with Killian. It's so final and drastic and yet it's possibly the only way out of this mess.

Killian means the world to me. The question is, does he mean more to me than my own family?

## 16

## KILLIAN

"This is certifiably insane."

Rourke nods. "I know, but what choice do we have?"

"No choice, it would seem," Kieran says, tossing his keys up in the air. "Shall I drive?"

I raise a brow. "You know I always drive."

Kieran shakes his head. "Not today."

Rourke nods. "I prefer Kieran driving."

I sigh heavily, narrowing my eyes as Kieran sticks his tongue out at me. "Whatever. You two just can't handle the speed."

"I want to be alive for the birth of my child, if that's too much to ask," Rourke says.

I tilt my head. "Then we shouldn't be going to this meeting."

A muscle in Rourke's jaw clenches. "You know it

can't be avoided. Spartak has to be part of the plan. It just turns out Remy arranged it before we could."

I rub a hand across the back of my neck. As when we approached the Morrone family, we always knew Spartak would need to be brought into the loop if we were going to stop his nephew. We just didn't expect for Remy to arrange it first. At first it felt like we were in control of this situation, but the Italians have seized the control from us and it's unnerving.

"I have a bad feeling about this," I mutter.

Kieran sighs. "Don't we all. Let's get the show on the road."

I swallow hard, contemplating the last time I saw Spartak Volkov. It was at the engagement announcement Father made for Maeve and Maxim. That event feels like a lifetime ago, considering everything that has happened since. The man is a sadistic son of a bitch, but I fear we may have been too rash to act when we found out about Father's death.

I slide into the back of the Mustang as Rourke takes the passenger's seat. "Make sure you get us there in time," I say, glaring at my brother in the rearview mirror.

He shakes his head and turns the key in the ignition as his car roars to life. An eerie silence fills the car as we head toward our reckoning. Spartak Volkov isn't known for playing nice with people who stand against him, and the war between us has been raging for months now.

It's a short fifteen minute drive to the docks, where

we agreed to meet at a vacant warehouse, since it's neutral territory. Kieran parks just outside it and cuts off the engine. "It looks like the Russians are here, but not the Italians," he says, glancing at Spartak's town car, which is vacant.

"They must be inside, then." I open the door and slide out. "What are you two cowards waiting for?"

There's no way I'm sitting outside waiting for the Morrone family to arrive. The last thing we want is our enemies thinking we're soft.

Rourke appears to agree as he gets out and heads toward the door, but Kieran looks reluctant, staring at the warehouse. "Are you sure that's a good idea?"

"Whats wrong, little bro, scared of the Russians?"

He glares at me. "They killed our father."

I grab his shoulder and look him right in the eye. "They wouldn't dare attack us on neutral ground." I squeeze lightly. "Now get your shit together."

His Adam's apple bobs as he swallows, but he nods and slips out of the car. Rourke leads us into the old warehouse and Kieran remains by my side. He's always differed from the two of us since he's the baby of the family, sheltered from the danger of our world until they killed Father.

Spartak has his back turned to us, speaking in Russian with Maxim as we enter. Maxim's expression turns sinister the moment he sets eyes on us and he nods his head, forcing his Father to turn and face us.

"Well, look who the cat dragged in," Spartak says, glaring at us menacingly.

Rourke's jaw flexes as he steps forward. "Are we going to be civil about this or not?" he asks, acting like the more mature of the two. Ironic, really, considering Spartak is at least sixteen years older than Rourke.

Maxim steps forward and crosses his arms over his chest. "Of course, we agreed to a peace talk."

Spartak smiles, but it's the most unnerving expression. "And unlike the people who called this meeting, we don't attack our enemies during a peace talk."

The tension heightens as he's talking about the peace talks he had with the Morrone family, which resulted in Maxim being shot. It only serves to remind just volatile the relationships are between us all. One wrong move could spell disaster.

I glance at my watch. "Where the fuck is Morrone, anyway?"

Spartak's eyes narrow. "How the fuck would we know?"

I clench my jaw and all three of us glare at the two men opposite. There's no way that this will go well if the Morrone family doesn't turn up soon.

And then, as if summoned by the mention of their name, Luca enters the warehouse alone. I'm surprised when I don't see any other Morrone.

"You," Spartak snarls, eyes flashing and fists clenching. "Where are the rest of your family?"

Maxim places a hand on his father's shoulder.

"On the way." Luca crosses his arms over his chest and gives him a cocky smirk. "Massimo will be here any moment." He glances at his watch. "After all, you guys are early."

I grit my teeth as Luca is right. We're early but then I expected everyone to be early for a meeting like this.

After another couple of tense, silent minutes, Massimo strides in alone. My brow furrows, as I wonder whether the fuck Remy is. After all, he's the don of the family. He should be here for such an important meeting. Massimo stands by his brother and they talk in hushed tones. The tension in the room has only mounted the longer we waited and Spartak keeps flexing his fingers like he's ready for a fight.

Not to mention, Rourke hasn't taken his hand off his gun for at least five minutes.

Massimo clears his throat, drawing everyone's attention. "Since we're all here, shall we get to it?"

Spartak smirks. "So now you are taking control, are you, Massimo?" His brow furrows. "Where is your father?"

"He's unwell," Massimo replies, running a hand across the back of his neck. "And somehow Adrik knew about it and accosted me only fifteen minutes ago outside the hospital."

Rourke's eyes narrow. "How would he know that?"

Massimo shrugs. "Beats me, maybe the Cartel?"

"What hospital is he at?" Spartak asks.

"Mercy, why?" he replies.

Spartak nods. "That's how they know, as Hernandez owns shares in the hospital."

Massimo's jaw clenches. "I'll have him moved."

Maxim steps forward. "Bad idea. If you move him, they might get suspicious."

"Fine." The Italian crosses his arms over my chest. "The question is, what are we going to do about Adrik and the Cartel?"

"Have you learned anything new since we last spoke?" Rourke asks.

"We found out one of our caporegime was leaking information to him. I have him strung up in my basement."

Spartak clears his throat. "If you need a hand interrogating him, I'd be happy to help."

Trust the sadistic son of a bitch to offer help to his fucking enemy just so he can torture someone. The guy is not right in the head and never fucking has been. It's hard to believe my father really wanted to go into business with someone so unhinged.

"I've got it handled, thanks," Massimo says.

Spartak nods.

"Apparently, Adrik isn't ready to strike yet." Massimo glares in our direction and I can't help but feel hatred toward him, even though we're trying to put the past behind us. "The bombs he's working on need another couple of months."

I breathe a sigh of relief at the news. "That's grand news if I ever I heard it."

Massimo nods. "Yes, but it doesn't solve the issue that if we take down Adrik, we have to take down the Cartel too."

"We get our supplies from the Vasquez Cartel in Mexico. If the Estrada Cartel cuts us off, we're screwed." Kieran says.

"All of us get our supply from the south of the border. They control all drugs coming in and out of Mexico," Maxim says.

Massimo clears his throat. "We don't get our supply from Mexico."

I glare at him, brow furrowing. This is news to me that the Italians don't get their product from the south of the border.

"Then where the fuck do you get it from?" Spartak asks what all of us are thinking.

He shakes his head. "That's not something I'm going to disclose, no offense intended."

"Great, so you're the only ones who won't lose out if we piss off the cartel?" Kieran asks, stepping forward so he's standing shoulder to shoulder with me and Rourke. "Why should we trust you aren't just trying to screw us?"

"You forget that your brother is the one who approached me with this, not the other way around," Massimo replies.

That seems to shut Kieran up as his head bows slightly.

"To answer your question about how we do this

without pissing off the cartel, I think we need to go over Adrik's head."

Spartak runs a hand through his hair. "How exactly are we going to do that?"

"Hernandez has had all of us running around for his loyalty, when he never intended to give it to any of us." Massimo crosses his arms over his chest, glancing at each of us individually. "We change it up and invite him to another meeting, but this time, all three of our families will be in attendance."

"We tell him we know about his plan with Adrik and persuade him to back out of it," Maxim says.

"Exactly. Hernandez is greedy, but he's not stupid. The bombs aren't ready and he can't hold off all three of our families alone, even with the power of Mexico behind him."

Rourke clears his throat. "It's a sound plan, but we'll have to offer him something. He won't back out for nothing."

"We'll come to that bridge when it happens," Massimo says, his attention on Spartak. "What do you think?"

"I think it's fucking risky." He shrugs. "How do you know your man was telling you the truth about the bombs?"

Massimo's jaw clenches. "I've known the guy my entire life. He was telling the truth."

"Fair enough." Spartak nods. "Who will call the meeting with the Estrada family?"

"I will. At the casino," Massimo says.

Spartak's eyes flash. "The last time I stepped foot in that fucking casino, my son got shot."

"Things are different now. If we are going to work together, we need to have some level of trust."

"Trust?" Spartak's eyes widen. "Your brother." He glares at Luca. "Shot me on my wedding day and you expect me to trust you?" He laughs.

The tension heightens again, and it feels like we're right back at square one.

Massimo grabs hold of his younger brother's arm. "This won't work if we're at each other's throats."

Rourke nods. "I agree with the Italian, unfortunately." He glances at Spartak. "My father was murdered by your—"

"Don't go there again. I've told you countless times I was not behind the death of Ronan. What good would it do me killing the man I expected to partner with?" His eyes narrow. "I don't break my deals, Callaghan."

Rage coils through me, but I know that it's probably the truth. Whoever killed our father was clever and intended to drive a wedge between the families of Chicago. And the more we learn, the more certain I am that Adrik was behind it.

"I thought we already deduced it's quite possible that Adrik was behind your father's death. It would make sense," Massimo points out.

Rourke nods. "It would, but if you'd have let me finish, I was going to say that he was murdered by someone in your organization, even if it was Adrik, and I'm still willing to put it aside and work with you." His eyes narrow. "Neither you nor your son are dead, so I don't really see what you're whining about."

Spartak's jaw clenches, his fists bunching as he makes a move toward my brother.

I reach for my gun, but Maxim stops him. "He's right."

The rage in Spartak's eyes is dangerous as he glares at our family.

"Shall I make the arrangements?" Massimo asks.

"No, I will." Spartak's eyes narrow. "You will all come to Podolka, and I will arrange for Hernandez to be there."

All three of us tense up at the mention of the club where our father was found dead. I'm about to protest, but Rourke agrees before I can say a word. "It's a deal."

I look at my elder brother, wondering why on earth he'd agree to set foot in that place.

"Fine, Podolka it is," Massimo agrees.

It appears to be the end of the meeting, as everyone disperses except for me, Rourke, and Killian. "Why the fuck did you agree to go to that place?" I ask through gritted teeth.

Rourke looks me dead in the eye. "Because if we want to survive this, we have to make sacrifices, brother." He claps me on the shoulder. "We don't have a choice."

I clench my fist by my side, angry that we let the Russians push us around. It's bad enough having to work with the Italians, but now we're letting Spartak call the fucking shots. The only possible positive about this entire shit show is that if the Morrone family and the Callaghan family are working together, perhaps there's hope, after all, for me and Mia.

## 17

## MIA

*I* walk into the kitchen and gasp when I see Leo's face. "What the hell happened to you?" He has a dark bruise over his right eye and a cut just beneath the left one and his nose is bruised.

His jaw works, and he glares at me. "Massimo."

"Boys." I shake my head. "What was it this time?"

"I don't want to talk about it."

I slide onto a stool at the kitchen island opposite him and cross my arms over my chest. "When are you two ever going to learn that fighting gets you nowhere?"

Leo doesn't answer me, merely takes a long sip from what I assume is a glass of scotch.

"A bit early for alcohol, isn't it?" I ask.

"It's never too early."

I sigh. "Is there anything I can do to stop you mopping about?"

"Leaving me alone might help."

Leo can be a nightmare when he's in one of these moods, but the one thing I know he can't refuse, no matter how foul a mood he's in, is ice cream.

I stand and head to the refrigerator, opening the freezer compartment and digging out a pot of his favorite flavor, peanut butter. "How about sharing some ice cream?"

He rolls his eyes, but there's a faint whisper of a smile on his lips as I return with two spoons.

I dig in first and soon enough Leo is cheering up as we talk about the first time he and Massimo had a serious fight. They broke a priceless vase and Father lost it.

However, the mention of Father puts a dampener on the atmosphere.

"Do you think he'll make it?" Leo asks.

I have to believe that there's a chance he can fight this. He's only fifty years old, which is too young to die. I always thought he'd be around forever. "He'll fight," I say.

Leo nods. "Of course, he's the strongest man I know."

I set my hand on top of Leo's and squeeze. "We'll all be okay, no matter what happens." I give him a weak smile. "We've got each other."

He smiles back, but it's tinged with sadness. "True." He delves in for a large scoop of ice cream as silence falls between us again.

Someone clears their throat in the doorway, and I turn to see Carter, our butler, standing there. "Mia, there's a gentleman here to see you."

My brow furrows and butterflies ignite as I wonder if Killian would be crazy enough to come here. "Who is it?"

"Alejandro De León."

Fuck.

Why the hell is he here?

"Oh, I see." I glance at Leo, wondering if he has any idea why Alejandro would be here.

Leo shrugs. "Don't look at me. Father arranged all of that."

I sigh heavily and get off my stool. "Thanks Carter, I'll see what he wants."

My stomach churns as I head toward the entrance hall, as I don't know why he'd be here. He's standing with his back to me, looking at an oil painting on the wall.

I clear my throat. "Not to sound rude, but what are you doing here?"

Alejandro spins around and smiles at me. "Hey, fiancée."

I wince at that, shaking my head. "I can't marry you, Alejandro."

His brow furrows. "What?"

"You're like a brother to me." I twist my fingers together in front of me. "It's just not right."

He paces toward me and grabs my shoulders,

searching my eyes. "Don't tell me you're still hung up over that piece of shit, Callaghan?"

I step back, freeing myself of his grasp. "So what if I am?"

"Listen, Mia. It's done. My father has agreed to a lucrative deal for your hand with your father, and there's no breaking it."

Rage coils through me as even a man I thought was my friend will happily force me into a marriage I don't want.

"We will be happy, I'm sure of it." He reaches for my hand. "I can make you happy."

I pull my hand away and take a step back. "No."

His jaw clenches. "What do you mean, no?"

I shake my head. "I don't want to marry you. It's that simple."

"Where is your father?" Alejandro demands.

It feels like a slap in the face as he wants to go over my head and speak with him about it. "In a coma in hospital." I reply, placing my hands on my hips.

Alejandro's eyes soften. "What happened?"

"Cancer," I reply, my voice cracking slightly.

He moves toward me to comfort me and places a hand gently on my arm. "I'm sorry, Mia. Is it bad?"

I nod. "They're not hopeful, but I think he can fight it."

At that moment, Massimo walks through the front door, and I breathe a sigh of relief. I hate being alone with Alejandro, especially as he insists we have to marry. "Massimo, Alejandro is here."

He smirks slightly. "I can see that. What's the occasion, De León?"

"I came to see my fiancée." His expression turns serious. "However, she insists she won't marry me."

Massimo's jaw clenches as he glares at me and that's when I notice the bruise on his right cheek. Turns out Leo must have got a punch in, too. "Did she now?" He shakes his head. "Why don't the three of us head to the study to discuss the matter?"

I don't like the look in my brother's eyes. It scares me and suggests that he has every intention of forcing me to go ahead with Father's plan to marry me off to Alejandro. I follow the two of them reluctantly into the back of the house and our father's study.

"Have a seat," Massimo says, then turning to me. "Both of you."

I swallow hard and then take a seat as far away from Alejandro as possible.

"Mia, you are unaware of the terms concerning your engagement to Alejandro."

"As always," I quip, as the fact is, no one tells me anything about this fucking family.

Massimo runs a hand across the back of his neck. "Alejandro's father has a lot of connections in Puerto Rico. He's agreed to bolster our supply of goods should we have any trouble with the Albanians. It's one of the terms of your engagement."

"And how does that concern me?" I ask, irritated that the main reason for selling me off to this man is just to secure more trade.

"You are part of the famiglia, and you need to do your duty."

Alejandro clears his throat. "Your father approached us with the deal, not the other way around." His eyes narrow. "He said he wanted to find a husband who he knew would protect and care for his daughter."

I swallow hard, as I know my father's intentions were in the right place, but none of these men can understand. I love Killian so much it hurts. I've loved him for years, and the thought of being with another man churns my stomach.

"Exactly, there's no breaking the deal, Mia." Massimo's tone is firm and hard and so different from anything I've heard him use with me before. I guess that's because while Father is too unwell, he's the head of the family. "You will marry Alejandro." He meets my fiancé's gaze. "I'd say it would be prudent to move the wedding up, don't you?"

Alejandro nods. "Yes, as soon as possible."

"Why does it need to be moved up?" I ask.

They both look at me as if I'm stupid, but it's Alejandro who replies. "To ensure you don't try to find a way out of it, of course."

It feels like I'm numb as I glance between my brother and Alejandro. "When will it be?"

Massimo shrugs. "I'll speak with your father and we'll work out a date."

Alejandro stands. "Sounds good." He holds a hand out to my brother. "See you soon." The look he gives me as he leaves the study is chilling and makes my skin crawl. I've always known he's wanted me in that way, but I never thought he'd be this ruthless about it.

Once he's gone, I turn my attention to my eldest brother. "Are you serious?"

One of his brows arches. "Serious about fulfilling our father's wishes. Yes. Give me one good reason why you can't marry Alejandro?"

I grit my teeth. "He's like a brother to me." I shudder. "It's just wrong."

Massimo shakes his head and walks toward me, kneeling down so he's at eye-level with me as if I'm a kid. "Mia, I know it doesn't seem fair, but believe me, Alejandro is a far better choice than most."

"I don't love him, though."

Massimo's eyes flash. "You can grow to."

I shake my head. "I can't." I know I can't because my heart well and truly belongs to another man.

Massimo squeezes my hand. "It won't be so bad." He stands and returns to the other side of father's desk, taking a seat. "I'd imagine we'll move the wedding up to within a week or two."

"A week?" I scoff, unable to believe that they could bring it forward that fast.

He nods. "It's best for everyone if it's done quickly, especially when you've got cold feet."

I glare at him. "Why are you being such an asshole?"

Massimo tilts his head. "I'm telling you what Father would say if he were here and able."

A flood of guilt kicks me in the stomach, as it appears as if I'm using Father's absence to try to break the engagement, which is not the case.

He's still in a coma, but they say he's responding well to the expensive and experimental treatment Massimo has paid for.

"So, you are going to make me get married when he's not even here to walk me down the aisle?"

Massimo's jaw clenches. "I will walk you down the aisle, piccola."

I draw in a deep, shaky breath and force away the ache in my chest. "I don't love him." I meet Massimo's gaze. "How is it fair that you get to be with the woman you love?"

Massimo's shoulders tense. "Who says I love her?"

I roll my eyes. "It's obvious, Massimo. Why else would you force her to marry you?"

"And who is it you love, Mia?"

The question which is impossible to answer, at least to my brother. "It's not important."

"So there is someone?" he asks.

I nod in response.

He sighs heavily. "I'm sorry. I don't know what else

to tell you. Alejandro will be a good and fair husband to you."

I frown at him. "You don't even know him."

"I know you were friends at the academy. And if I know my sister, I know she wouldn't be friends with an asshole."

I chuckle at that, despite the heaviness resting on my chest. "But one week?"

"Would two be better?" he asks.

I nod in response.

"Fine, we'll make it two, but you must promise me something."

"Anything," I reply, as one week isn't long enough to come up with a plan. Two might not be either, but it gives me a chance.

"You can't try anything to get out of this engagement."

I swallow hard, as I'm not someone who makes promises I don't intend to keep. "I promise," I murmur, knowing that if it's Killian getting me out of it, then I still keep my promise.

He's sure he can find a way, and I trust him with my life.

Camilla's words return to the forefront of my mind, *If you are meant to be together, then you have to find a way.*

She's right. If we are meant to be, then it will work out in the end. I have to trust that there's hope, even if it feels impossible right now.

## KILLIAN

*M*ia is late.

I pace the floor of the little wine bar I booked out for our private dinner, feeling increasingly anxious.

She promised she'd be here and hasn't let me down since I accosted her in the dressing room of bloomingdales.

Something feels off, but I don't know what it is.

A text comes through.

**On my way, got held up.**

A flood of relief courses through me the moment I see her text and I take a deep breath, taking a seat at the table in the center of the room.

"Is everything alright, Mr. Callaghan?" the head waiter asks.

I nod. "Yes, my date is just running a bit behind."

He smiles. "Shall I get you a drink while you wait? Maybe a few appetizers?"

"Sure, I'll have a beer, thanks." I loosen the tie around my neck, questioning why I even wore a suit tonight.

It's habit, wearing a suit and ensuring I look that part as my brother's right-hand man all the time. I find suits stuffy and irritating, though.

The waiter returns with a pint of beer and a few appetizers, but I can't actually think about eating, not until Mia is here.

Instead, I take a long swig of my drink and wait, staring at the door.

After another five minutes, which feels more like fifty, she comes rushing through the door, her cheeks a little red as if she's been running.

"Sorry I'm late."

I shake my head. "I was going out of my mind, baby girl." I stand and approach her, grabbing her hips and pulling her toward me. "I'll have to punish you later for your tardiness."

A shudder races through her, and I can't help but smirk at how easily I affect her.

"I had a good reason, unfortunately." Her tone sounds broken.

"What is it?"

Her throat bobs. "So much has happened since I saw you a week ago."

"Such as?"

"My father is in the hospital in a coma. He has cancer."

The heartbroken look in her eyes makes my chest ache. All I want to do is pick up the pieces and put them back together. "I'm sorry, Mia."

"He'll fight it. I know he will." Her chestnut eyes turn determined. "But that's not all." She fidgets with her hair and doesn't look me in the eye. "Alejandro visited today, and I told him I didn't want to marry him."

I clench my fist by my side at the thought of her even being in the same room as that snake. He's been after her for years. "What happened?" I ask, unable to keep the rage out of my voice.

"Massimo returned home, and he told me he's moving the wedding forward because he doesn't want me getting cold feet." Tears fill her eyes, but they don't fall. "What are we going to do?"

"When is the wedding?" I ask.

"Two weeks," she replies.

Fuck. It makes the challenge ahead of us far more difficult, but I hate the way she's looking at me. Mia wants me to sort this out for her, and I'll be damned if I let her down. I cup her cheeks in my hands and look her in the eye. "Don't worry about it and leave it to me."

"But, what—"

I kiss her to silence the next question out of her

mouth. "I said don't worry about it, baby girl." I give her a stern look. "Be a good girl and do as I say."

She tilts her head slightly. "You can be a bit overly bossy, you know?"

I chuckle. "And I know you like it. Now come and enjoy a meal with me."

She sighs heavily. "I fear that sooner or later, I'm going to get caught sneaking off at night all the time."

I raise a brow. "What makes you say that?"

"Sandro has been acting weird. I think he suspects something because I tell him I'm going to bed so early."

Sandro is her bodyguard and one of the biggest obstacles between us, as when she's out, he's always there. "Well, we've got two weeks, and then all of this sneaking around will be over."

"You really believe that?" she asks.

I nod in response, even though I'm still not entirely sure how I'm going to stop the wedding without causing havoc for our family. "Yes, I do."

She smiles at me and it's the sweetest smile I've ever seen. "Thank you."

I pull out her chair and she sits down.

"What do you want to drink?"

"Do they do cocktails?"

I smile. "They'll do anything you want."

Her cheeks flush pink and she clears her throat. "I'll have a Mai Thai, then."

I call the waiter over and order her drink.

Once he's gone and we're alone, that palpable tension floods the air.

"I've missed you," I say softly.

"I've missed you too," she replies.

"Why don't you come over here?" I ask, patting my lap.

Her cheeks blaze a deeper shade of red and she glances around. "Surely not in here."

"I rented the place. If I want you to sit on my lap, then you can."

Mia's tongue darts out across her bottom lip, driving me wild with need. "What about the waiter?"

"He won't care. I'm not telling you to ride my cock." I shrug. "At least, not yet."

"Killian," she hisses, shaking her head. "I really never knew how crude you can be."

"I know. You've already told me as much." I pat my lap again. "Come here." I infuse my tone with dominance and she stands almost on instinct.

I love how naturally submissive she is.

"This is crazy," she mutters as she sits on my lap, wrapping her arms around my neck.

I kiss her neck and she lets out a soft little moan. "Much better."

My cock is hard against her ass cheeks and she wriggles slightly, making me groan. "Careful, baby girl. I might end up fucking you after all if you don't hold still."

Her eyes flash and she moves again, as if challenging me.

"Is that what you want?" I ask, my cock leaking into my underwear now. "Do you want me to fuck you right here where the waiters can listen and watch?"

Her cheeks are so red now, but there's something dangerous sparking in her eyes. "I want you," she mutters.

"Not hungry for dinner, then?" I nod at the appetizers that are already on the table.

She shakes her head. "Not right now."

I reach beneath the skirt of her dress and find she's not even wearing underwear. "You dirty girl," I murmur, thrusting a finger into her already drenched pussy.

Mia gasps, wriggling more in my lap.

"If I didn't know any better, I'd say you planned this."

The look on her face is down right devious.

I unzip my pants and release my cock, knowing that there's no holding me back. She wants me and I want her. Strike that. I need her.

It's like the way I need air to breathe and water to hydrate. Mia is like oxygen and it feels like I'll die if I don't get enough of her.

I position her so she's straddling my thighs and looking right at me, and she moans softly as the head of my cock rests against her wet entrance. "Killian, what are—"

I thrust my hips upward and bury myself inside of her, groaning at how tight she is. "Fuck, baby girl," I murmur, grabbing a fistful of her beautiful brown hair and pulling her neck back to kiss it. "I can't ever get enough of your sweet little pussy."

Mia gasps. "Killian, they'll hear you."

"I don't care," I growl, tightening my grasp on her hips and lifting her harder and faster over my shaft. "I booked the place out, which means I can do what the fuck I want in here."

Mia moans as I grab her throat, squeezing softly.

"If I want to fuck you hard at the table before our entrees, then that's what I'll do."

She arches her back as she tries to get more from me.

"Now, ride my cock like a good girl," I murmur, releasing her throat.

Her hips being to move on demand and she starts to fuck herself on me, forgetting her inhibitions and where we are.

It's a beautiful fucking sight, watching her chase her own pleasure like a sex goddess.

"You are doing so well, Mia." I can't believe how much awe is in my voice, but it's the truth.

She's true female perfection if ever I'd seen it, the embodiment of femininity as her hips move so softly.

"Oh God," I groan, struggling to hold myself back from the edge. "Just like that, Mia."

She moans, her thick lips parting as she looks me right in the eye.

Her eyes look like they're alight and flecked with gold as she watches me. "Fuck, Killian. Choke me," she orders.

I can't deny that her request surprises me, but I'm quick to oblige.

"Do you like my hand around your neck like a collar, controlling how much oxygen you can breathe?" I ask.

"Yes, sir. Choke me," she murmurs.

I grab her throat hard and her eyes widen slightly. "As you wish. Now come on my cock like a good girl."

Her eyes are slightly wide as she adapts to the pressure around her throat, but she continues her thrusts up and down my shaft, coating me in her arousal.

Every one of her movements becomes jerkier and more uneven as she gets closer to the edge.

I watch her carefully, ensuring I'm not starving her of too much oxygen as she fucks herself on me.

"Killian," she cries as I feel her muscles tighten like a vise around me.

"Fuck, make that pretty cunt come for me," I growl, my own release rushing toward me hard and fast.

Her entire body shakes above me as she comes apart, and a gush of arousal soaks the front of my pants again. I love it though. I love how fucking well she comes.

I pull her forward and bit her collarbone hard as I

shoot my cum deep inside of her. A dark desire clawing at the forefront of my mind to get her pregnant with my baby.

If she has my baby in her, then she can't possible marry another man.

The thought makes me crazy as I thrust my hips into her over and over, long after I've spent every drop of my cum.

"Killian," she whimpers softly, lacing her fingers softly through my hair. "Stop," she gasps.

I do as she says and collapse back in my chair, looking at the woman splayed over my lap.

She looks utterly divine, like an angel who's fallen from heaven right into the devil's lap.

"Fuck, that was amazing," I murmur.

She jumps off of my cock and smooths down her dress, eyes darting from side to side. "Do you think the staff saw?"

"I hope so," I say, smirking at her.

She shakes her head. "How can you be so brazen?"

I shrug. "Because I'm a Callaghan, which means I can do what I want."

She walks to the other side of the table and sits down, smoothing down her messy hair.

I adjust myself and thrust my cock back into my pants, zipping them up. "Let be honest here, you were the one that started it."

Her eyes narrow. "That is a complete and utter lie. You started it by making me sit on your lap."

"I asked you to sit on my lap, not wiggle around and make me harder than a rock." I shrug. "And then you were the one that said you were hungry for my cock rather than food."

She leans forward and grabs an olive off one of the plates, popping it in her mouth. "I think you are mistaken."

"I think you are trying to ensure you get a stern punishment when we leave here, baby girl."

Her lips purse slightly, as if she's excited by the idea.

And then the waiter appears, looking rather red-faced, proving he had indeed heard or perhaps even seen us fucking. "Sorry to interrupt, but I wondered if you are ready for your entrees?"

I smirk as Mia's cheeks turn the same color as his. "Yes, thanks."

He bows slightly and then scurries off to get the food I ordered.

"What is on the menu?" Mia asks.

"If you're not careful, you will be."

Her nostrils flare and I just sit back and take a long swig of my beer, enjoying the way she glares at me and how it makes my cock hard even after I just fucked her.

Mia is going to be the death of me, and I wouldn't have it any other way.

## 19

# MIA

*A*fter we've eaten, Killian drags me out onto the street and smiles down at me. "Time for me to punish you."

I shake my head and glance at the time on my watch, realizing it's almost midnight already. "I will get caught if I keep staying out so late."

Killian growls softly. "I'm not letting you go yet. I've got the same room booked at the Waldorf."

It hurts to even consider shooting him down, as all I really want is to spend every waking moment wrapped in this man's arms.

"It's too risky."

"No, it's not." He yanks me toward a cab and pushes me into the back forcefully. "The Waldorf, please."

I swallow hard as it moves. "Were you always this pushy?" I ask.

He smirks, and it's a devilish smile that makes my insides flip. "Yes, I guess you just never got to see this side of me."

I can't understand why a flash of jealous heat washes over me. "No doubt Kimberley did."

He raises a brow. "Perhaps. Were you jealous of her?" he asks, as if he's enjoying this.

"I didn't like seeing you with her, if that's what you mean."

Killian kisses me. "If it makes you feel any better, I never really wanted her. Not the way I wanted you."

It feels like my heart skips a beat at that as he kisses my neck, instantly turning me into lava. "Killian," I breathe his name.

The cab comes to a stop, jerking both of us out of our daze. "The Waldorf, sir."

"Thanks. How much do I owe you?"

"Fifteen dollars."

Killian grabs a twenty-dollar bill and passes it to him. "Keep the change."

And then he slips out and drags me with him. "What about being spotted?" I ask.

He shrugs. "It's late and I already have the key." He holds the key card up. "Stop worrying."

I swallow hard, as it's risky for us to walk in there together. Anyone could see us and I fear he's getting too careless.

We walk through the large doors into the lobby, which is pretty quiet, and head for the elevator.

"Are you sure I shouldn't take the stairs?" I ask.

He shakes his head. "I'm sure." He pulls me tighter against his side.

The elevator opens, and to my relief, it's empty. He pulls me against him, kissing me once the doors are shut. "Would you quit being so uptight? Chicago is a big city."

I raise a brow. "Yes, and we know many people here."

He sighs heavily. "I can't wait to give you a good spanking."

My thighs clench at the thought, which makes me wonder if I'm a masochist. Why do I enjoy the mix of pleasure and pain that Killian doles out?

"What are you thinking?" he asks.

I shrug. "I'm thinking there's something wrong with me for getting so excited about being spanked."

He chuckles. "No, there's nothing wrong with you." his hand moves lower to cup my ass cheeks. "But we're going to see just how far you will go tonight."

My brow furrows. "What's that supposed to mean?"

"Let's just say I set up the room before our date."

I swallow hard, unsure what to make of that. It was pretty clear from our first sexual encounter that Killian is into pretty kinky sex, but I fear I've hardly seen anything yet.

The elevator dings, signaling we've made it to the fifth floor before I can ask what he means.

And he grabs my hand and yanks me down the corridor toward the hotel room.

Once we're inside, my anxiety eases until I see all the things Killian has set up in the room.

"What the hell?" I ask, glancing at him.

He shrugs. "I can't take you to my bedroom, so I had to bring it here."

I swallow hard as I walk toward the bed, which is already fitted with chains to hold me down.

He has whips, paddles and other devices the likes I've never seen before resting on the bed.

"What is all this stuff?" I ask.

He shrugs. "My toys."

I swallow hard as I move toward the bed, picking up a pair of odd looking clips. "What are they for?"

He smirks and moves toward me. "Nipple clamps."

I wince at the thought of him putting them on me. "Ouch."

"Don't knock it until you've tried it, baby girl." His hand moves to my nipples, which are hard against the fabric of my dress, and he pinches. "It can be fun to push the boundaries."

I pick up an oddly shaped silicone toy and glances at him. "Dare I ask?"

"Butt plug," he says simply, and I feel my thighs dampen.

"Oh," I murmur, remembering just how good it felt when he stuck his finger in my ass. It was dirty, but so fucking hot. "I wouldn't mind trying that."

He chuckles and moves toward me. "I'm going to make you come so hard you won't remember your own name, Mia."

I gasp as he grabs hold of my hips hard and forces me to turn around, pressing the length of his hard erection against my ass.

"Do you feel what you do to me?"

I nod in response.

"Let me hear you," he growls.

"Yes, sir."

He makes a satisfied sound as he unfastens my dress from the back and allows it to drop to the floor, leaving me in nothing.

I didn't wear a bra with the dress as it would have been visible.

His hands find my breasts and he squeezes them together, groaning. "No bra and no panties. Such a dirty little girl."

I moan as he plays with my nipples roughly, making them hard beneath his fingers.

His lips are brushing against my earlobe as he murmurs, "So sensitive, I think you'll love it when I put that clamp on your nipples."

My thighs squeeze together at the thought, and a soft moan tumbles from my lips.

"Now, it's time for me to tie you up." He pushes me roughly onto my back on the bed.

I watch the man I've longed for all these years grab holds of the restraints affixed to the bed and clamp my wrists in to them.

He steps back and admires me naked and restrained for him. "There's something missing, baby girl."

"What's that?" I ask.

His smirk widens as he reaches for some more restraints and affixes the cuffs to my ankles. "I want you spread wide open for me." The restraints affix to the other ones around my wrists, forcing my hips back and my legs high in the air.

"Oh," I murmur as they make it impossible for me to shut my legs.

"Perfect," he growls, grabbing the nipple clamps. "Now, for a bit of pain."

I swallow hard, uncertain about him using them on me, and yet there's a tingle of excitement racing over every inch of my body.

"Take a deep breath for me, Mia." He approaches and clamps one of them onto my right nipple.

I yelp in pain, eyes wide. "Fuck, that hurts!"

He kisses me, swallowing my cries of pain. "It will feel good soon. Just relax."

It's hard to relax as my heart beats unevenly in my chest and he clamps the second one on.

The shock is less, but the pain is just as intense as I cry out again, tears prickling at my eyes.

And then Killian's mouth is between my thighs as he feasts on me.

I shudder, the intensity of the pleasure somehow heightened by the pain.

I writhe against the restrictive restraints, unable to regain any control of the situation.

Killian groans against my arousal, the vibration coursing right through my body.

And then he moves lower, licking my back hole ferociously. "You taste so fucking good," he rumbles.

I swallow hard, my body tensing at the new sensation of his tongue against my ass.

"I'm going to plug this ass up and then fuck your tight little cunt," he groans, his hand fisting his cock through the fabric of his pants.

"Killian," I breathe his name, unable to believe how good it feels with his tongue against my ass.

He thrusts two fingers of his free hand into my pussy as he continues to tongue my sensitive ring of muscles.

My body shudders against the coming storm as he pushes me toward orgasm faster than ever before.

"Oh fuck," I scream as he pushes me right over the edge, his fingers thrusting harder into my dripping wet pussy.

His tongue continues to probe at my ass as he doesn't let up at all, leaving me panting and rushing right toward another cliff edge.

Finally, he stops and grabs the thick flared silicone toy he told me he was going to put in my ass. "Time to stretch that ass, baby girl."

I swallow hard, but feel eager to try it. "Okay," I reply.

He smirks as he grabs a bottle of lube and squirts it into my hole. "Your ass is very sensitive. You've never come that fucking fast before." And then he lubes up the plug and presses the tip of it to my hole.

I tense as it eases inside.

"Relax, or it will hurt," he advises.

I take in a deep breath and try to relax, even though it feels so unnatural having something shoved in my ass.

Killian forces it through the muscles and then suddenly it pops inside, the flared base tight against my skin. "That's it, you've taken it right inside that virgin asshole," he murmurs, his voice infused with desire. "And now I'm going to fuck that pretty little cunt and see how tight it feels while your ass is filled."

I watch him as he removes his pants and boxer briefs. And then his shirt, revealing the beautiful ink scrolling across his skin. My mouth waters at the sight.

Killian kneels between my legs, spanking me hard. Then he rubs the head of his cock through my eager entrance, coating himself in my arousal. "Is that what you want, Mia?"

"Yes, please fuck me," I beg.

The look in his eyes is pure evil as he shakes his head. "But wait, I haven't punished you yet."

"What for?" I ask.

"Being late to our date and teasing me into fucking you before dinner, both are punishable offences." He gets off the bed, which makes me whimper in protest.

I watch as he walks over to the other implements

he's put out on a side table, running his fingers over them. "The question is, which should I use?"

"I don't know what you are talking about."

"Which implement should I punish you with?"

I swallow hard, unsure whether I like the devilish look in Killian's beautiful green eyes.

He returns holding an odd looking implement with strands of leather attached.

"What is that?" I ask.

"A flogger," he murmurs, shrugging. "It's not the most painful, but it can be rather arousing if used correctly."

He brings the leather strips down right onto my pussy, sending a mix of pain and pleasure arching through my body.

"Fuck!" I cry.

Killian's eyes darken. "Perhaps I need to gag you, too. You've got a real filthy mouth on you, baby girl."

I draw in a deep breath as he reaches for some kind of gagging device. "What about the safe word?"

He pauses then and looks at me malevolently. "Click your fingers if you need me to stop. Try it now."

I try it, just about able to click them.

"Okay?"

I nod, but I can't deny that I'm starting to wonder whether I know the man I've got into bed with.

My scolding of Camilla for falling for a sadist may be rather hypocritical, as I'm starting to think that's what Killian is, too.

He affixes the gag to my mouth and watches me with predatory glee as he fists his huge cock in his hand. The way he looks at me makes all my worries melt away.

And then he lifts the flogger and brings it down hard against my back legs, making me shriek into the gag.

He's a sadist, that's for sure. The question is, can I be what he wants?

## 20

### KILLIAN

*M*ia watches me with an intoxicating mix of fear and desire. Her legs are shackled to her arms in a way that bares her to me deliciously.

I know that how wrong it is that her fear turns me on, especially since all I want is to protect her.

It's all I've wanted for as long as I've known her, but the fear makes my cock ache.

"How does it feel to be at my mercy?" I ask, knowing she can't answer because she's gagged.

Her brow furrows adorably as she glares at me and makes a strange grunting sound.

I chuckle. "Oh right, you can't tell me, can you, baby girl?" I tilt my head slightly and then bring the flogger down right over her glistening cunt.

She jolts, a cry of pain muffled behind the gag.

"I love having you at my mercy like this." I move

forward and grab her pussy, groaning at how wet she is. "And I love how fucking wet you are."

My cock jerks of its own free will as her pussy gushes more.

"I bet you are gagging for my cock. Aren't you?"

Her eyes turn furious as I strike her with the flogger again, winding her up.

She is so wet that her arousal is leaking all over her ass and the plug and it's a beautiful sight indeed.

"Don't worry, you don't need to answer." I step forward and thrust two fingers deep inside her cunt, groaning at the way her muscles tighten. "Your pussy is doing all the talking for you."

She makes a muffled moan as her eyes flicker shut and her back attempts to arch against the restraints.

"Such a beautiful cunt and all mine," I muse, thrusting deeper and harder with my fingers. "I wonder if I've punished you enough yet."

Her eyes fly open as she searches mine, wondering what on earth else I could do to her. Mia has no idea of the things I'm capable of.

I chose the flogger because it's light and not too painful, but I have far more painful implements. My cane, for instance, but I know it's too soon to use it.

Instead, I reach for a small vibrator, which I placed on the nightstand.

"Perhaps a bit more torture just to be sure you've learned your lesson."

Her eyes widen as the device beings to buzz and I

press it an inch away from her clit, making her body shudder.

"Do you want to feel it against your clit, baby?" I ask.

She manages to nod her head despite the awkward angle her body forced into.

"I bet you do." I move it around her labia instead, never quite giving her that buzz she needs where she needs it.

It's intoxicating having so much power over the woman I've longed for all these years. I've dreamed of having her at my mercy like this countless times, but it's so much better in reality.

Her chest heaves as her breathing becomes more labored and intense. I notice the way her beautiful brown eyes are so dilated. There's barely a centimeter of brown left.

And then just when it looks like she might pass out from frustration, I push the device against her clit and she screams into the gag.

Her pussy squirts as she comes apart just like that, some of her arousal hitting my abs and cock.

"You come so fucking well, Mia," I groan, rubbing her arousal on my cock and using it to jerk myself off. "I don't think I would ever get tired of making you come."

My cock is so hard it hurts and I know I can't keep teasing her forever, so without a word of warning I push my hips forward and seat myself all the way inside of her.

Her eyes widen and she growls behind the gag, nostrils flaring as she tries to regain her composure. For the first time in her life, she's filled in both her ass and her cunt and it feels like fucking heaven.

"Oh fuck, you are tight with that plug in your ass." I keep the device against her clit as I fuck her, knowing it will driver her mad with need.

Her eyes roll back in her head as I fuck her hard and deep, enjoying the way her muscles cling to my cock like a second skin.

It's as if we were made to fit perfectly. Two halves of a fucking whole.

"Take that cock deep in your cunt," I growl, my own handle on control beginning to slip as I rut into her more forcefully. "You are such a good girl, taking my cock all the way inside while that plug is in your tight little ass."

I spank her thighs and she groans again. Her nipples look painful in the clamps.

My hands reach for the clamps and I unfasten them, resulting in a shriek that is barely muffled by the gag in Mia's mouth.

I unclasp the gag from the back and then swallow her cries of pain, feeding off of them like the sick of son of a bitch I am.

"It's alright, baby girl. I'm here," I murmur, my fingers gently caressing the painful flesh.

She shudders, her pussy clenching around my cock

in a warning. Mia is on the edge of no return, and I want her to come. I want her to come so many times she can hardly think.

"That's it, come for me. I want to feel that tight little cunt come for me." I hardly recognize my own voice as I fuck her harder, sweat pooling over my chest as I fuck her harder than I've ever fucked in my life.

Her body bends to my will as she shatters, arousal pooling around my cock and dripping onto the hotel's sheets.

It will be a fucking mess by the morning, but I don't give a shit.

Mia is going to come so many times it will look like someone dropped an entire bathtub's worth of water on the damn mattress.

I groan, knowing I'm not ready yet to spill inside of her.

"Killian," she breathes my name over and over. "No more, please."

I smirk and bite her bottom lip, my hips still rocking into her softly. "I'm not done with you yet, Mia." I bite her collarbone and she groans, eyes fluttering shut. "I need you to come once more before I let you have my cum. Do you understand?"

She whimpers. "I don't think I can."

I wrap my hand around her throat and squeeze softly. "Don't make me gag you again, baby girl. Of course you can." I reach for the vibrator again and push it against her clit.

She cries out, bitting her lip. "Oh God, you are going to kill me."

"I'm pretty sure you can't die of multiple orgasms." I kiss her, my tongue thrusting into her mouth with demanding strokes. "Now be a good girl and let me fuck you to climax."

Her beautiful brown eyes are so hazy with lust, it drives me crazy as she nods. "Okay, sir."

"Fuck," I growl, tightening my hands on her bound legs and pushing them closer to her head so she's almost folded in half. "Such a good girl," I purr, as my cock pounds into her with so much force it's as if I'm trying to break her in half.

She takes it though, like a fucking champ.

Her nipples are red and sore and yet as hard as stone as I suck on one, making her moan incoherent words.

"You are perfect," I murmur, moving between her two nipples despite the fact that she's restrained in such an awkward position. It's a good thing she's so flexible.

And then I pull back and grab her thighs hard, sinking my fingertips into them as I fuck her harder.

Our bodies becoming one as she moans my name, spurring me on with even more force.

I've never felt desire or need like it. It takes over my body and infects me like a disease.

Before I know what is happening, she's crying my name and coming for the third time, and this time I know I can't hold it.

The force of her muscles clamping down around my shaft is so tight it drags me right over the edge.

"Fuck," I roar, my cock exploding as deep as physically possible inside of her. I empty my balls, spilling over and over again until every drop of my cum is released.

That odd clawing sensation prickles over my mind as the image of Mia growing big and round with my baby appears again.

*What the fuck is that all about?*

I've never really been one to think much about having kids, but there's something about being with Mia that makes me want to get her pregnant.

Perhaps it's the fact that she's still not secured as mine, but if my child was in her belly, she soon would be.

I remain seated in her long after my orgasm passes, keeping my cum deep inside of her in the hope it will take root.

Mia finally makes a little plea of protest. "You are crushing me."

I chuckle and pull out of her, unfastening her legs from the wrist clamps and allowing her some reprieve. Once she's completely unrestrained, I fall onto my back and pull her against my chest. "That was fucking amazing, lass," I say.

She shakes her head. "I'm exhausted, and I didn't even move."

A deep laugh resonates through me, and I realize in that moment I haven't felt this happy in years.

I kiss the top of her head. "It's because you orgasmed four times."

Her eyes are shut but she murmurs, "Five if you count the restaurant."

"True," I say, smiling as I take in the vision of her lying in my arms, looking so peaceful. "Have a nap and I'll wake you up for round two shortly."

Her eyes shoot open and find mine. "You have got to be kidding, right?"

I shake my head. "No, but I'm happy to fuck you while you sleep if you're that tired," I suggest, the idea instantly making my cock semi-hard.

"You are going to kill me, I'm sure of it," she says, but there's a hint of humor in her tone.

"Why would I do that when I love fucking you so much?" I pull her closer, my hands tightening around her hips.

She sighs and nestles closer to me. "Because you are crazy."

"Do you like playing with my toys, Mia?" I ask, kissing her neck.

She shrugs, but her cheeks darken in color. "I think so."

"Do you realize you still have that plug in your ass?" I ask.

Her body grows tense and her eyes open. "No, I forgot."

I smirk. "Leave it in until I'm finished with you," I murmur.

She falls silent, and then her eyes flutter shut as she rests her head on my chest.

I feel pressure increasing in my chest as I watch her, knowing that this is how I want to spend the rest of my life, wrapped up with the woman of my dreams. There's always been this tenable connection between us, even since we were kids. Her breathing becomes even and heavier as she drifts asleep in my arms.

Somehow, I have to find a way to stop her upcoming wedding and claim her for myself. If she's marrying anyone, it will be me. I'd risk my life to ensure she ends up with me. Hell, I'd tear the world down to have her. And that's exactly what I plan to do.

---

THE NEXT DAY I'm exhausted as I finally haul myself out of bed well past midday and make my way down to the kitchen to find some breakfast.

Rourke and Viki are sitting at the kitchen island having lunch when I enter. "Where have you been?" Rourke asks the moment he sees me, shaking his head. "I've been calling you since last night."

I run a hand through my hair. "My cell phone died while I was out." I shrug. "What's up?"

"What's up?" he scoffs, glancing at Viki. "What's up

is that the meeting with Hernandez was last night and you didn't show up."

"Shit." I totally forgot that was last night. "How did it go?" I pull open the fridge and grab my carton of orange juice, drinking right out of it.

"Hernandez is dead."

I spit some of my orange juice out, shutting the fridge. "What?"

"You heard me. Adrik Volkov killed him in cold blood and claimed the crown."

"He can't claim the crown. He's not an Estrada." I shake my head. "And how the fuck did he find out about the meeting?"

Viki speaks next. "He can because he married Eliza just before killing him. Adrik is ruthless and he'll stop at nothing to get what he wants." She shrugs. "At least he believes he can."

"I thought the lad was a waste of space." I take a seat on a stool at the island, feeling a little numb at the insane news.

Viki shakes her head. "Our family has always underestimated him, and I think we turned him into a monster."

"And we don't know how he found out. We're assuming he had a spy who was close to Hernandez," Rourke says.

"Have you spoken with Spartak and Massimo since?"

"Not in person." He sighs heavily. "We all agreed

we need to change tactics to handle Adrik. He's proving more resilient than we expected."

"No shit." I rub my face in my hands. "Do you need me to do anything?"

Rourke shakes his head. "Just be ready to head to a meeting once it's setup. I'll need you and Kieran by my side while we handle this."

"No worries," I reply, swallowing hard.

If it wasn't enough that I have to worry about breaking off Mia's wedding in such a short time, the situation between the mafia families of our city is on a knife's edge.

I am painfully aware that my actions concerning Mia could cause more headaches for the clan, but at least I have two weeks to figure it out. Not as good as two months, but I know I have to find a solution. Allowing Mia to walk down the aisle and marry another man isn't an option.

## 21

## MIA

*a* bang on my bedroom door startles me awake as I sit up suddenly, glancing at the clock on the nightstand.

It's eleven o'clock in the morning, but I'm exhausted. Perhaps it's because I didn't get back until after five this morning, after Killian had finished with me. I stretch my arms above my head and swing my legs out of the bed, grabbing my robe off the seat next to it. Once I'm decent, I open the door only to wish I hadn't.

Alejandro is standing on the other side, eyes blazing with barely contained rage.

"What the fuck—"

He forces the door all the way open and storms inside, cutting off the question I was about to ask. "Don't say a fucking word, Mia." He paces the floor of the room and then looks me dead in the eye. "How long has it been going on?"

"What?" I ask, crossing my arms over my chest. I don't like being in only my nightwear in his presence. It makes me feel vulnerable.

"You and Killian," he hisses, nostrils flaring. "I saw the two of you walk hand in hand into the fucking Waldorf Hotel last night."

The blood drains from my face as I had a bad feeling the moment we stepped out of that cab. "You were watching us?" I question.

He shakes his head. "I'm staying there and was having a late night drink at the bar." His jaw clenches. "Only to see my fiancée stroll through the fucking lobby and into an elevator with Killian Callaghan." He walks toward me and grabs me by the shoulders. "How long?"

"It doesn't matter. I told you I don't want to marry you." I try to shrug him off, but he just grips me tighter. "Why don't you accept I'll never care for you that way?"

"Because I can't. You belong to me."

I shake my head. "No, I belong to Killian."

He growls and his hands find my throat as they tighten around it. "Listen to me. It doesn't matter who you think you belong to. Our wedding is going ahead." His nostrils flare as he moves his face to within an inch of mine. "You will marry me and I will insist that the wedding is within a week." His grip is so tight on my throat it feels like he's trying to kill me. Finally, he releases it and steps away. "I will have men watching the house until the wedding. If you even think about going anywhere near Killian, I'll know, and I'll drag you right back home myself. Do you understand?"

A hot and new hatred bubbles like lava beneath an active volcano in my gut for a man I thought was my friend. "I hate you," I murmur.

He glares at me. "Bullshit. Once I'm through with you, you will forget all about Killian Callaghan."

"Impossible since I love him and always have."

He looks wounded by my admittance that I love Killian, but I can't understand why he's so hellbent on pursuing me.

"Why do you want me, anyway? Is it because you've always been jealous of Killian?"

His eyes narrow. "You don't know what you are talking about, Mia." He steps away from me. "I'll be watching. If you put one step wrong, I'll tell your family who you've been fucking behind their backs." His eyes are full of malicious intent. "And then we'll see how they react. They won't let you leave the house until you're married to me." Without another word, he turns and leaves the room.

I stare at the doorway, numbness spreading through every inch of my body.

We were too careless last night and now it's going to come back to bite us in the ass. It feels like the world is against us and yet I can't give up, not yet.

Killian is the love of my life, and I'll be damned if some jealous bastard comes between us.

---

A WOMAN's wedding day is supposed to be the happiest day of her life, but I'm dying inside. None of my family will listen to me when I tell them I don't want this, and Massimo obliged Alejandro and brought it forward to five days after he visited me in my room. For the first time in my life, I'm understanding how the men of my family view women, even ones that share their own blood.

We're a commodity. A bargaining chip that can be used to further the famiglia's status and power. They are the only things that matter to the Morrone family, and I'm sick of it.

The worst part of it is that Alejandro spotted me and Killian at the Waldorf. He knows my secret and he'll use it against me if I try to get out of this. The man was supposed to be my friend, but I'm thinking he's just as sick and twisted as the rest of them.

He doesn't care about me, he just likes the idea of having me. Throughout our years at the academy, he was jealous of Killian. Even if he was three years older; he was the king of the academy while he was there.

Alejandro envied him, and now he wants to take me away from him.

I stare at my reflection in the mirror and feel numb.

Somehow, despite all my protests to every one of my family members, no one cares enough to stop this wedding, except for Camilla, but she has as little power as I do in this situation.

My father would be the same if he weren't in a coma. He'd tell me it's my duty to the famiglia.

*Fuck duty.*

Even though Alejandro didn't tell my family the reason for moving the wedding up, he's threatened he will do if I do anything to stop it.

Killian has been ringing me non-stop since I text him to tell him we are too late.

The door swings open and I turn around, my stomach sinking when I see it's Massimo standing there. "Hey, Mia." He smiles, but it doesn't quite reach his eyes. "How are you feeling?"

I glare at him. "Like shit. I don't want to do this."

Massimo sighs and approaches me. "Well, you look beautiful, if that's any consolation."

"It not," I murmur, almost to myself. I've never felt so powerless as I watch my brother behind me in the mirror.

"You know I'm not doing this to punish you." He squeezes my shoulder. "I wish it could be different."

"It could be," I say, looking him in the eye through the mirror. "You know it could."

Massimo shakes his head. "What message would I send if one of the first things I do as acting don of the family is undo one of Father's deals?"

I shrug. "That you aren't as much of an asshole as him."

"Mia!" Massimo's eyes flash with anger. "Don't speak of him like that, especially not when he's..." Massimo trails off as if he can't even say the word.

"What? When he's dying of cancer," I mutter.

"He still has a chance," he says, shaking his head. "He's not dying."

I clench my fists by my side as I know I'm speaking out of anger. Most of the time I've been positive, but I can't help but feel gloomy today.

"I will walk you down the aisle," he says, turning me around to face him. "Okay?"

I bite my lip. "Fine, but I'd rather not walk down it at all."

He chuckles softly. "Unfortunately, that's not an option."

A heaviness settles on my chest as I'd really hoped that he'd change his mind, but here we are an hour before my wedding and he's still making me go through with it.

I always expected this from our father, but not from Massimo or my two other brothers.

"I'll see you shortly, Mia," Massimo says, giving me a wistful smile before turning to leave.

"Is Camilla here yet?" I ask.

He stops by the door and shakes his head. "Not yet, but I'll send her to you the moment she arrives."

I roll my eyes. "Trust Camilla to be late."

He smiles. "Try to relax." He opens the door and disappears out of it, leaving me feeling even more hopeless.

As I stare at myself in the reflection of the mirror again, I know deep down I'd been hoping that Killian might be able to stop it before it happens.

Even with only one hour until I become Mrs. De León. I shudder at the thought and turn away from the mirror, unable to look at myself any longer. I had hoped that there was still a chance. However, with every minute that ticks by, it's slowly fading into nothing.

The worst part of it is that I'm pretty sure I'm carrying Killian's baby. I'm ten days late for my period, and I'm never late. My stomach churns as I wonder if I'm going to puke, and then the door swings open and Camilla comes rushing in.

"Hey, sorry I'm late."

I shake my head. "Don't worry about it," I mutter.

Her eyes turn pitiful and she stands in front of me, grabbing my hand and squeezing. "I must admit, you look like the saddest bride I've ever seen."

I force a smile just to stop myself from sobbing. "Maybe that's because I am."

Camilla shakes her head. "Run away, Mia."

I give her a questioning look. "Run where?"

"To him," she says, shrugging. "If you are with him, they can't make you do anything."

I sigh, as it's probably not that easy. "I wish that were true, but the war could get worse if I do that."

"Fuck the war," Camilla says, setting her hands on her hips. "This is your life we're talking about."

I raise a brow, as she sounds so passionate about it. "What would you do in my shoes?"

"I'd run."

She says it with such certainty, but I fear it's because she's not in my shoes.

The door to the dressing room opens again and this time, standing in the doorway, is Killian.

I blink a few times, wondering if I'm imagining it.

His brow furrows when he sees Camilla, and he holds his hands up. "Don't scream. I'm not here to hurt you."

Camilla shakes her head, laughing. "I know. Thank fuck you are here."

Killian looks confused.

"I was just trying to convince her to run away and find you."

"You told her?" he asks, glancing at me.

I shrug. "She's my sister. I tell her everything."

"What's your plan?" Camilla demands.

It's almost impossible not to smile at the look on Killian's face as he rubs a hand across the back of his neck. "I don't really have one, to be honest."

Camilla makes a tutting sound, glancing at me. "Are you sure about this one?"

I laugh at the comical scene in front of me. "Yes, I'm sure." My eyes meet Killian's and there's such passion in them.

"Well, how the fuck are you getting her out of here without being seen?"

Killian rubs a hand across the back of his neck. "I'd hoped to just race her out of the back entrance."

Camilla rolls her eyes. "You'll need a diversion." A wicked smile twists onto her lips. "Luckily, I'm all for getting Mia out of this wedding, so I'll create one."

"What do you have in mind?" I ask.

She taps her chin lightly and then, as if a light bulb goes off in her head, she smiles. "I'm going to go into the church and tell them I think I saw the Russians lurking outside the front."

I shake my head. "Will it work?"

"It will send them into high alert and while they go to check it out, you can head out the back and escape."

Killian looks uncertain, but nods. "I think it's the best we've got."

"Of course it is, because you came in here without a plan," Camilla says, walking up to me and pulling me into a long hug. "I don't know when we'll see each other again."

I shake my head, tears prickling at my eyes. "We will find a way."

She gives me a sad smile and nods. "Right, I better get this show on the road."

I watch as my sister leaves the room, ready to distract my family to ensure I can escape safely with Killian.

He chuckles once the door shuts behind her. "I like your sister better than the rest of your siblings."

I glance at him. "You came."

"Of course I fucking came. I told you, Mia. You belong to me." He storms toward me and grabs my hips, pulling me hard against him. "And when you get married, it will be walking down the aisle with me at the end."

I raise a brow. "Is that right?"

His eyes narrow. "Yes."

"What if I don't want to marry you?"

"Bullshit," he says, grip tightening on my hips. "Of course you want to marry me, baby girl."

I roll my eyes. "Arrogant."

He chuckles as heavy footsteps rush past the door, no doubt in response to Camilla's distraction. "I think that's our cue."

I smile and take his hand, allowing him to lead me out of the dressing room at the back of the church.

It's not a long walk down the corridor to the back exit, and I sigh a breath of relief the moment we open the door and step outside.

"Where the fuck do you think you're going?" Alejandro's voice cuts through me like a knife.

My heart pounds frantically as I turn to face the man I once called a friend. He's glaring between me and Killian, rage in his eyes.

"I can't marry you, Alejandro," I say, hoping that he will finally accept that we were never meant to be.

He shakes his head. "You have to." His eyes dart to Killian, who is glaring at him hatefully. "You didn't think I'd fall for Camilla's half-assed distraction, did you?"

"She belongs to me, De León. She always has and always will," Killian says.

Alejandro's jaw clenches. "Then why is she engaged to me?"

"Because you are a sad son of a bitch who roped his father into making a deal for her hand, all because you couldn't win her the right way." Killian pushes me behind him and draws a gun, aiming it at Alejandro.

"Killian," I murmur his name, trying to ease his rage as I press my hand to his back. "No violence."

"Let us leave, Alejandro."

I can't see his face, as Killian is blocking me with his body.

"Or I'll blow your brains out."

I swallow hard, wondering if Killian would actually kill Alejandro over this.

"You'll regret this, Callaghan," Alejandro says, but I sense he's backing off for now.

"I'll never regret taking what belongs to me." With that, he pushes me toward his Porsche parked nearby. "Get in, Mia."

I get into the passenger's side fast as Killian turns on the engine, but Alejandro is quick to react as bullets ricochet off the body of the car. "Fuck!" I shout.

"Don't worry, and keep your head down," he instructs.

I do as he says, keeping my head down as he drives out of the parking lot, bullets continuing to bounce off the body of his car.

"Motherfucker is messing up my paintwork."

"Is that really what you are worried about right now?" I ask, shaking my head. "Not the fact that we could get shot."

"The car has bulletproof glass and body, Mia."

I relax slightly at that as Killian speeds away from the church and the bullets cease hitting the car, but then I realize what I've done.

My family will never forgive me for not marrying Alejandro, which means I may have won what my heart desires, but I've lost my famiglia. As I stare out of the window at the buildings rushing past, I can't help feel solemn even though I got what I really wanted.

Killian wants to marry me. He wants me forever, and that's all I've really ever wanted. I just wish it didn't have to be at the expense of the relationship with my family.

But that was a fantasy, because a Morrone can't be with a Callaghan without changing sides, and it looks like that's exactly what has happened. I'm now an enemy and my family will view me as a traitor.

## 22

## KILLIAN

"What have you done?" Rourke growls, eyes full of manic rage.

I cross my arms over my chest and glare at him. "I did what I had to do."

He shakes his head. "Massimo is at my throat. He says he'll make us pay for this. I need an explanation right now."

I run a hand across the back of my neck, knowing that taking Mia half an hour before her wedding was a risky move. "I can't let her marry him."

Rourke's eyes look even more frantic at that rather vague response. "Explain," he barks.

"I love her."

"Motherfucker," he growls, throwing a glass paperweight across the room.

It smashes into the wall and shatters into pieces.

I hold my hands up as he spins on me, eyes full of

rage. "And you didn't think to even give us a heads up? Your own fucking family."

"They moved the wedding up suddenly." I shrug. "I had to act off instinct."

Rourke growls and paces back to his desk, sitting down and holding his head in his hands. "How are we going to make amends now?"

"I don't know," I admit, knowing that I've thrown the clan into turmoil. "Maybe if I marry her, then it could be the bridge we need between our two families," I suggest.

Rourke looks at me as if I've lost my mind, and perhaps I have. "You want to marry a Morrone?"

I nod in response. "It's not about her name."

"And what about the fact her father killed our mother three years ago?" he asks, eyes wild. "Does that not matter?"

"You know that it was an unfortunate incident that could have been avoided." I glare at him, as I'm not letting him shame me when he's harbored the secret over threatening Remy all these years.

"What is that supposed to mean?"

"I mean, the threat you sent Remy the morning our mother was murdered." I cross my arms over my chest.

Rourke pales and his eyes widen slightly. "How long have you known?"

"Ever since you sent it."

He shakes his head and stands, moving toward me. "Why the fuck didn't you say anything?"

I shrug. "Because I could tell the guilt was tearing you up."

Rourke's Adam's apple bobs as he swallows. "She died because of me."

I shake my head. "She died because the Morrone family killed her, but your threat may not have helped."

He sags against the edge of the table, cupping his face in his hands. "I didn't know how to tell any of you." He looks at me, such emotion blazing in his crystal blue eyes. "Least of all, Father, and then…" He can't finish the sentence.

"And then he died too," I murmur.

Rourke nods. "I reignited the feud with the Morrone family."

"Something would have in the end." I stand and set a hand on his shoulder. "It's not your fault, brother."

He meets my gaze. "But how did you expect us to survive such a blatant attack on the Morrone family while we're trying to work with them?"

"I couldn't think about it. What would you have done if it were Viki?" I ask.

Rourke searches my eyes. "I fell for Viki after kidnapping her. It's a completely different situation. Not to mention, she's a fucking Morrone." The way he growls that makes my blood heat.

"Not for long. I intend to make her a Callaghan and quickly."

"You've lost the plot. How are we going to work with the Morrone family now?" He shakes his head.

"Adrik is the head of the cartel and wants to blow us away, and now we're potentially isolated with no allies?" His nostrils flare. "There's no other way to say this, but you are being a selfish asshole."

I cross my arms over my chest. "I don't care."

He growls and I can tell he's about to attack me as he rushes forward, only for Torin to appear at that very moment.

"Enough," our uncle growls.

As always, out of habit, we listen to our uncle.

He walks toward the two of us, eyes darting between me and Rourke. "What Killian did was reckless, but the fact is, it is done." He claps Rourke on the shoulder. "We now need to find a way to amend the rift it has caused."

Torin is level-headed and sometimes I wonder why he didn't volunteer to take our father's place. Granted, it isn't his birth right, but he'd make a fine clan leader.

"Now sit down, lads, and let's discuss this like competent adults."

Rourke glares at me, but he does sit behind his desk.

I sit down on the chair opposite and Torin perches on the desk, watching us both.

"Do you have a plan, Killian?" he asks first.

"I plan to marry Mia, so surely our joining could be a more finite peace offering between our two families?" I suggest.

He sighs. "I'm not sure the Morrone family will see

it like that after you stole her from the church on her wedding day to another man."

"Damn right they won't," Rourke growls, fists bunching on his desk. "He's ruined everything."

Torin shoots him a look, and he shuts up. "But it might be our only course of action to at least offer some kind of deal for her." His eyes move to me. "After all, you fucked up what was going to be quite a lucrative partnership with the De León family, as far as I hear."

"So basically it's going to cost the clan for his mistakes," Rourke says.

I don't rise to Rourke's taunting, instead I just look at my uncle. "I couldn't let her marry him."

"I know, lad." He claps me on the shoulder. "We'll make arrangements for you and Mia to meet with Massimo and discuss it."

"Is that wise?" Rourke asks.

Torin's brow creases as he frowns. "What else do you suggest?"

"He shouldn't take Mia with him. It's too much of a temptation for Massimo to try to steal her back."

It's true that I wouldn't trust Massimo not to pull something if I took her with me. "Fine. I'll go alone."

"Not alone." Rourke glares at me. "I will be attending too, since he'll have demands of the clan, which I need to approve."

I sigh. "Fine, we'll go."

Torin clears his throat. "Perhaps I should be there

too, to make sure you two don't kill each other instead."

"Rourke and I may not always see eye to eye, but we're not stupid enough to squabble in front of our enemy." I glance at my uncle. "But you may come if you wish. I'll make the arrangements with Massimo."

"You better clean up this mess, Killian," Rourke warns.

I nod in response and rise from my chair. "Don't worry about it." I walk out of the study and head toward my room, knowing that all I want to do right now is to be with Mia. She was silent when I brought her in here, and I know her mind must be reeling right now.

Fleeing her own wedding with an enemy of their family won't have gone down well with her siblings, other than Camilla, who orchestrated the escape. I take two steps at a time as I rush toward Mia, my heart pounding in my ears. We've done something about the problem. The question is, can we survive the fallout?

I open the door to find Mia sat on the edge of the bed with her head in her hands. "Are you alright, baby girl?" I ask.

Mia looks at me, her eyes red and puffy from crying. She still looks achingly beautiful. "Not really."

I walk over to the bed and perch next to her, wrapping my arm around her back to pull her close. "I know it's hard, Mia, but everything will be okay." I press my lips to the top of her head and kiss her softly. "I'm going to fix it."

"How?" she asks, beautiful brown eyes staring up at me.

"I'm going to arrange a meeting with your brother."

Her eyes widen. "It's too dangerous. He'll kill you."

"He won't hurt me during a peaceful sitdown, even if I stole you."

Mia shakes her head. "You don't know what he's capable of." Her hand moves to mine and she squeezes. "I'll have to come with you, otherwise he'll never believe this is what I wanted."

I clench my jaw, as my initial instinct was to take her to the meeting. Rourke, however, didn't believe it wise. "I can't, Mia."

Her eyes narrow. "Don't tell me you are as chauvinistic as the rest of them?" She stands, looking furious. "I'm fed up with being treated like a second-rate citizen."

If it weren't for the circumstances, I'd probably find her little tantrum cute. At the moment, it is just another problem.

"Rourke won't allow it. He says it's too much of a temptation for your brother to steal you back."

Her lips purse, and she sets her hands on her hips. "If you don't take me, he will kill you." She says it with such certainty.

"How do you know that?"

"Because you telling him that his sister wants to be with you isn't the same as him hearing it from me." She shakes her head. "It's the only option. Make arrangements to ensure he couldn't possibly steal me." She shrugs. "Meet somewhere public."

*Public.*

It's rare that we agree to have meetings in public with enemies, as the risk of being outed is high.

"Are you crazy?" I ask.

Her eyes flash. "No, sensible."

"It's risky to meet with an enemy publicly."

Mia tilts her head. "It's safe. You will just be meeting my brother for a meal with me in a restaurant. What could be more simple?"

"Come here," I order, tapping my lap to show her where I want her.

She regards me with suspicion, but in the end walks over to me and sits on my lap. "Will you at least consider it?"

"Yes, I'll run it by Rourke."

She sighs and leans against me, eyes flickering shut. "I can't believe I ran away from my own wedding."

I growl softly. "A wedding you never agreed to." My hands tighten on her hips as I adjust her so she's straddling me, looking at me with those beautiful brown eyes. "They had what was coming to them."

Mia's throat bobs. "I love my family, but they are so out of touch." She shakes her head. "I've always hated the fact they're so involved in trafficking. It's one thing I could never get my head around."

I nod in response, as trafficking is the most disgusting aspect of the crime world. The Callaghan Clan has never even considered entering trading in flesh. "It's wrong, even by a criminal's standards."

"I think I've just always turned a blind eye to it." Her eyes turn determined. "But not anymore."

I chuckle. "What are you going to do? Become an activist?"

"Maybe," she says, arching a brow.

It's crazy the way my stomach flips at the look in her eyes. She's so perfect and so beautiful and I can't believe she's here with me.

"I love you, baby girl," I murmur, my voice quiet and uncertain, because never before have I uttered those three words to another human. Except maybe my mom when I was little, but not recently.

Her eyes widen slightly and then glisten with unshed tears. "I love you too," she replies, her voice cracking with emotion.

I pull her closer and kiss her soft, pouty lips. They part for me and my tongue delves inside as the desperation between us hitches.

She was so close to marrying another man. So close to slipping through my fingers.

And now she's here, with me, in my room. I won't let her get away again. This time I'm holding her close and never letting go.

## 23

## MIA

*T*wo days have passed since Killian stole me away from the church and still no word from my brother.

It figures he would be difficult, but I can't ease the guilt clawing at my gut.

Camilla rang me and told me she took off for the academy early, because she couldn't stand being around our brothers at the moment.

Apparently, they blamed her for being complicit in the entire thing.

I walk through the house toward the kitchen, admiring the art on the walls as I pass by.

It's less extravagant than our home and more homely, and I like it a lot.

As I enter the kitchen, I notice a young woman sitting on a stool at the island eating her lunch. "Oh, sorry to interrupt."

She smiles at me and shakes her head. "No worries, come on it. Mia right?"

I nod in response.

"I'm Viki, Rourke's wife."

I swallow hard as I realize Viki is also Spartak's daughter, the same daughter he shot. "Nice to meet you. I just wanted to fix a sandwich."

Viki holds up a plate. "Have one of these. I made too many thinking Rourke would be home for lunch, but he's at a meeting."

I gratefully sit down and grab one of the salami sandwiches. "I assume Rourke is with Killian, then?" I take a bite out of the sandwich, only then realizing how hungry I was. "He was gone when I woke."

"Yes, I believe they're meeting with your brother."

I almost choke on the sandwich and set it down. "What?"

Her eyes widen. "Was I not supposed to tell you?"

I clench my fists on the island. "Killian promised he'd consider bringing me with him."

"Oh, sorry." She gives me a pitiful glance. "If it's any consolation, I doubt my husband would have allowed it."

"Men are fools," I mutter.

She laughs at that. "I'd have to agree with that sentiment."

"My brother won't just take Killian's word for it that I want to be with him." She shakes her head. "He'll kill him instead."

"Unlikely," Viki says, brow furrowing. "They're meeting at the Oriole. It's very public."

"At least he listened to one of my ideas." I realize at that moment that Viki fucked up by telling me where they're meeting. "I'm sorry, I've suddenly lost my appetite," I say, setting down the half-eaten sandwich on my plate. "Maybe I'll save it for later." I pop it in the refrigerator and then head toward the door. "It was nice to meet you."

"You too," she says, her attention on her sandwich.

I slip out of the kitchen and head for the front door, knowing that I have to get to the restaurant before it's too late.

Massimo may not be crazy enough to kill Killian in public, but it doesn't change the fact that he won't believe Killian.

If we are going to find a way to be together, then we have to work together.

I call up the Uber app on my phone and order one, impatiently tapping my feet on the sidewalk as I wait.

After five excruciatingly long minutes, the driver pulls up to the curb and rolls down his window. "Mia?"

I nod. "Yep, that's me." I slide into the back of the car and rest my head on the headrest as he drives me toward the restaurant.

I'll never forgive Massimo if something happens to Killian, which is why I need to get there before it's too late. Somehow, there has to be a way out of this where everyone is happy. I fear that is wishful thinking.

THE RESTAURANT IS BUSY, which is a good sign.

If it were quiet, I couldn't be confident that the lack of people would keep my family from attacking the Callaghans out in the open.

Once I get to the host, he looks down his nose at me. "Name?"

"I'm here with the Morrone party." I grit my teeth, as I don't like the way he's looking at me.

Granted, I'm not exactly dressed for one of the fanciest restaurants in Chicago, given that I rushed out of the house without a second thought.

His brow furrows. "All guests have arrived for that dinner."

"Last minute addition," I say, crossing my arms over my chest. "You wouldn't want to upset my brother, Massimo, would you?"

His eyes narrow, but he shakes his head. "Of course not, Miss Morrone, right this way."

My heart thuds against my rib cage as he leads me across the busy restaurant floor toward a table near the back.

Trust my brother to ensure he got the most private table in the entire place. It makes my stomach churn with unease.

He clears his throat. "A Miss Morrone to join you," he announces, drawing everyone's eyes to me.

Massimo stands suddenly, eyes narrowing. "Mia, why are you here?"

The host leaves as I shrug. "I found out about the meeting and had to come. You have to know that leaving with Killian was my choice."

Killian is glaring daggers at me right now, so I elect not to look at him.

Massimo looks irritated as he tugs at the tie around his neck and that's when I notice Paisley sat at the table.

I give her a wave and then take a seat next to her, leaning over. "What did I miss?"

"A hell of a lot of tension."

I swallow hard. "Tension I created, no doubt." I glance at my brother, who has taken his seat again.

"Why didn't you tell me about Killian?" he demands.

I shrug. "What good would it have done?" I glance at Killian. "I told you there was someone else. You told me it didn't matter."

Massimo sighs heavily, looking me in the eye. "You've put the famiglia in a tough position with the De León family."

"Fuck the famiglia," I say, anger clawing at my insides.

"Mia!" Luca says, eyes wide. "You know that family is the most important thing to us."

"Right, so important that you just sell me off to the highest bidder?"

A muscle in his jaw tenses, but he nods. "She has a point," he says, glancing at Massimo.

"Enough," Massimo growls, nostrils flaring as he looks across the table at Killian. "Do you expect me to agree on a deal for my sister's hand in marriage to you after you so blatantly disrespected us?"

Killian grits his teeth before nodding once. "Yes, because we will give you something you want."

"And what is that?" he asks, eyes narrowing.

"Territory. If you agree to Killian marrying Mia, we will offer you a chuck of territory as a peace offering." Rourke runs a hand across the back of his neck. "We need to work together, and their marriage could be the final nail in the coffin, so to speak. New generation, new peace treaty between our families." He shrugs and his eyes remain fixed on my brother. It's an offer that isn't disrespectful, but I fear it's rather one-sided in that it benefits the Morrone family more than the Callaghan Clan.

After a few moments of silence, Massimo nods. "It's a deal." He doesn't sound too thrilled about it as he glares at me. "Mia will marry Killian. We will agree to the specifics tomorrow over dinner at the Morrone residence, and to anyone not at this table, it was an agreement brought about mutually, not because Killian stole Mia."

"He didn't steal me. I ran away," I say, glaring at my brother.

Massimo shakes his head. "Whatever, you get what

you want, little sister." All the tension in my body eases, but as I glance over at Killian in glee, he doesn't look so happy. He's angry that I came here, but he's the asshole that kept the meeting from me. I should feel sheer elation, but because Killian looks so angry, it tempers the happiness.

Rourke clears his throat. "It is settled then."

"Shall we eat?" Massimo asks, calling over the waiter.

It seems a little odd that we'd share a meal together considering how tense the atmosphere is, but Massimo doesn't seem to let it phase him.

"What can I get you, sir?" the waiter asks.

"I'll have the fillet steak, medium-rare with pepper sauce."

He nods, jotting down the order. The waiter then goes around the entire table before leaving to get our orders. And then silence ensues.

"So, this isn't awkward in the slightest," Luca jokes, as always being the clown.

I shoot him an irritated glare. "if our families are going to work together, we have to get used to being in each other's company. Don't you think?"

"Aye," Rourke says, running a hand through his light brown hair. "But it'll take some getting used to."

"No shit," Massimo mutters.

I roll my eyes and grab the bottle of wine in the center of the table, pouring myself a glass. "All of you need to lighten up. After all, it's Adrik that is our real enemy, right?"

The mention of Adrik seems to make it worse. All the men at the table grimace. "Don't say that name," Luca snaps.

I raise a brow, as Luca is always the most laid back. "Well, what are you going to do about him?"

"He's put himself in a powerful position, if the Estrada family in Mexico back his succession." Rourke shrugs. "They will believe Hernandez was weak and sloppy." He takes a sip of his beer. "It's rather brilliant the way he's handled it."

"The biggest issue is how we're going to stop him using those fucking missiles," Kieran mutters.

I swallow hard at the thought as it's been weighing heavily on my mind ever since I found out about Adrik's plan. The psycho threatens to destroy everyone I love in this world. Somehow, we have to stop him in his tracks, even if he has the cartel behind him.

There's a tense silence as everyone thinks about the question Killian's brother just posed.

"We have no choice but to negotiate with him," Massimo says, his jaw clenching. "I don't like it, but we need him to decommission those missiles and eliminate the threat, and that's the only way to do it."

"Aye, I hate to say that I have to agree," Rourke says, eyes narrowing as he glares at Massimo. "Which of us should reach out to him?"

It's odd to be privy to these kinds of conversations,

since as a woman I'm mainly left in the dark. I watch as the men discuss who will be the one to invite Adrik to a truce meeting. "Surely Spartak makes the most sense?" I say, instantly regretting speaking when all eyes turn to me.

"Spartak?" Killian scoffs, eyes wide. "He's the least objective of the three. Don't you think?"

"Aye, Spartak wants Adrik's head for his betrayal," Kieran adds.

I shake my head. "They're family."

Everyone just looks at me like I'm being naïve. "And that matters how?" Massimo asks, rolling his eyes.

"Surely he's more likely to trust his own family than one of you."

"He knows how insane his uncle can be, so no." Rourke shakes his head. "I think you'll find it would have the opposite effect."

Paisley leans toward me. "He seems a little insane. I met him at Podolka."

I swallow hard and shut my mouth, feeling useless as always. It's loathsome the way women are treated by my own family and my future family, it would seem.

"I know he's crazy, but I'm sure if Adrik were to agree to a peaceful meeting that Spartak isn't foolish enough to break it." My brow furrows as I glance at each face around the table. "He's not that stupid, considering what is at stake."

"Mia has a point," Luca says, raising a brow as he looks at me.

"Of course I have a fucking point. I'm fed up with you treating me like a second-rate citizen." I point my knife at Massimo and then at Luca. "Stop it."

Massimo chuckles at that and then the rest of the table starts laughing, even Killian.

"What's so funny?" I ask, crossing my arms over my chest.

Luca shakes his head. "You, piccola. Born and raised in this world and still you fight back." He glances at Killian, amusement in his eyes. "I think you'll have your work cut out with her."

A whisper of a smirk twists onto Killian's lips. "I'm betting on it."

It's strange that a veil of tension seems to lift from the table as my family and Killian's begin to talk tentatively, dare I say, almost enjoying each other's company. My heart swells slightly as I glance at Killian, finding him looking right back at me with an odd glint in his beautiful green eyes. Hope is what I feel. Hope that somehow, despite our secret affair being revealed, we can make it out of this together, side by side as I always dreamed.

The question is, how realistic is that dream?

## 24

## KILLIAN

*M*ia is brilliant, but she's also a naughty little brat who needs punishing.

Somehow, we were getting nowhere with Massimo until she arrived. I guess she was right all along. Massimo needed to hear it from her to believe it.

Now, we're in the back of a town car with Rourke, who is furious that Viki let the location of the meeting slip.

"You know I'm going to punish you when I get you home?" I whisper into her ear.

She stiffens beside me. "What for?" Her jaw clenches. "For saving the fucking day?"

I clench my fists to stop myself from grabbing her here, in front of my brother. "Watch that mouth, baby girl."

Her eyes narrow, and she blows out an irritated breath before shaking her head. "Unbelievable."

"What's so unbelievable?" I question.

"You kept this meeting a secret from me after promising to consider bringing me along."

Rourke meets my gaze. One brow arched. "He was never going to bring you, Mia. I had told him no."

Her brown eyes dart to my brother, who she appeared to forget was sitting there. "Why? If I hadn't turned up when I did, I doubt the meeting would have gone so well."

"She has a point," I say.

Rourke shoots me a sharp look. "It was dangerous, as Massimo could have tried to kidnap you." His gaze moves to Mia. "Just like when he kidnapped Imalia off of Spartak on their wedding day." He shrugs. "History can help predict a lot."

Mia turns quiet at that and stares out of the window, clearly not wanting to continue the conversation. The rest of the way back to the house, we all remain silent. Once we get back, Rourke is the first to exit the car and head toward the house. Mia moves to get out, but I grab her hand and yank her back toward me.

"Where do you think you are going?" I ask, wrapping my palm around her slender throat.

Her body turns tense against mine. "Inside," she rasps.

"Did I tell you to leave the car?" Her eyes dart to the rearview mirror as the driver is still sitting up front. "Thanks, Derrick, I'll take it from here."

He nods and meets my gaze in the mirror. "Of course." He gets out, leaving us alone.

"Killian, let go," she protests, trying to twist away from me.

I tighten my grasp on her. "You are a naughty little brat for crashing a dangerous meeting like that, aren't you?"

Her tongue slides over her bottom lip, wetting it. "You're an asshole at times."

I smirk. "And you love it." I grab her hips and lift her to position her over my lap, her ass facing upwards.

"What are you—"

I lift the hem of her dress and then spank her hard on the right cheek, groaning as my cock stiffens against her stomach. "Punishing you, baby girl."

She wriggles on my lap, which only makes me harder. "Why here?" she gasps.

I don't answer, instead I slam the palm of my hand into her other ass cheek. And then I knead the already reddening skin.

"Beautiful," I muse.

Mia glares at me over her shoulder. "Killian."

I spank her again, even harder.

She yelps at the sudden pain, and then I spank her a few more times for good measure.

"By the time I'm through with you, you'll think again about being so naughty."

Her brow furrows as she looks at me over her shoulder. "I'm not a kid."

"No, but you are my submissive, Mia."

Her eyes narrow. "What?"

"And a submissive should do as they're told."

I grab the fabric of her panties, which are bunched against her wet pussy, groaning when I feel just how soaked she is. "You are gagging for this, baby girl." I thrust three fingers inside of her, which results in a cock-aching moan. "Such a dirty girl getting off on being spanked. Do you like being punished, Mia?"

There's no response as I continue to thrust my fingers harder and deeper inside of her, pushing her toward the edge.

"I asked you a question," I growl.

"Yes, sir," Mia rasps, glancing at me over her shoulder with such desire glazing her beautiful brown irises. "I love it."

"Good girl," I say, fucking her harder now.

"Oh God," she mutters, her thighs shaking as the pressure inside her builds.

I pull my fingers out, smirking as it results in an irritated whimper from the woman over my lap.

"What the hell?" she asks, glaring at me over her shoulder.

"Naughty girls don't get to come, Mia. This is a punishment, not a reward." I push her off of my lap and open the door to the car. "And I'm only just getting started." I hold my hand out to help her down from the car, but she just jumps out on her own.

The look in her eyes is one of pure rage as she glares at me. "I'm wondering if I made a mistake."

I chuckle. "What kind of mistake?"

"Choosing you," she says, nostrils flaring. "You can act like a real self-entitled, arrogant dick."

"And yet only a minute ago you were telling me how much you love being spanked."

She blows out an exasperated breath and then rushes off toward the house, as if she can escape me.

There is no escape. Mia Morrone is mine, and there's no going back now.

I intend to claim her in every way, first by making sure she's getting big and round with my baby.

My cock swells in my pants at the thought and I groan as I follow my beautiful baby girl into the house, knowing that I'll never get enough of her.

"You can't escape me, Mia," I say as I follow her into the entrance hall.

She spins around and points at me. "You are the one that needs punishing for not telling me about the meeting."

I tilt my head. "If I'd told you it was happening but I couldn't bring you, what would you have done?" I'm pretty confident about her answer.

Her shoulders slump slightly. "That's not the point."

I walk toward her and cup her cheeks in my hand. "It's exactly the point. You would have gone anyway, wouldn't you?"

She bites her bottom lip in the most delicious way. "Possibly."

"So, I didn't tell you, because Rourke told me you couldn't come." I shrug. "It's not up to me to call the shots, although I can't deny your presence helped."

A little triumph shines in those brown eyes of hers. "You admit you wouldn't have got where you did without me?"

I kiss her quickly and then shake my head. "I don't believe we would have, but don't let it go to your head."

She smiles, and it lights a fire blazing in my gut as I grab her hand and drag her toward the stairs.

"Now, where were we?" I ask, glancing at her over my shoulder. "Oh yes, I need to continue punishing you."

She doesn't look as irritated this time as I lead her to the bedroom and shut the door behind us, locking it.

"On the bed," I order.

There's hesitation before she finally sighs and goes to lie on the bed.

It's amusing how she can't deny any of my orders. No matter what, she always wants to please.

The sign of a true submissive—a submissive who I've been in love with for years.

It's hard to believe she loves me back, but I sense we've always been on this path since the academy.

She mistook the kiss during my last night at the academy as a quick attempt to get into her pants before I left, but it wasn't that at all.

I'd known there was something about her ever since we met as kids. I remember thinking to myself if I ever marry I'd marry her.

Mia watches me with interest as I stand in the same spot, mesmerized by her utter beauty. "What am I to do on the bed, exactly?" she questions.

I hold a finger up to my lips to tell her to be quiet and approach, running my hands gently down the length of her legs.

She shudders, eyes dilating with desire. "Killian."

I love hearing her say my name. "Yes, lass?"

Her nostrils flare as my finger don't stop, moving higher until they skate over her inner thigh. "Please," she begs.

"Please what?" I push, wanting her to tell me what she wants.

"Please fuck me," she says, her cheeks turning a little pinker as she watches me cautiously.

I groan at the thought. But she hasn't earned it yet. "On your hands and knees," I order.

Her eyes flash with a mix of desire and fear as she does as she's told, positioning herself in front of me.

I push the hem of her skirt higher and then grab the gusset of her panties, tearing them apart.

Mia gasps, glancing at me over her shoulder. "Do you have to ruin all my best underwear?"

"I rather enjoy it, yes." I spank her firm ass. "I'll take you shopping for more."

That seems to shut her up along with my finger as it

skates lightly over her swollen clit. She shudders, arching her back further.

I tease her with the pad of my finger, running it roughly over her clit.

She moans, her pussy getting wetter with each movement. "Please, Killian," she begs, her voice breathless.

"Please what, baby?"

"Fuck me," she grits out, arching her back and glaring at me over her shoulder.

"That's not a nice way to ask."

Mia's cheeks turn red with frustration as she blows out a breath. "Please fuck me, sir," she grits out.

I groan and spank her already red ass cheeks, holding myself back from ripping my clothes off and plowing into her with all that I've got.

"Do you really believe I've punished you enough?"

She doesn't say a word, because she knows how dark my desires are. The light spanking in the car was nothing, and I'm ready to take this to another level.

After all, Mia is to be my wife. She needs to know what kind of man she's dealing with. "Come with me," I say, grabbing her wrist and yanking her off the bed.

She stumbles after me, struggling to get her footing. "Where are we going?"

I stop in front of the bookcase on the far wall and give her a sly smirk. "My den."

"Den?" she asks, looking adorably confused.

I flick a switch and the secret door opens to reveal my sex dungeon.

Mia gasps when the lights illuminate the kinky room full of all my favorite toys.

"I want to play with you, baby girl."

Her throat bobs as she swallows. "What the hell is this?"

I push her inside and don't answer. "Now, be a good girl and get your ass on that bench." I point at my spanking bench.

Mia glances at me and then the bench and then me again, before swallowing hard. "Why are you showing me this now?"

"Because if we're going to be married, you need to know everything about me." I spank her ass. "On the bench, now."

She does as she's told, walking over to the bench and climbing onto it. The bench pushes her ass high in the air and I love the sight, as her still torn panties lay in tatters around her thighs.

"Such a beautiful girl," I murmur as I move toward the equipment hung up on the wall. I want to push every one of her boundaries tonight and see if she breaks.

I grab a blindfold and o ring gag first and walk back to her.

She shudders when she looks up at me. "What are you going to do to me?"

"Drive you fucking wild, baby." I tilt my head slightly. "Do you trust me?"

She nods. "Of course."

"Then relax." I put the blindfold on her first and then the gag so both her eyesight and speech are completely gone. "If you need me to stop, remember to click your fingers," I murmur, as I clasp her wrist into the fixings fitted to the bench. "Can you do that for me?"

She clicks her fingers with no issue despite the restraints around her wrists.

"Good girl." I run the pad of my finger down her spine, making her shudder. And then I fix her ankles in too, ensuring she can't move a muscle.

I step back, enjoying the sight of the woman I've wanted for so long at my mercy in this room.

My cock is leaking into my boxer briefs as I walk around the bench and stand in front of her, unzipping my pants. "Now, I'm going to fuck that pretty little throat."

Mia whimpers as I thrust my cock through the hole in the gag and right into the back of her throat. "Fuck," I grunt, as I grab a fistful of her hair, taking what I want from Mia. "Your throat feels like heaven."

I glare down at her as saliva spills over her chin and tears wet the fabric of the blindfold. "Take that cock like a good girl, Mia," I growl.

She moans around my shaft and then chokes some more, her throat contracting around my shaft.

"I want you to swallow every drop of my cum, baby girl," I groan, my rhythm getting jerkier and more frantic as I rush toward my climax. There's no holding back as I push myself right over the edge and then spill my cum down it, groaning as her throat feels like heaven around my shaft.

"Fuck, that was perfect," I murmur, grabbing hold of her chin. "Did you swallow every drop?"

I know she can't answer me, but she sticks her tongue out through the ring in the gag as her reply, showing me there's not a drop of cum left.

"Good girl," I reply, kissing her deeply as I thrust my tongue in and out of her gagged open mouth. "Such a good girl."

She moans, but it's muffled by the gag.

"Now, I want to see just how much of a good girl you are."

Her entire body shudders as I drop her chin and move around to the back of the bench, spanking her bare ass cheek with my palm.

I walk to the wall again, selecting a paddle from it and a large butt plug and bottle of lube.

My cock aches and hardens almost instantly at the thought of fucking her ass.

Mia's innocence is going to be corrupted by me and I can't find it in myself to care, because she was always meant to be mine.

I return and rub the flat paddle across her skin and

she shudders deliciously. "I'm going to make you cry from both pain and pleasure, baby girl."

Mia makes a whimpering sound again, but it's even more tortured. I pour some lube onto her beautiful asshole and thrust a finger inside, making her jerk forward. "First, I'm going to plug this tight virgin ass up." I add another finger, stretching her slowly.

Her pussy is so wet that her thighs are glistening with her arousal, and I love seeing that she's as in to this as me.

"Such a greedy girl," I murmur as her hips start to rotate backwards and she fucks herself on my fingers. "So fucking needy."

I grab the paddle and spank her ass with it. The thought of leaving my bruises only driving me crazier.

Her strangled cry of pain is audible despite the ring gag in her mouth.

Her ass grips me like a vise as I reach for the butt plug and lube it up, slipping my fingers out and pressing the large tip at her hole.

"Relax for me, Mia. I want that greedy ass to swallow this plug." I spank her with the paddle again in my other hand. "And then your desperate cunt is going to swallow my cock."

Her body relaxes and practically swallows the plug. Once it pops through the tight ring of muscles, she moans loudly.

More arousal spills from her pussy, making a mess of the bench.

"Fuck," I groan, unzipping my pants and dropping them to the floor. I can't even wait to step out of them, as I shuffle forward and rub the head in her arousal. "You are so wet, baby girl."

She moans, back arching.

"Do you like being at my mercy?"

Her head nods up and down frantically—the only way she can answer me.

"Such a good eager slut," I mutter, grabbing her hair and pulling on it. "My eager slut."

I push forward and bury my cock inside of her with one hard stroke.

Her muscles clamp around me instantly and I can hardly believe it as she comes apart, her body convulsing with the force of her orgasm.

She screams so loud I'm sure the entire house must hear her, but I don't care.

I fuck her right through it and build her toward the next, never once missing a beat. "All mine," I growl, chanting it as I take my baby girl to new heights.

And all the while, I can feel myself hoping that she gets pregnant this time. I want my baby in her belly before the night is through.

# MIA

*I*t feels like I've died as I shudder on the bench, my body feeling as though it's entirely liquid.

Never in my wildest dreams did I ever imagine anything like this. Killian has corrupted me and turned me into someone I can hardly even recognize anymore. The way he controls every aspect of this situation is so fucking hot as he deprives me of my senses and fucks me like an animal.

My jaw aches, and yet every ounce of pain only feeds the pleasure coursing through my body.

"My dirty little slut," he groans, spanking my ass with the paddle again.

I know he's going to leave bruises on my skin, and I relish the thought. It hurts like hell and yet it feels better than anything I've ever experienced. I moan as he drives into me harder, as if he's trying to break me apart. The lack of vision only seems to heighten every sensation, but I wish I could see his expression while he's fucking me like this.

As if he hears my mental plea, he yanks the blindfold from my face.

"Look at me," he growls.

I glance over my shoulder, my mouth still forced open by the gag.

The look in his eyes steals what little oxygen is left in my body. It's manic and possessive and almost impossible to describe. My stomach flutters.

"I want to breed this tight little pussy. Do you understand?"

I swallow hard at his dirty words, understanding he's suggesting he wants to get me pregnant. Problem is, I'm pretty sure I already am. I've just been too scared to buy a test and find out for sure.

"Do you understand?" he growls.

I realize then he wants a response to his question, and it snaps me out of it, nodding in reply.

"Good girl," he says, slamming into me with even more force.

My body feels so spent as he continues to use me. I've never felt more used and yet more aroused when he fucked my throat through this gag. It was degrading, and yet I loved it. Clearly, sex and enjoyment during it is very subjective and I feel like an asshole for ever judging my sister over her choices.

Killian is clearly sadistic and loves doling out pain

and taking control. I love bending to his will and being taken by him.

I watch him over my shoulder as sweat coats his muscled and inked torso, and I know in that moment I've seen nothing so beautiful before. He's a powerful, damaged, and dark man who I've loved for years. And most important of all, he's mine.

"That's it, baby," he murmurs, holding my gaze. "Watch me fuck that pretty little cunt of yours and breed it with my cum."

I feel the tension inside of me building like the lava bubbling under the earth's surface, preparing to erupt. It's the most intense sensation I've ever felt as I continue to watch him. The sight of him makes me crazy with need and I know I couldn't look away even if I wanted to.

The emotion flooding me at that moment is impossible to comprehend.

He holds my gaze, and it feels like he's looking right into the core of my being, seeing through everything.

I swallow hard, my mouth dry from being held open by the gag.

Killian spanks me again, but with his hand, my flesh so sore it sends a spark of pleasure right to my core.

Every muscle in my body becomes taut as I come apart from the most explosive orgasm I've ever had.

I scream, even though it's muffled by the gag, every part of my body feeling more sensitive than it has ever felt.

"Good girl," Killian purrs, his cock still spearing into me with hard, heavy thrusts. "Come on my cock and milk my cum into that tight little cunt," he growls.

His dirty talk heightens my pleasure as I moan through it, struggling to see through my hazy vision. I fall forward, my head down on the bench as my climax drains me.

He holds his cock deep inside of me, spilling all of his seed.

And then, he unfastens the gag at the back of my head, allowing me to shut my mouth. I can't bring myself to speak, as I'm still overwhelmed by what we just did and how much I loved it. My breathing is heavy and labored as I remain affixed to the bench, Killian's cock still lodged deep inside of me.

He leans over my back and kisses my spine, sending shivers through me. "That was fucking amazing, Mia."

I swallow hard, unable to find the words to explain just how good it was.

After a few moments of silence, he adds, "Did you enjoy it?"

I nod my head. "Very much," I say, my voice hoarse.

He chuckles. "That's because you are as kinky as me, baby girl."

Finally, he pulls his cock out of me and then unfastens the restraints around my ankles, before walking around to unfasten the restraints around my wrists. He then lifts me and takes me over to the bed in the center of the room, which is a four poster and affixed with all sorts of odd devices.

"Stay on your back for me, Mia. I don't want you wasting any of my cum."

I swallow hard as I look into his gorgeous green eyes. "And why is that?"

"I told you, I want to breed you." He kisses me, his tongue thrusting into my mouth. "I'm going to get your pregnant, baby girl."

A shudder races up my spine as I shake my head. "Isn't it a little soon?"

"Soon?" he asks, arching a brow. "No, because I'm spending the rest of my life with you and I want to watch you grow big and round with my baby." He kisses me again with such passion it makes my entire body tingle. And I decide at that moment I'll have to get a test and find out tomorrow without fail. It's scary at my age, but I can't think of anyone I'd rather have a baby with. Killian has always been my dream man and somehow, it seems like that dream is finally coming true.

---

I sit in front of the mirror at Killian's dressing table, fixing my makeup. It's weird to think I'm about to attend a dinner with my family almost as an outsider. After Killian made his desire for a baby clear last night, I brought a test and find out if I'm pregnant. The test was positive.

We are having a baby.

It's all a bit much to process as it's happened so fast, but I guess we've been reckless. After Killian's declaration of wanting to breed me, I've wondered if he didn't use protection on purpose. Before the meal tonight, I have to tell him I'm pregnant. I can't stand keeping it from him any longer. Even though I've only just found out for certain, I've been pretty sure for a little while.

The door to the bedroom swings open and he walks in, smiling. "Hey, baby girl."

"Hey," I say, smiling at him in the mirror, but I can't help the nerves twisting my stomach. "You're late." I'm not sure how to drop the bomb on him that I'm pregnant.

He shrugs. "A meeting ran over. Couldn't be helped." He walks over to me and kisses my neck softly, sending shivers right down my spine. "How was your day?"

"Boring," I say, although it's been rather eventful, finding out I'm pregnant. "I was so exhausted and sore I could hardly get out of bed." That is true, even though I got up so that Sandro could drive me to the drugstore. And I realize I just missed my opportunity to break the news.

He laughs. "Get used to it, as I enjoy having you in my dungeon." He licks a path up my neck and pleasure sparks deep in my core, making me moan.

"You need to get showered," I say, nodding my head toward the adjoining bathroom.

"Shame you've already had one." The look in his eyes is devilish. "I would have liked to have some fun with you."

I shake my head. "You shouldn't have been late then."

His eyes flash with a challenge. "Perhaps you need a second shower."

I shake my head. "No fucking chance. I've just finished my makeup."

He watches me for a moment, increasing the nerves knotting together in my stomach. "Fair enough. I'll be quick." He kisses the back of my neck softly.

A shudder races down my spine at his lips on me, and I hate how little control I have around him.

And then he gives me a cocky little wink and walks toward the bathroom.

I clench my thighs together, feeling needy despite the fact we have no time to do anything. The last thing I want is to be late for the dinner with my family. The rush of water from the shower echoes through the room, and I glance toward the bathroom.

I can't deny I'm tempted to go and spy on him. The need coursing through my veins as I push myself up from the dressing table and walk toward the bathroom door, which he's left ajar.

I peer through the crack in the door and moan softly when I see him with his cock in his hand. It's hard and erect, and my thighs dampen instantly. Killian's eyes are clamped shut as he works the shaft up and down, soap covering his beautiful skin and the ink covering it.

I lick my lips, wanting nothing more than to feel his cock deep inside of me, despite how sore I felt earlier. Instead, I reach under the skirt of my dress and shove my fingers deep inside of me, thrusting in and out hard. My teeth sink into my bottom lip as I force myself not to moan, watching Killian as he pleasures himself.

Suddenly, his eyes shoot open and my heart skips a beat. They connect with mine almost instantly, and a smirk pulls at his lips.

"Come in here where I can see you," he orders.

I open the door and move inside, my fingers still inside of my pussy.

"Such a dirty girl, watching me and fingering that beautiful pussy." He continues to stroke his cock with hard, forceful strokes. "Show me how wet you are."

Excitement pulses through my veins as I lift my skirt and show him my pussy, which is ridiculously wet.

He growls softly and nods to the bathtub. "Sit on the edge with those legs spread wide and fuck yourself in front of me."

"Yes, sir," I say softly, walking over to the edge of the tub, which is set opposite the shower and sitting down. I hoist my dress up to my hips and spread my legs wide apart, my fingers still deep inside.

"Such a good girl," he purrs, his cock leaking precum as he continues to take himself in hand. "Now, fuck that pussy the way you love me fucking it."

I thrust my fingers in and out with hard, forceful movements, watching Killian as he matches them with his hand.

"I bet you wish my cock was deep inside of you, don't you?"

"Yes, so badly," I moan.

"Too bad that you will have to be satisfied with watching."

My nipples harden as I continue to push myself higher, watching him.

"Fuck yourself with four fingers, Mia."

I swallow hard and add my two other fingers, moaning as they stretch my sore pussy more. The red-hot desire pulsing through my veins outweighs the ache from last night's rough fucking.

"You're tight little cunt is dripping everywhere," he growls, his hand movements becoming stronger and faster. "I bet it's dripping right down onto that beautiful asshole, which I intend to fuck sooner rather than later."

Fluttering ignites in the pit of my stomach at the thought of trying to fit his huge cock in such a tight, tiny hole. He may have got that butt-plug in, but his cock is longer and wider.

"Would you like that, Mia?"

I nod in response. Despite knowing how crazy it is, I want to experience it with him. This man has opened my eyes to pleasure I never knew existed. A world far beyond what I'd imagined, and I love how good it feels to be kinky with him. "Yes," I rasp.

The smile that twists onto his lips is downright wicked. "Good, because I'm going to take that virgin ass and stretch it over my dick. But I'm also going to get my fuck machine out and it's going to plow into your pussy while I do." His breathing becomes more labored and the thrusts of his hand up and down his thick shaft faster. "You'll be stuffed full with two big cocks at the same time, fucking you. How about that?"

I can hardly speak at the thought, as it's surely impossible to fit his cock in my ass and a dildo in my pussy. And yet, it makes me wetter. I moan loud, thrusting harder as my orgasm comes rushing toward me. "I'd love it," I breathe, barely louder than a whisper, but he hears me.

"Good, now make that pussy come while thinking about it. I want to see you squirt for me, Mia, just like you did before."

I draw in a shuddering breath as I hit the spot inside of me that turns me into liquid. And then I squeal at the top of my lungs. The force of release so intense I find it hard to believe it feels so good, especially since I brought myself to climax.

As I pull my fingers out and rub my clit, a flood of liquid shoots out of my pussy and onto the floor, making a mess.

Killian growls, drawing my attention back to him as he shoots load after load of thick cum onto the shower screen, watching me with such intensity it's almost fear inspiring. "You are my dirty little slut, Mia," he says, his voice gravelly. "Aren't you?"

I nod. "Yes, I'm your slut, sir."

He groans as he continues to stroke his cock until every drop is spent. "Now, be a good girl and get cleaned up." His eyes narrow. "You are going to make us late."

I grit my teeth. "The only reason we'll be late is because of you."

"I don't think so, Mia." He stops stroking himself and shuts off the water, pushing open the shower door. "You are the one that was fingering yourself and watching me jerk off." He grabs a towel and wraps it around his waist. "Such a naughty girl."

He walks toward me and grabs the hand I'd been fingering myself with.

I watch, my heart racing as he lifts the fingers to his mouth and sucks each one clean individually, groaning as he does. "My naughty girl."

He yanks me toward him and kisses me, stealing the oxygen from my lungs. And then he breaks away, walking into the bedroom and leaving me breathless and needy again despite having just climaxed.

I fear tonight is going to be uncomfortable if I can't control my earth shattering desire for the man I'm trying to convince my family to let me marry.

## KILLIAN

The last time I came to the Morrone's house, I broke into Mia's bedroom. Luckily, I was never caught crashing either party.

It feels a little odd being here by invitation, along with Rourke, Viki, Kieran Maeve, Gael, and Torin. We didn't want to come with an army, but at the same time, it's stupid to walk into an enemy's home without backup. We kept it to the family only. After all, the Morrone family is a large one, too.

"Let me do all the talking when it comes to territory," Rourke says, glaring at me.

I hold my hands up. "Of course."

He's been angry ever since Mia turned up at Oriole and he's taking it out on everyone. Giving territory to the Morrone family will be one of our biggest setbacks in years, and it's under his watch. It may not be his fault since it was my actions that lead us here, but it won't look good that he's giving over territory within a year of taking leadership.

He presses the bell at the door, and within minutes, a housekeeper comes to open the door. "Mr. Callaghan?" She confirms, brow furrowing slightly as she gazes at the rest of us.

"Yes."

She nods and ushers us inside. "Please wait here while I fetch Mr. Morrone."

I tap my foot on the fancy marble floor, glancing around at the lavish interior. "Do you find our house dowdy?" I ask, leaning close to Mia.

Her brow furrows. "What?"

I shrug. "Well, it's not as fancy and lavish as this place."

"It's far more homely at your home."

I nod. It's true there's a coldness to the home with all its marble and pomp. It's not a kind of place I could imagine growing up. "True."

A thud of footsteps echoes through the entrance hall and Massimo appears with his wife, two brothers, cousins and uncle.

It feels a bit like a standoff as they line up in front of us, eyes narrowed slightly. "I'm a little surprised you turned up," Massimo says, his eyes pausing a few beats on his sister, Mia.

Rourke's muscles bunch under his tight suit jacket as he glares at the acting don. "Of course we turned up. We have business to discuss."

Massimo smirks slightly. "Indeed, shall we?" He signals to the corridor they all appeared from.

Rourke nods, and Massimo leads the tense dinner party visitors through a wide corridor and left into the most pretensions dining room I've ever seen. The room is painted in cream with gilt decorative baroque style details all over the walls and ceiling. Expensive and ancient looking paintings hang on the walls and the floors are covered in that same fine Amalfi marble.

I lean toward Mia and whisper in her ear, "This definitely isn't homely. It's intimidating."

She glances at me, a small smirk on her lips. "Don't let my family hear you say that, as they'll never let you forget it."

I shake my head and keep my hand on the small of her back as we approach the stupidly long dining table.

Mia appears to know her place and takes a seat, so I sit on the right of her. The rest of my family is shown where to sit, as Massimo takes his place at the head of the table.

The atmosphere is tense and I can't imagine it will be a very pleasurable meal if it's like this the entire time.

"We need to discuss the territory before we even consider announcing Mia and Killian's engagement," Massimo says, cutting straight to the point.

Rourke nods. "Aye."

"What do you propose?" Massimo asks.

I know how much cutting a slice of our territory off

and giving it to the Morrone family hurts him, but I couldn't allow Mia to be married off. She is mine.

"My proposal is a take it or leave it proposition."

Massimo nods as if in understanding, but we all know that if his proposal isn't what Massimo expects, then this meeting could turn sour quickly.

"I will give you Bridge Port, Armor square, Douglas, Fuller Park and Grand Boulevard." Rourke's eyes narrow. "It's my best and final offer, as well as a peace treaty between our families."

There's silence as Massimo regards my brother carefully, giving nothing away in his expression. "Deal."

It feels like a veil of tension has been lifted from the room as everyone seems to exhale at the same time.

"When and how shall we announce Mia's engagement?" Massimo glances at her, irritation still clear in his eyes. "Second engagement, I might add."

Mia stiffens slightly next to me. "And whose fault is that?" she says, glaring at her brother.

"It does not matter." He waves his hand dismissively. "Father came out of his coma yesterday," he says, eyes fixed on her. "We've yet to break the news to him. Do you want to be the one to do it?"

Mia's throat bobs as she swallows, but she gives him a quick nod in reply.

"Fair enough. You can visit the hospital tomorrow." His attention moves back to Rourke. "Any ideas for the announcement?"

"We can hold a small party at The Shamrock?" Rourke suggests.

Massimo glances at me and then Killian. "What do you say?"

I look at Mia. "It's up to you."

She sinks her teeth into her bottom lip, glancing between me, Rourke, and Massimo. "The Shamrock sounds good."

Massimo nods. "Then I'll leave it to you to make arrangements, Callaghan."

Rourke's jaw tightens slightly, but he nods.

"Great, can we eat now?" Luca says, smirking slightly. "I'm fucking starving."

I smile at that and the temperature in the room eases from frosty to chilly. Mia's brother seems alright, even if he can be a bit of a hot head. I mean, the guy shot Spartak Volkov for fuck's sake. That act alone deserves my respect.

Leo, the middle brother, shakes his head. "Always thinking about your stomach, aren't you?"

Rico clears his throat. "I could do with a fucking drink first."

"Aye," Torin adds. "I'm parched."

Everyone chuckles in response and the atmosphere warms further, as Massimo calls over one of the servers waiting near the door.

"Get everyone drinks. Whatever they want," he says.

She walks around the table taking people's drinks

orders and as I glance around the people sitting around it, I wonder if this could be the future. A Morrone and Callaghan Clan alliance, after years of feuding. It would be ironic that all it took was me and Mia to find each other to bring the two families together.

The past is behind us now, even if it's full of blood shed. Could love really win out?

I may have been ruthless in my pursuit of her, but I never believed it could bring about peace.

We may have had to give up a slice of territory, but it would be worth it just to stop the violence.

Mateo, Massimo's cousin, is sitting next to me and turns. "So you are going to be part of the family then, Callaghan?" he asks, eyes narrowing.

I shrug. "I guess so."

"I never thought I'd see the day we'd welcome an alliance with the Irish." His nose turns up.

"That's because you are a closed minded idiot, Mateo," Mia quips, glaring at him.

He chuckles. "Always have been so feisty, Mia."

She huffs and shakes her head. "Ignore him," she says to me.

"That's exactly what I intend to do," I say, smiling at my fiancée, who I've yet to buy a ring for. Our engagement came rather suddenly, and I hate that it didn't happen the way I wanted it to. It was part of a bargain with our families, rather than romantic.

Mateo observes me for a few beats before nodding. "I've decided that you two are perfect for each other."

Both of us laugh as neither of us wanted his blessing.

Rico, his brother, shakes his head. "You can be a real idiot, brother."

They start to squabble as the woman returns with our drinks. She sets down a pint of Guinness in front of me and I take a long sip, savoring the flavor. "At least you Italians have good beer in, even if it is Irish."

Torin nods. "Aye, it's appreciated." He takes a long sip, too.

Mia leans towards me. "Can you believe how well everyone is getting on?"

I shake my head. "Not really."

Her throat bobs slightly. "I'm not sure it would be the same if my father were here."

I'm not sure it would be either. In fact, I'm fairly confident that the deal wouldn't have been anywhere near as easy.

The difference is that both Massimo and my brother, unlike their fathers, want an end to this historical feud.

"Will you come with me to the hospital tomorrow?" she asks, her voice almost cracking.

I squeeze her thigh beneath the table and nod. "Of course, baby girl. I'll do anything for you."

Her smile could set the world ablaze. "Thank you," she murmurs, squeezing my hand.

Maeve has been oddly quiet tonight. In fact, she hasn't been herself since she found out the truth about our uncle and what he did to her. I guess scars like that take a long time to heal. Gael, however much I dislike him, has been her saving grace through it all.

"Mia, I don't think you've met my sister, Maeve," I say, smiling at her as she sits directly opposite me.

Mia shakes her head. "No, I haven't."

Maeve smiles, but as always lately, it doesn't reach her eyes. "It's nice to meet you, Mia." She sighs. "It will be good to even up the balance of females in the family. With you and Viki, we'll be a little less male dominated."

Mia nods. "I can't imagine growing up with just my brothers." She glares at Massimo, Leo and Luca. "They would have driven me insane, but luckily I had Camilla." She glances at Massimo. "Will Camilla be able to attend the wedding?"

He nods. "Of course, once we know a date, I'll put in a request with the academy."

She visibly relaxes next to me. "Good, she has to be my maid of honor."

Gael clears his throat. "Since our alliance is strengthening, I propose we try to strike Adrik as a unit."

Some of the tension returns at the mention of Adrik.

"Is that not what we're doing?" Massimo asks, regarding him warily.

Gael nods. "Yes, but we could combine forces in a more literal sense."

Rourke turns tense, and I sense that Gael didn't run this idea past him. "What are you getting at, Ryan?" he asks, calling him by his second name.

Gael shrugs. "If we were one unit, rather than two, it would be more effective against the cartel. It's merely a suggestion."

"You are suggesting that the Morrone family and Callaghan family join forces on the streets?" I confirm, the idea is rather far-fetched, even if I'm about to marry into the family.

"Yes," he says simply.

Massimo glances at Rourke. "Is this your idea?"

Rourke shakes his head. "I fear it's a step too far for our men and yours."

"Agreed," Massimo says. "If we get desperate, we can consider it."

Rourke nods in accord and it seems that is the end of that.

Kieran clears his throat. "What is this?" he asks, holding up some kind of breaded ball.

Luca shakes his head. "It's a stuffed rice ball. We call it Arancini."

Kier nods and takes a bite and then his eyes widen. "Tastes delicious."

It seems to mark the end of any more business talk as the rest of the party chat amongst themselves in quiet conversation. The tension that had been there at the start eases and I lean toward Mia. "This is going better than I expected."

Mia sighs. "Don't get ahead of yourself. We haven't got to the entrees yet." Her expression looks a little pained, which is surprising considering.

My brow furrows. "Are you okay?" I ask.

She nods, swallowing hard in a way that suggests she's lying.

"What's wrong, Mia? Tell me."

"Not here," she murmurs, shaking her head.

I grit my teeth, wanting to know what's bothering her. "Where, then?"

"Later," she hisses back.

I move closer to her so my lips are within an inch of her ear. "No, Mia. You tell me right now what is wrong, or I swear to God I'll drag you right out of here in front of everyone and cause a scene."

Her brown eyes flash with anger. "This is not how I wanted to tell you, but you are being a complete and utter jerk." She leans toward me and whispers, "There's nothing wrong other than the fact I'm pregnant."

It feels like she slaps me in the face as she pulls away, glaring at me angrily. Not because she's pregnant, which is exactly what I wanted, but because I was an ass for forcing her to tell me that way. "Sorry, baby girl," I mutter, grabbing her hand and kissing the back of it. "I didn't mean to force it like that, but this is amazing news."

"What news is that?" Maeve asks, clearly catching the end of our conversation.

"It's just amazing news that me and Mia will be getting married," I say, shrugging.

Maeve looks a little confused but nods. "Fair enough."

When she looks away, I give Mia a wink, which seems to soften her anger.

"You are such an idiot at times," she mutters.

I smile. "And despite that, you love me anyway."

She rolls her eyes. "Yes, for some unknown reason."

I nudge her gently and move closer again. "I can't wait to start a family with you," I whisper into her ear.

It seems that breaks her anger entirely as she beams at me with the most beautiful smile I've ever seen. "Me neither." I watch her in awe, struggling to believe that I'm actually lucky enough to call her mine. Mia is pregnant with my child and our engagement has been agreed on.

It's hard to believe that this isn't just a fantasy anymore. We've managed to make it out the other side, with both our families tentatively agreeing to it. It's miraculous considering how bad the history is between the Morrone family and my family, and yet I can't shake the sense of unease that until Adrik is dealt with, our happy ending is under threat.

# MIA

*I* feel sick as I walk the corridors of Mercy Hospital, even with Killian right by my side.

Father is going to get a shock when he sees me with a Callaghan and I can't help but feel guilty that I'm telling him while he's so unwell. Although, we've both agreed not to tell anyone about the baby until we have no choice. It's going to remain between the two of us for now.

I stop a few paces from the door, and Killian stops next to me. "I think it best I go in alone at first. It would be a bit of a shock for him to see us together."

Killian gives me a sad smile. "You'll be fine, baby girl." He kisses me softly. "I'll be waiting right outside."

I nod and move away from him, my heart pounding at a thousand miles an hour. Once I get to the door, I see he's sleeping soundly in bed. It's hard to see him like this, a man so great turn so sickly. He's survived so many things over the years, but now he's been brought to his knees by a disease.

I gently push open the door and step inside, drawing a deep breath to steady my nerves.

"Father," I murmur softly.

His eyes flicker open the moment I speak. "Mia." He smiles weakly. "It's good to see you."

Guilt coils through my gut as I move closer. "I've got some news." If I don't just rip off the bandaid, I know I'm going to chicken out.

He sits up slightly straighter in the bed and then coughs from the exertion.

"Don't move. Rest." I take his hand and sink into the chair next to his bed.

"What news do you have?" He asks.

I swallow hard. "My engagement to Alejandro is off."

His brow furrows. "What do you mean? It was all done."

I swallow hard. "I love Killian Callaghan, Father, and we are to be married."

He drops my hand then, eyes narrowing. "Not over my dead body," he growls, the fierce and ruthless don showing through despite how sick he is.

I play with the ends of my hair. "It's all arranged. Massimo has agreed to their offer of territory for me."

His brow arches slightly. "Territory? The Callaghan family gave us territory?"

He sounds as if he doesn't believe it as I nod. "Yes,

Bridge Port, Armor square, Douglas, Fuller Park and Grand Boulevard."

He falls silent then, staring off into the distance. "How did this happen, Mia?"

"How did I fall for Killian?" I confirm.

He nods, eyes flickering shut for a moment as if the nodding is putting too much strain on him.

"I've loved him since the academy." I shrug. "He's always held my heart, and I had no control over it."

There's a tense silence that falls over the room.

"You know I love you Mia and I want you to be happy, but a Callaghan." He shakes his head. "Do you realize his grandfather murdered your mother?"

I nod. "Of course, and you were behind his mother's death."

His jaw clenches. "Indeed."

"But should a man and an entire family be tarnished with the same brush because of one person's actions?"

He regards me for a while and then shakes his head. "I assume that the entire famiglia is aware of this?"

I shake my head. "Not everyone, just blood family at the moment. Rourke Callaghan has arranged an announcement for tomorrow evening at The Shamrock."

Father nods. "I wish I was strong enough to attend."

I swallow hard and reach for his hand, squeezingly lightly. "You will fight this off."

He smiles, but it doesn't quite reach his eyes. "I'll sure as hell try. How is Massimo coping?"

I shrug. "On the outside, he's as strong as always. He has taken to his role well, but I'm sure it is difficult for him."

Father nods and then coughs deeply from the slight movement, spluttering everywhere. My heart skips a beat as he coughs up some blood. "Oh dear," he murmurs, grabbing a tissue to clean it up. "That's been happening a lot lately."

I hate the way my gut twists, as I'm sure it's not a good sign. Glancing back at the window, I notice Killian lingering outside. "Killian is here right now. Do you wish to meet him?"

His brow furrows as his dark eyes snap to the window. "I think I will." He beckons him in and Killian obliges, opening the door and walking into the room. A tension clouds the air as Killian walks closer. "Do we have your blessing?" he asks.

Father just gives him the slightest of nods, but I can see the anger in his eyes. "You better look after her."

"Always," Killian says, his eyes finding mine. "I'd give my life for hers."

Father's jaw clenches. "And that is all a father wants for his daughter. A man that is devoted enough to risk everything for her."

I raise a brow. "Then why did you want to sell me off to Alejandro?" I question.

His brow furrows. "I believed he was that man."

I shake my head, as it's laughable, really. If Alejandro was that man, he wouldn't have wanted to marry me against my will. He would have put my desires and wants ahead of his own.

"Sit down," Father says, nodding at the chair next to me. "I'd like to get to know you a bit before you marry my daughter."

Killian looks a little hesitant, but takes a seat as my father questions him. I sit back, thankful that somehow it seems the fallout from our secret wasn't half as bad as I expected. We could head into a new era for the city of Chicago, one where violence and feuding aren't a normal, every day occurrence. Is it possible that the mafia organizations of the city could live in relative harmony?

---

"I'M PROUD OF YOU," Camilla says, smiling at me in the mirror.

I raise a brow. "Proud, why?"

She shrugs. "For telling them to fuck off and going after what you deserve. To be happy."

I sigh and look at myself in the mirror, feeling nervous about the announcement. Camilla wanted to come back for it, even though the wedding won't be for another week. "I really didn't want to marry Alejandro."

She chuckles. "Poor guy, there's nothing wrong with him."

I nod. "No, I just didn't love him."

Camilla nods. "And that's the most important thing." She sets her hands on my shoulders.

"How is everything with Professor Nitkin?"

Her eyes fill with what appears to be sadness. "Complicated."

I sense she doesn't want to talk about it and I will not push her to, even though I want to. "Isn't it always?"

She shakes her head. "It turns out not so complicated for you in the end."

I raise a brow. "I'd say having to run away from my wedding whilst being shot at is rather complicated, wouldn't you?"

"I guess so." She shrugs. "It just all worked out for you, is what I mean." There's a sad tone to her voice, which makes me wonder what has happened between her and Nitkin, but I don't push it.

I smile at her. "Perhaps it will all work out for you in the end, too."

She shrugs. "Perhaps."

I swallow hard as I look at myself in the mirror, feeling nervous. This is the first time Killian and I are going to appear in public as engaged. The famiglia includes many people I've grown up around who might judge me for it. After all, the feud between the Callaghan family and the Morrone family dates back to well before I was born. I decided to get ready at home, as this is where all my clothes and shoes are and Camilla could help me.

I stand up and do a twirl in the beautiful golden lace applique a-line gown I picked out for tonight. "How do I look?"

"Gorgeous as always," she says, smiling at me with such warmth.

"You would say that because you are my sister." I nudge her gently.

She shakes her head. "Bullshit. I'd tell you the truth if you looked like shit because you are my sister."

I laugh and hook my arm with her. "Shall we?"

"We shall," she says.

And then we walk out of my bedroom and into the corridor, heading toward the stairs. Killian is already at The Shamrock, helping to set up for the party. The Russians have been invited to the party out of goodwill to ensure they don't feel like the Italians and Irish are plotting against them. After all, Spartak can be a highly suspicious individual.

"It will be nice to see Imalia tonight," I say.

Camilla nods. "Yeah, I hate the way Father and our brothers wanted to shun her entirely."

It's what I'd expected to happen to me, but I guess perhaps my family is learning their lesson. Only time will tell as the war progresses whether Massimo has learned from past mistakes made by the dons before him. I've always thought my brother would make a more sensible leader than my father, even if Father has always been so strong. A balance is better and Massimo is smart and calculated, but can be ruthless when he needs to be.

All the family is gathered already in the entryway, and as always, me and Camilla are ready at last. Luca approaches us first, shaking his head. "I can't say I'll miss your tardiness, Mia."

I glare at him. "And I can't say I'll miss your smart remarks."

He chuckles and shakes his head. "You don't mean that."

"Maybe I do," I say, smirking. "And besides, Camilla takes just as long as me, so it will make no difference."

Camilla clears her throat. "That isn't true. You definitely take longer."

I stare at her wide eyed. "No, we always get ready together, and—"

"And I'm always ready and waiting for you at least a half an hour before you are."

I frown at her, but realize that perhaps she's right. After all, we did just spend the last twenty minutes chatting while I did my makeup. "I always just assumed you took as long as me." I shrug. "Ah, well, you'll all miss me when I'm gone."

Luca nods. "I will. Strange to think within a week you won't be living here anymore."

Leo approaches. "Strange. Mia Callaghan." He

scrunches up his nose. "Doesn't have as good a ring to it as Mia Morrone, does it?"

"I like it," I say.

"You would," Massimo says behind me, approaching us. "Are you done chatting as we're going to be late?"

I smile and realize it is going to be odd not living here with my siblings. In one week, this chapter of my life will close. I'll miss my siblings' antics every day, but I can't deny I'm excited to start a new chapter with Killian. One full of love, laughter, and children.

## 28

# KILLIAN

*T*he Shamrock is getting busier by the minute and the tension is increasing.

It never occurred to any of us it might be a bad idea to bring Morrone men and Callaghan clan members under one roof, without it being clear that we're agreeing to a truce. Add the Volkov Bratva into the mix, and you have the most tense atmosphere I've ever experienced.

Rourke approaches me, brow furrowed. "Where the fuck are they?"

I run a hand through my hair. "Late."

He glances at his watch. "How can they be late for something so important?"

"Mia is always late."

"Great," he mutters, tapping his foot impatiently on the floor. "There's an odd tension in here tonight."

Torin approaches, eyes darting nervously around

the room. "This is like a time bomb waiting to go off, lads."

I nod. "Well, we have invited three rival mafia organizations to come together under one roof with no explanation." I shrug. "What do you expect? Everyone to have a jig together and celebrate? They've got no idea what the fuck this is all about."

Torin sighs heavily. "It would help if the Morrone family were here. Their men are on edge."

The Morrone family have invited many members of their organization here, as have we, and the Russians have a few people here too, so there's a strange feeling in the air. It's tense, as if a fight could break out at any moment, and the Morrone family not being here doesn't help. I know why they're late, though. Mia is always late. It's one thing I learned about her while following her around the city as my obsession with her grew.

"I fear if they don't arrive soon, we'll have more serious problems on our hands." He nods toward a couple of our men and Morrone men having a heated argument.

Kieran claps me on the shoulder. "Where the fuck is your girl?"

I clench my jaw. "I don't know."

Rourke nods toward the men who are about to have a fight that could turn bloody. "I best sort that out before it turns into a fight."

"Aye, we don't want anyone dying tonight," I reply,

pulling my cellphone out of my pocket. "I'll found out when they'll be here."

Rourke nods and marches over to the men to break up the pending fight as I dial Mia's number.

She picks up on the second dial tone. "Hey."

"Hey, where are you?"

"Just parking now. We'll be in shortly."

I shake my head, even though she can't see me. "It's tense in here. A lot of Morrone men are here and there's no boss, which is making them antsy."

"Sorry, you can blame me for that. I took a little too long getting ready."

"I figured, baby girl. Now get your ass in here, pronto."

"See you in a minute." She cancels the call, and I can't help but smile as I stow my phone in my pocket. Just talking to her makes me smile. It's crazy that one person can have such a positive effect on my mood, as I've always been a rather grumpy guy. I'm not the kind of guy to go about smiling all the time, but since Mia's come back into my life, I can't help it.

"What you smirking at?" Torin says, amusement in his eyes.

"Nothing." I shake my head. "What's so funny?"

"Baby girl? You really have fallen for this Morrone girl, haven't you?"

I clench my fists by my side, irritated by my uncle's teasing. "Aye, why the fuck do you think I'm marrying her?"

Kieran shrugs. "Because she's hot."

I growl and glare at him. "Don't you ever call her that again." I grab the lapel of my little brother's jacket. "She belongs to me and I don't even want to see you looking at her, got it?"

Kieran's brow arches. "Got it loud and clear."

Rourke returns to my side, running a hand through his hair. "Any news?"

"They're parking now," I reply.

"Thank God, it feels like the place is going to explode at any moment." He glances at Spartak. "At least the Russians are keeping their guys in check."

At that moment, Massimo walks through the door first with his wife, Paisley, on his arm. The rest of the family follows and I hold my breath, waiting to see my fiancée walk through.

Mia appears wearing the most stunning gold lace gown with a plunging neckline that accentuates her perfect breasts. I'm star struck whenever I see her, but right now, she looks like a gilded goddess that just landed on earth from heaven. She is too fucking good for me and yet I can't find it in me to care because I know she belongs by my side.

"Quit gawping," Rourke says, elbowing me in the ribs.

I glare at my brother, shaking my head. "I wasn't gawping."

Mia scans the room and then smiles when she sees me, heading straight toward me. The rest of my family scatter, giving me some privacy with my soon to be wife.

I swallow hard, as it's kind of impossible to believe that we're actually going to announce our engagement publicly.

"Sorry I'm late," Mia says, a soft pink blush staining her tanned cheeks.

I hold her hand and pull her close, but refrain from kissing her. At least until we have made the announcement. "I expected nothing else. You always were tardy, even at the academy."

Her nose crinkles slightly as she pulls a face. "That's not true."

I chuckle. "Believe what you want. Are you going to tell me it was your brother that held you up, doing his hair?" I nod toward Luca, who has always taken great care with his hair.

"No, I took a little too long today getting ready, but I wasn't always late at the academy."

Rourke clears his throat. "Sorry to break up this little lovers' tiff, but Massimo and I want to get the announcement done and dusted straight away."

I nod. "Who is making the announcement?"

"Rourke," Massimo says as he walks up behind him. "He's the host and leader, so it must come from him."

I clench my jaw and meet Rourke's gaze, nodding. "Let's get it done."

Rourke leads the way to the stage, and Mia follows me. The last time an announcement was made on it, my father stood there and told those closest to us that Maeve was to marry Maxim Volkov. It feels like a lifetime ago, now. I remember the look on Maeve's face at the mere thought of being married to Maxim.

My brother taps the mic and tests it's working, before clearing his throat. "Can I have everyone's attention?"

His voice cuts through the room and right through the tension as everyone glances in his direction. I remain standing by his side and Mia remains a few paces behind me, looking nervous. After all, we're about to shake up the city like no one has in years.

"You lads are probably all wondering why we are all here together, Callaghan, Morrone, and Volkov."

Quiet murmurs break out in response to that comment.

"We are here to announce a truce and agreement between the Callaghan Clan and the Morrone family. Killian, my brother, will marry Mia Morrone next Saturday. All of you are, of course, invited. The following territory will switch to Morrone territory effective immediately."

It feels like everyone holds their breath, waiting to hear. A few of our guys are going to be pissed to be moved off their patch of turf, but they'll get over it.

"Bridge Port, Armor square, Douglas, Fuller Park and Grand Boulevard."

Louder chatter breaks out amongst our men.

"Silence," Rourke growls.

Everyone in the pub shuts up.

"Our organizations will live in harmony from here on in." Rourke glances across the room toward Spartak. "Including the Volkov Bratva, as we all have a common enemy we need to overcome." He looks toward Massimo, who gives him a nod. "The cartel is threatening all of us and our existence in this city. Their new leader, Adrik Volkov, is ruthless and wants to take over the entire city."

There are a few beats of stunned silence until a distinctly evil laugh echoes from the back of the room. Everyone's attention moves toward the source and I squint, trying to see who it is that's laughing. A shiver races down my spine as I have an inkling, but hope to God I'm wrong.

"Is that right?"

Unfortunately, my inkling was right. My heart stops beating in my chest as the voice coming from the back belongs to the enemy my brother just mentioned. Adrik Volkov is here. How the fuck did he find out about this announcement?

"Show yourself," Rourke demands, eyes scanning the crowd for any sign of the man who intends to ruin us all.

Adrik strolls forward from the back of the room with his wife on his arm. Eliza Estrada, now Volkov, looks infinitely uncomfortable as he drags her forward. "I guess you all forgot to invite me, but that's alright I came, anyway." His eyes narrow slightly. "Perhaps it's because you are spewing lies about me to your men."

A few Cartel members flank him and as I scan the perimeter of the room, I count about ten of them. He isn't stupid enough to walk into a den full of enemies alone. I feel my fingers itching to reach for my gun, as this man poses a threat to my family and the woman I love.

"We did not invite you for good reason," Spartak practically growls, trying to move forward as his son holds him back.

Rourke clears his throat. "I haven't lied about a thing. You are the one that murdered Hernandez in cold blood."

Spartak manages to free himself from his son's hold and walks toward his nephew, standing in front of him. "What do you want, Adrik?"

"I want in on the action. After all, you can't deny the power our organization holds over all of yours."

"And what power is that?" Spartak asks.

"I control the borders. If I want to stop your product coming through, I can." A cold and calculated smirk spreads onto his lips, and I can't deny that in that moment it's very clear he's related to Spartak. He's got the same dark look in his eyes and reckless instincts that could get us all killed.

Spartak moves suddenly, grabbing his nephew and holding a knife to his neck. "Give me one good reason not to bleed you out right here and now." A tiny speck of blood forms on his neck where Spartak presses the knife too tightly to his skin.

The men Adrik brought in here all draw and cock their guns, pointing them at Spartak. It feels like you could hear a pin drop in the silence until Adrik breaks it.

His chuckle sounds almost manic. I study his face, surprised to find he doesn't look worried at all at being helped by his psycho of an uncle at knife point. "I'd like to see you try, but my men will shoot you dead in the process."

Spartak's nostrils flare and he growls softly. "You will regret this, Adrik." He still doesn't move the knife, but he eases the pressure.

All the men in the room are on edge, hands reaching for guns as they gaze around the room. We've got four fucking organizations in one room and a maniac driving the tension through the roof. One wrong move could spell disaster for all of us.

It looks like our happy ending could still be ruined yet.

I pull Mia behind me out of instinct, knowing that the man who just walked in here is potentially the most dangerous man in Chicago. After all, he killed Hernandez in cold blood, apparently in front of every-one. An act I didn't witness but have heard about enough.

Who knows what this man is truly capable of?

## 29

# MIA

*K*illian is tense as he pulls me behind him, blocking my view of Adrik.

Spartak is still holding the knife to his throat, and it feels like everyone in the room is holding their breath, waiting on a knife's edge to act.

I peer around Killian's arm to see Spartak release his nephew. "You are a piece of shit," he spits, eyes furious as he moves away. "What the fuck do you want?"

"Aye, why are you here, Adrik?" Rourke asks.

Adrik's unusual hazel eyes move between Rourke and Spartak, and then he shakes his head. "You didn't expect me to sit around while the three of you collude against me, did you?" He stretches out his neck and then cracks his fingers. "We can come to an arrangement that we're all satisfied with, I'm sure. After all, this is a meeting for the Mafia organizations of Chicago, and I'm the leader of the cartel."

Massimo shakes his head. "This is a meeting for an alliance between three families of which you don't belong. An alliance against you and your psychopathic plans."

He tilts his head. "Now that's not very fair, is it?" He waves his hand in the air dismissively. "Don't mind me and continue your announcement. It's very interesting to hear that Callaghan Clan are such wusses they're giving up territory to their longest standing enemy." His cold eyes dance with amusement as he watches Rourke's reaction.

Rourke's body bunches up as he clenches his fists by his side. "Careful, Adrik."

It's clear that this man is trying to stir things up, and I notice my eyes drawn to the woman on his arm. Eliza Estrada. She looks uncomfortable and is completely out of her element. It's hard to believe Adrik has thrust her into such a terrible position, considering she was attending the academy with Camilla recently. Adrik forced her down the aisle early and then shot her father dead in front of her.

I feel sympathy for the poor girl being shackled to a man so evil. Her eyes look haunted and a shudder races down my spine as I wonder how a man could kill his own wife's father and even look her in the eye, let alone force her into a room on his arm.

"Careful of what, Callaghan?" He shakes his head.

"Are you going to give me territory, too?" He tilts his head, smirking.

The tension hikes up even more and terror seeps into my blood, as I wonder if any of us are going to make it out of here alive. Four mob bosses are going head-to-head right now and they're renowned for dick measuring. After all, if one disrespects the other, they'll look weak for not reacting. It's as if Adrik wants a fight and he's trying to rile everyone up in the room into shooting first.

I step forward, pushing past Killian, and reach for the microphone on the stand. "Don't listen to him. Can't you see he's trying to drive a wedge between everyone?"

Adrik's eyes move to me and light up. "Is that what I'm doing?"

Spartak miraculously seems to come to his senses the moment I say that, as he takes a step back. "She's right," he says.

Killian grabs my wrist and tries to pull me away. "Mia," he hisses.

I shake him off and continue. "If you want to negotiate, then arrange a meeting with us rather than crashing a party you weren't invited to." My eyes narrow as I glare at him. "Clearly, you have different motives for being here than what you claim."

His smirk widens. "Perhaps." He waves his hand and nods toward his men. "Put the guns away."

I breathe a sigh of relief as the men stow their guns

back in their holsters, but I'm well aware this isn't over. Adrik Volkov is more unpredictable than his uncle and fucking crazy for coming into his enemy's pub as if he has the right.

"Since I'm here, why don't the four of us have a chat?" Adrik suggests.

Killian pulls me tighter against him as if he's worried I'll be snatched away at any moment. "What are you doing?"

I swallow and look him in the eye. "His words are poison, and he's trying to undo any good we've done so far."

"It's dangerous to get involved."

Rourke speaks. "We will sit with you for a discussion, but only two of your men can accompany you."

Adrik nods. "Done. Little Mia has to come, since this was her idea."

Killian growls. "Over my dead body."

"That can be arranged," Adrik says, his voice so cold and unemotional.

"I'll be fine," I say, prizing Killian's hand off my wrist.

Rourke squeezes Killian's shoulder. "You can come in as well. As my second."

He visibly relaxes then, nodding. "Thanks."

Rourke looks me in the eye. "Good move, Morrone."

I smile. "I simply saw what he was trying to do and called him out on it."

304

Spartak approaches, shaking his head. "This is a mistake. There's no reasoning with him."

"What choice do we have?" Rourke asks.

Maxim is close behind. "None. We need to listen, even if he's just here to taunt us."

Massimo and Luca approach us wordlessly, and the look in my brothers' eyes is one of irritation as they regard me. "That was reckless, sister," Luca finally says.

"Reckless how?" I ask, shaking my head. "You weren't doing anything, just listening to his toxic words."

A muscle ticks in Massimo's jaw. "Let's get this over with." He glances at Rourke. "Lead the way, Callaghan."

Adrik stands a few yards away, but he's watching me in an unnerving way that puts me on edge.

I draw my eyes away from him and wrap my hand around Killian's, squeezing. "I fear he's up to something."

"You don't say," he says through gritted teeth. "The last thing I wanted was for you and him to be in the same room together."

We follow Rourke toward the back of the pub, where there's a small meeting room with a boardroom table in the middle.

Rourke sits at the head of the table with Killian to his right, and I sit next to him. The rest of the men flood into the room, taking seats around the table.

Until it's just Adrik left with two of his men. They don't take a seat, which only heightens the tension.

"Have a seat, Adrik," Rourke orders, eyes narrowing.

He cracks his neck. "I think I'll stand, thanks."

The tension rises the moment he refuses to sit.

"Sit down, Adrik," Spartak says, eyes fixed on him. "Or I will slit your fucking throat."

Adrik smirks. "Always so bossy, uncle." He shakes his head. "If you insist." He pulls out a seat at the other end of the table and sits down, lazing back casually as if he's not in a room full of enemies.

I realize at that moment that I'm the only woman in the room, and the reason is that Adrik insisted on it.

"So, Mia." Adrik, saying my name, snaps my attention to him. "What is it you think I'm here to do, exactly?"

I sit up straighter. "Cause a rift in an already precarious relationship," I say simply.

"Smart." He taps his fingers in rhythm on the boardroom table. "And how do you propose we settle our differences?"

Rourke clears his throat. "Mia isn't in charge of that. We need to settle them ourselves. It would help if you destroyed those fucking missiles for a start."

Adrik's smirk widens. "Missiles?" He chuckles then. "Such fools."

"What the fuck are you chuckling about?" Massimo asks, impatience growing in his dark eyes.

"Hernandez believed that shit, but I didn't really think you would all be swayed so easily." He shrugs. "It was my ploy to secure my position in the Estrada Cartel. There are no missiles."

Rourke shakes his head. "We've seen the photos."

Adrik laughs harder. "You mean the photos of the empty shells I tricked that idiot Hernandez with?" He shakes his head. "So gullible, all of you." He runs a hand through his dark hair. "Maybe I should have sourced missiles and blown you all away. The lot of you are fucking idiots and this city would thrive under me." I can't help but feel relief hearing him say they're empty. It wouldn't surprise me if Adrik were telling the truth about that, but we'll obviously need proof.

Spartak stands, his fists bunched by his side. "You traitorous little—"

"Save it, uncle." Adrik stands too and I notice some of the men reach for their guns. "The family deserved no allegiance from me. After all, I've only ever been the black sheep of the family." He bares his teeth angrily, the first sign of anger on his part. "You and my father brought this on yourselves."

Maxim calms his father, who returns to his seat. "So, what is it you want?" he asks, glaring at his cousin.

"I want recognition in this city, but I also want the same deal you agreed with my predecessor."

Rourke shakes his head. "You want us to buy our product from you?"

He shrugs. "It was a deal you agreed on."

"Yes, when we believed there were missiles that could destroy us."

Adrik chuckles to himself softly again and his eyes move to me. "What do you think, Mia?"

I swallow hard. "About what?"

He shrugs. "Do you think they should honor the agreement made with my predecessor?"

"I think that they should if you can prove that there are no missiles."

His smirk widens. "You are very smart, aren't you?"

Killian growls, his hand moving under his jacket as he reaches for his gun.

"And your fiancé needs to be kept on a tighter leash," he says, glaring at him.

I reach for his hand and squeeze, trying to calm him. "So, will you prove it?"

He taps his chin, thinking about it. "I'm not sure there'd be much fun in that. I'd rather let the bunch of you sweat for a bit longer. Make you pay for your inadequacies." He pulls out his gun suddenly and aims for me. "No hard feelings, princess."

Killian moves so fast I hardly see it as he grabs the back of my chair and tips it backward, forcing me to the ground with his body slumped over me. The impact knocks the air from my lungs for a moment and the weight of him over me makes it almost impossible to draw the oxygen back in.

I hear people shouting as gun shots go off.

Killian groans and shifts a little on top of me.

"Are you okay?" I ask, trying to get out from under his heavy weight.

"I'll live, but it hurts like hell."

"What does?" I ask, panic clawing through my chest.

"He hit me."

"Where?" I say, trying desperately to shift him off me so I can get a look.

"Stay still," he growls. "Until the shooting stops, I'm not fucking moving."

"Killian," I say his name sternly, but I know he won't listen to me. "Let me see the gunshot wound."

"See you later, fuckers," Adrik says, followed by a few more shots as the gunshots grow more distant.

"Killian!"

He finally moves off of me, shaking his head. "It's only a flesh wound. Look." He shows me where the bullet hit the edge of his arm, thankfully. "It's basically a graze."

"You could have been killed."

"Gladly so, baby girl," he murmurs, grabbing my hand and squeezing. "I'd die any day to save you and our baby." He places a hand gently on my lower abdomen.

Tears prickle at my eyes as I shake my head. "But how would we survive without you?"

He smiles, and it makes his light green eyes look more vibrant. "You are the strongest woman I know, Mia. You'd do just fine." His smile turns a little devious.

"But as it happens, that's not the case." He drags me toward him and kisses me passionately, his tongue searching my mouth with desperation. "We're together, we're going to get married, we're going to have a baby, and if Adrik isn't lying, he's not intending to blow us all up." He shrugs. "I'd say today has been rather positive."

I move away from him. "Other than the fact you got shot!"

He chuckles. "Honestly, it's a fucking graze." He kisses me again, driving me wild with need at the most inappropriate moment.

I break the kiss. "Shit, we should check on everyone else." Guilt coils through me as I wonder if my two brothers are okay.

"Or we could stay here," he says, shrugging.

"What if our family are hurt?"

Killian sighs and nods. "You're right." He gets to his feet, wincing slightly as he moves. "Let's go and check on everyone." He holds his hand out.

I take it and we walk toward the main pub together, hoping that everyone we love is safe and well. Adrik is a bastard for what he did and I can't believe he didn't just agree to the deal. Something tells me dealing with him is going to be far harder than any of us anticipate, even if he doesn't have missiles.

## 30

# KILLIAN

*R*ourke is bent over a table, clutching his side while Viki looks panicked, trying to help him.

"Are you alright?" I ask.

He shakes his head. "Got hit by that son of a bitch, but thankfully Luca sunk a bullet in his leg. That's when he went off squealing."

"If it makes you feel any better, I got hit, too." I signal to my arm.

He glances at it and then shakes his head. "That's a fucking graze." He removes his hand and my stomach churns when I see the bloody wound on the side of his abdomen. "I need to get to a fucking hospital fast."

"Aye," I agree. "Shall I drive you?"

Rourke shakes his head. "Ambulance is already on its way."

Mia tightens her grasp on my hand, gazing around

for her brothers. "Where's Massimo and Luca?" she asks.

Rourke's jaw clenches. "They went after the son of a bitch. So did Spartak." He winces as he moves. "I would have been with them if I hadn't been shot."

Viki clears her throat. "You wanted to go with them even though you had."

I chuckle at that. "Right, because that would have been a good idea. You can barely stand."

Rourke pales slightly.

"Wouldn't it be best if you sit?" Mia asks.

"I've been telling him to sit. He won't listen to me."

He nods. "I think I will sit, actually." He slumps into the chair and suddenly panic claws through me, as the wound he's sustained could be life-threatening. I can't lose my big brother.

"Are you going to be alright?" I ask.

Rourke looks me in the eye and shrugs. "Fuck knows. If not, you get the crown. Isn't that what you wanted?"

"No," I growl, angry that he'd even suggest that. "Don't fucking talk like that."

Rourke smiles weakly. "I'm jesting, little bro."

I roll my eyes. "Well, it's not funny."

Kieran rushes toward us. "Ambulance is here." He glances at me. "Help me get him up."

Rourke practically roars when we try to help him out of the seat. "I've been shot, but I'm not an invalid."

Torin approaches, looking skeptical. "Let him try, lads."

We move away and my stubborn older brother attempts to claw himself out of the chair and fails. "Fuck," he curses.

Kieran shakes his head. "Idiot." He steps forward. "Stop being a martyr and let us help you."

I offer him my arm and he nods, allowing us to support him out of the chair. We have to lift him across the floor to the entrance of the pub where a paramedic greets us, eyes wide when they see he's been shot.

"What happened?" they ask.

"Gunshot. Some thugs tried to rob us," I lie.

They nod and take over from me and Kier.

Viki rushes up to them. "I need to go with him. I'm his wife."

They nod and get Rourke onto a stretcher in the back of the ambulance as Viki climbs in next to him.

I glance at Kier. "We'll have to follow the ambulance."

"Aye," he says, chucking me the keys to his mustang. "On this occasion, you can drive. But don't even get a scratch on her."

I smirk. "I won't."

Mia squeezes my hand. "Shall I come to the hospital with you?"

I nod. "Yes, I want you there."

She smiles, but it doesn't reach her eyes. "Of course."

I tighten my grasp on her hand and lead her toward the mustang, allowing her to get in the back. And then I make the journey across the city behind the ambulance to the hospital. All of us are silent as we head there, none of us knowing yet how bad Rourke's injury is. Gunshot wounds can be unpredictable and life threatening, especially where he was hit.

All we can hope is that he makes it through. The alternative isn't worth thinking about.

---

ONE MONTH LATER...

I'm nervous, even though that's a very rare occurrence for me.

I guess it's natural for any man to be nervous about his wedding day. A day that I postponed after it was clear Rourke wouldn't be able to attend considering how bad his gunshot wound was. Thankfully, the surgeons worked fast and saved his life, but it was touch and go at one point. After a long night waiting for news, Viki finally came to get us to see him.

It was the most nerve-wracking night of my life. Knowing that we could have lost him still scares me to this day, even if I wouldn't admit it out loud. I fidget with my fingers as I stand at the end of the aisle, Rourke by my side. The wait feels excruciating, as even though I know how much Mia loves me, I still fear she'll change her mind and realize she can do better.

There were times I thought we'd never make it to our own wedding, but thankfully, we did.

"Stop fidgeting," Rourke says, shaking his head. "Why are you nervous when you are marrying the woman of your dreams?"

I shrug. "Because she can still change her mind."

Rourke laughs and claps me on the shoulder. "No chance in hell, lad. That girl is mad about you."

His words of encouragement soothe some of my anxiety, but I can't help but feel I won't relax until my ring is on her finger and we say I do. After all the shit we've been through the past few months, it's hard to believe anything will go smoothly.

"What time is it?" I ask.

"It's not half-past yet. Calm down." Rourke glances down the aisle. "You seriously need to relax. The girl is having your baby, Killian. She's not going to pull out of this wedding."

I clench my fists by my side and nod, calming my nerves. I've never felt like this before in my life. The odd clawing at my gut and the desire to be married to her about yesterday. Impatience isn't something I'm used to feeling either.

And then when it feels like I'm about to lose my mind, the band plays the wedding march and everyone's eyes are drawn to the end of the aisle. Camilla walks down it first, smiling widely as she leads her sister. Mia appears a short while later, accompanied by Massimo, looking like a true goddess in the most stunning white lace wedding gown that hugs her figure like a second skin.

My mouth dries, and every muscle in my body relaxes the moment our eyes meet. The love in those dark brown eyes almost bowls me over. She looks so utterly confident and sure about this, and I know my jitters were completely unfounded. We were always meant to end up here in a church, saying our vows to be together for the rest of our lives.

I knew it when we attended the academy and the impulse to be with her never left me. There's no one in this world that would accuse me of being a soppy romantic, but I know that what I have with Mia is true love. The kind of love that can't be broken or ignored. The kind of love that overcomes obstacles that seem impossible and yet it comes out stronger for it.

She stops in front of me and it feels like the rest of the world fades away as she looks into my eyes. I take her hand and squeeze, and the smile she gives me almost stops my heart.

The priest clears his throat, signaling he's ready to start to ceremony. I can't tear my eyes away from my wife to be. He addresses the crowd and talks a load of shit about God and martial obligation, but I don't listen. Our family may be Catholic traditionally, but I've never been one for tradition or religion. It's just not me.

I agreed to get married here because it's where every Callaghan has married for as long as we can remember. Instead of listening, I find myself lost in my baby girl's eyes, drowning in the beautiful brown hue of them. Until I hear the priest say my name and I realize he's at the vows.

Rourke nudges me and passes me the ring, and I take it, positioning it at the tip of Mia's finger.

"Killian, do you take Mia to be your wedded wife, to live together in marriage? Do you promise to love her, comfort her, honor and keep her for better or worse, for richer or poorer, in sickness and health, and forsaking all others, be faithful only to her, for as long as you both shall live?"

I smile at her and nod. "I do." I push the ring onto her finger, feeling a weight lifted the moment it's on there. A lawfully binding reminder to everyone in this world that this woman belongs to me and me alone.

"And Mia, do you take Killian to be your wedded husband to live together in marriage? Do you promise to love him, comfort him, honor and keep him for better or worse, for richer or poorer, in sickness and health and forsaking all others, be faithful only to him so long as you both shall live?"

"I do," she says, without a moment's hesitation, pushing the ring onto my finger.

"Then, by the power vested in me by the almighty lord, I now pronounce you husband and wife." He nods at me. "You may kiss the bride."

I step closer to her and wrap an arm around the small of her back, bringing her body flush against mine.

"You look so fucking gorgeous, baby girl," I murmur into her ear.

She gasps softly. "Don't swear in church."

I chuckle and then capture her lips with my own, pouring every ounce of love and passion into the kiss.

The guests all erupt into cheers and clapping as we kiss in front of them, unafraid to show the world how much we love each other. When I finally free her, her eyes are dilated with desire that she tries to shake off. I move my lips to her ear. "Don't worry, baby girl. I'll find a way to consummate the marriage quickly. I'm sure you must be gagging for your husband's cock."

Again she gasps, acting scandalized as she glances around to check the priest didn't hear. "Honestly, Killian. You shouldn't speak like that in a church."

He shakes his head. "I'll speak how I wish." I grab her hand and nod toward the aisle. "Shall we?"

She nods. "Yes, let's go and celebrate with the people we love."

"Sounds like a plan."

We walk together down the aisle and I know in that moment that I am the luckiest man on earth. I got the girl I always wanted, despite the mountain of obstacles that stood in our way. There's no doubt that not giving up is the key to success, and there was no way in hell I was giving up Mia Morrone. Now that I have her, I never intend to let go.

THE CELEBRATIONS ARE SLOWLY DRAWING to a close and I think my patience has been more or less saint like for not fucking my new wife in a bathroom stall at the pub.

Mia said that's not how she wants it to be, and I listened, even if my cock has been stiff all damn night. However, my patience is wearing thin and my cock is leaking into my boxer briefs as I stare at the beauty that is my wife.

"Are you ready to leave yet?" I whisper into her ear. "Because my cock is so fucking hard and needs to be deep inside my wife's pretty little cunt."

Mia draws in a breath and her cheeks turn a pretty pink as she wets her bottom lip. "I guess we can get out of here now."

I smirk at the eagerness in her eyes. "Yeah? Is that because your pussy is gagging for my cock?"

"Perhaps," she murmurs.

"I've got a real treat in store for you tonight, Mia."

"What kind of treat?"

"A very dirty one," I murmur, standing and grabbing her hand. "Let's say our farewells and get the fuck out of here."

She nods and we walk toward the stage, where I grab the microphone and tap the end to check it's on. That sound alone draws everyone's attention to us.

I clear my throat. "Thank you, everyone, for coming to celebrate our wedding. It meant a lot to us and all that shit."

People chuckle at that, but Mia gives me a nudge in the ribs.

"We are going to depart now, but continue drinking and eating and getting completely shit faced while dancing like your dad. I have a wife to take home." I wink and that also results in a lot of laughs, but Mia just turns the color of beetroot. "Thanks again."

With that, I put the mic back on the stand and people clap and cheer as we leave the room.

Mia glares at me the moment we're alone. "That wasn't a very heartfelt speech."

I shrug. "Sorry, baby girl. I'm no good at heartfelt, but I'll make you feel something alright." I grab her hips and pull her against me, allowing her to feel how hard I am. "Now stop messing around and get your ass in that car." I nod out the door where a car is waiting to take us back to the Callaghan residence.

She sighs heavily and then gets into the car. I slide in next to her, my hand instantly going up the hem of her dress and onto her thigh. It quivers under my touch.

"Thank God we're finally alone." I inch my hand higher and then run a finger around the very edge of her panties, teasing her but not touching her center. "Are you already wet for me?" I ask.

She nods, biting her bottom lip.

I remove my hand, which results in a whimper. "Too bad you'll have to wait until we get back for the surprise, isn't it?"

Her cheeks are red and her eyes turn furious as she

glares at me. "You can be a real ass at times. Did you know that?"

I smirk. "I'm pretty sure you've told me countless times."

She huffs and sits back in the chair as the driver takes us on the short journey to the house. It's hard to keep my hands off of her, but I want to wait until we're in my dungeon. I intend to fulfill a fantasy with my baby girl tonight. One I've teased about for a while, now.

The car pulls up in front of the house and I get out first, before helping her out onto the driveway. And then I lift her suddenly, making her yelp in surprise.

"What are you doing?" she asks.

I shrug. "Carrying you over the threshold. It's tradition."

She rolls her eyes, but I notice the way her lips curve up in a smile she can't help. The guard at the door opens it for us and I carry her inside. "Welcome, Mrs. Callaghan, to your new temporary home."

"Temporary?" she asks.

I nod. "Aye, now we're married and got a baby on the way. We'll want a place of our own." I wink at her. "After all, our fun can get very noisy."

Her cheeks redden even more and I find it utterly adorable as I carry her up the stairs toward my bedroom. I manage to open the door with one hand and then set her down on her feet in the bedroom. "For tonight, however, I intend to have some fun with you in my favorite room."

Her lip trembles as her eyes move to the bookcase, which hides my dungeon behind. "And what fun is that?"

"Come and find out," I say, holding a hand out to her.

She walks toward me and takes my hand and I lead her into the room, which I setup last night ready. The sex machine I've been promising to use on her while I fuck her ass is positioned behind my favorite bench. Her throat bobs slightly as her eyes are drawn straight to it. "Is that the…" she trails off, as if scared to say it.

I nod. "Yes, do you want to give it a go?"

Mia's teeth sink into her bottom lip as she nods. "I think so."

"Then let me take this beautiful dress off of you."

She nods and spins around, giving me access to the ties holding her in. I unfasten them slowly, taking my time and enjoying every inch of skin that comes visible to me, caressing it gently. Mia shudders at every light touch, and the power my touch has over her makes my cock even harder than I believed possible. Once the dress is undone, I let it pool at her ankles.

"Step out of it."

She does as I say and then turns toward me, standing there in nothing but a pair of red matching panties and bra and garter. And then I notice the way the panties are split in the center. "Are those crotchless, baby girl?"

She nods. "Yes, I thought you might like them." She

widens her stance and I can see her beautiful lips and clit framed between the split fabric.

I growl. "On the bench, now."

She walks over to it and climbs on, glancing at me over her shoulder. Her legs spread wide and her pretty cunt on show for me and her beautiful asshole. She got a pair that gives me access to both, which is perfect for what I have planned.

I rub a hand across my cock and then quickly get undressed, knowing that there will be no teasing or going slow tonight. I'm too wound up and ready to fuck her until she screams my name and comes all over my cock. Mia watches as I undress, her hand between her thighs as she plays with herself. "That's right, baby, get that pussy nice and wet for the machine."

Her brow furrows slightly. "What about you?"

"I'm going to stretch out that beautiful asshole of yours."

Her eyes widen and then turn dark with desire as she rubs herself harder.

"Do you like that idea?"

She nods. "Yes, sir."

"Good, because I'm going to breed that pretty little ass and then watch while my cum drips out of it."

She moans, eyes fluttering shut as she pictures it.

"Now, be a good girl and keep your eyes forward," I instruct.

She does as I say, looking forward as I walk to the machine and turn it on. Mia gasps as the thick dildo spears right into her pretty cunt, fucking her with slow precision. "Oh," she murmurs, wriggling her hips as she gets used to the new sensation.

I grab a bottle of lube off the stand nearby and squirt some onto her tight ring of muscles. This will be the first time I've ever fucked her ass, and I can't wait. If the way she reacted to butt play up to now is any indication, she's going to love it. As the machine slides into her wet pussy, I work my fingers into her ass, slowly stretching. "Keep rubbing your clit, baby girl. I want you turned on and relaxed, ready for my cock in that ass."

"Isn't it too big?" she asks.

I shake my head, even though she's looking forward. "No, it's just the right fit."

Once I'm satisfied she's well stretched, I climb onto the edge of the bench and angle my cock so that it's rested against her stretched hole.

She whimpers as she feels me press lightly.

"Relax, baby girl."

She does relax and I push forward, slowly sinking inch after inch of my cock into her virgin passage. It's so fucking tight and it looks so good seeing her cunt being stuffed while my cock slides into her ass. All the while, she's still wearing the sexy red crotchless panties.

Mia cries and moans, the sounds she makes a mix between pleasurable and painful.

"So fucking tight," I say, as my cock slides the last inch so my balls are rested between her ass and her pussy, which is still getting fucked by the machine. "It feels so good, baby girl."

She moans. "Killian, fuck," she murmurs.

"What is it?"

"I feel so full."

"Do you like it?" I ask.

There's a moment of hesitation before she nods. "I think I love it."

I groan, my cock throbbing in her tight ass as it sucks me in like a fucking vacuum, clinging to my shaft like a second skin. The thrusts of the dildo against my cock only add to the ridiculous pleasure.

"Fuck me," she moans, her back arching.

I spank her ass. "I'll fuck you when I'm good and ready, baby girl." I grab hold of her hips and sink my fingertips into them hard and then start to move with slow yet deep strokes, fucking her heavenly ass.

Mia moans and makes incoherent little pleas as I drive into her with all my strength, fucking my cock against the dildo in her pussy. It makes it so tight as I find the right rhythm with the machine, pushing her toward her limits as she's stuffed in a way she's never been stuffed before.

"Oh God," she cries, her back arching more. "It feels so fucking good."

I smirk and her pleasure only spurs me on as I fuck her harder and faster, driving her and myself toward a mutual explosion.

Her hand remains between her thighs as she rubs

her clit, and I feel her muscles start to spasm around my cock. The tightness around my cock is so overwhelming as I fight through it, thrusting into her with fierce strokes. "That's it, baby. I want you to come while you are stuffed with two cocks."

She moans so loud, her body shuddering more than it ever as she tips over the edge.

I roar as I come apart too, spending every drop of my cum deep in her ass. "Take every drop of my cum like the good girl I know you are."

Her back arches more and she cries my name, her orgasm spiking over and over. I keep thrusting long after I've come apart, making sure every drop is inside of her. Mia pants, her heavy breathing filling the room.

Finally, I come down from my high and slip my cock out of her gaping ass, groaning when I see my cum rush up and then out of her ass. "That's it, baby. I want to see the cum dripping out of your ass."

She moans and pushes it out, the result so fucking sexy as it drips down over her pussy and then onto the bench below.

I turn off the machine and then lift her off the bench, spinning her around to kiss her beautiful, pouty lips. My tongue thrusts into her mouth as I search it desperately, knowing I've never felt so needy for another person in all my life. "You are so fucking hot," I whisper against her lips. "Let's lie down." I nod to the four-poster bed and she jumps onto it, smiling at me as she waits for me to join.

I climb on it and lie down next to her. "Come here."

She moves over to me and throws her arm over my stomach. "That was crazy."

"It was heaven," I murmur, kissing her forehead. "I can't believe you are really my wife."

Mia looks up at me and smiles. "I know. It's the best thing ever, isn't it?" She shakes her head. "Who would have known we'd end up together after I ran away from you at the academy?"

"I did," I say softly.

Her brow furrows. "You did?"

"I always knew, Mia. I always knew you would be mine. I just didn't know how it would play out."

"I don't know how you were so certain. What if I didn't want you?"

I chuckle. "I knew that wasn't the case. You've loved me since the academy, and don't deny it."

She blows out a little breath and shakes her head. "Always so cocky."

"Aye, and you love it."

Mia nods. "I do, and I love you."

I smile and kiss her forehead again. "I love you, too, Mrs. Callaghan."

We fall into blissful silence as I hold her close, basking in our victory. Mia and I may have always been star-crossed, but perseverance led to success. She's mine and I'm hers, now and always.

# EPILOGUE

## MIA

*O*ne year later…

I hold our baby in my lap as I sit on the enormous bed in our room, smiling as he stares up at me. "Hey little Ronan, how are you doing today?" I ask, tickling under his chin. He's six months old now, and he looks just like his father. The same devilish good looks and green eyes. We named him after Killian's father.

It's crazy to think that somehow, after such a long time of uncertainty and chaos in the city of Chicago, there's a sense of calm that has fallen over it. Somehow, we made it through, and even Father is alive and has fought off the cancer despite the odds.

He'll never be the same. He gets tired easily, and it's why Massimo remains in control of the mafia.

"Did you have a nice day?" I ask, bouncing him a little more on my knee, as he's been with our nanny today, who is a godsend.

"You know it's too early for him to speak back, right?" Killian asks, entering our new apartment with a glint in his eyes.

I stick my tongue out at him. "It doesn't mean I can't speak to him."

He smiles and sits down on the bed next to me. "Of course not."

I watch as he looks adoringly down at our son, eyes full of emotion. "Hey, little buddy." I can't deny that I've never felt so happy.

"How was the meeting?" I ask.

He sighs heavily. "Tiresome." He shakes his head. "I get that after all the shit that happened last year. We need these meetings, but they never get easier."

I nod in response, as the families of Chicago have agreed to have once a month meetings to ensure we avoid any fallouts like last year. Avoiding war all together benefits all of us and that's all we really want. A city with relative peace.

Erin, our nanny, enters the room and gives us both a shy smile. "It's Ronan's bedtime, if you are ready?"

Killian reaches for him and I let him take our little boy. "Good night, little one." He kisses him on the head and I can't deny that seeing him and our son together melts my heart every single day. "Time for bed." He passes him into Erin's hands.

She carries him away, and I slump against Killian's shoulder, sighing. "I'm exhausted."

He sighs. "Why don't I give you a massage?"

I raise a brow. "What kind of massage?"

A wicked smirk spreads onto his lips. "Purely platonic, of course."

"You say that every time and it always ends up with me on my back, tied up and my legs spread for you."

He chuckles. "And isn't that just a wonderful position to be in?" he asks, pressing his lips to my neck and kissing me.

I groan as his tongue darts out over my skin, sending goosebumps prickling over every inch of my body. "Killian," I breathe his name. "The door is still open."

He pulls away and his brow arches. "Your point?"

"Erin might see us."

"I'm still failing to see what the problem is."

I punch him playfully in the chest and get off the bed, walking to the door and shutting it. "You can't start upsetting our nanny." I turn the lock on the door. "She's great, and I don't want her to leave." When I turn around, Killian is already behind me, eyes dark with lust.

"Is that right, baby girl?" He boxes me against the door with his arms and leans closer, his breath tickling my neck as he barely ghosts his lips over my skin. "And yet she's going to know exactly what we're doing in here anyway, as I'm going to make you scream."

I shudder, reaching out to steady myself with his shoulders. "And what exactly are you going to do?" I ask.

He kisses my neck then, pressing his lips to the juncture where it meets my shoulder. "Dirty things," he murmurs.

I clench my thighs together, struggling to control the raging inferno he lights inside of me.

"First," he murmurs, his lips moving to my collarbone. "I think I'll feast on that pretty little cunt." His fingers inch the hem of my skirt up and he groans when he feels I'm not wearing panties—I rarely do anymore, since it makes it easier for our impulsive moments together. "And then, I think I'll stretch your pretty ass hole out and shove my cock deep inside."

My eyes clamp shut at the thought and I feel him thrust a finger into my soaking wet pussy. "Is that all?" I ask, pushing him.

He bites my collarbone then. "No, I think while I fuck that pretty asshole, I'll have the fuck machine set up with two dildos affixed so it plows into that tight pussy."

I swallow hard, as he's done that once before, and the effects were magical. At first, it felt like he was trying to be break me apart from the inside, but once my body adapted to the fullness, it was the single most erotic sensation I've ever experienced, being stuffed so full.

"And you know what? I'll also tie you down to my bench while I do it. I'll put a blindfold over your eyes while you have three big cocks thrusting into your tight holes."

I moan then, the image in my mind so perverse and

yet so fucking good. Killian knows how to turn me on like nothing can.

"Do you like the sound of that, baby girl?"

"Yes, I like the sound of it very much."

He smiles against my skin. "And perhaps I'll even light a candle and pour the wax over your beautiful tanned skin."

"Stop talking about it and do it, then." I'm so needy, so utterly desperate, that it feels like I can hardly breathe.

"So impatient, Mia." He makes a tutting sound and moves back, wrapping a strong hand around my wrist and yanking me toward his secret room. When we bought this apartment, it was the first change he commissioned to have it fitted with a room matching the one at the Callaghan residence.

He pulls down the book on the shelf and the door slides open, revealing his new and improved sex dungeon. A place we spend a little too much time together.

I follow him into the room and strip before he asks me to.

When he turns around, he shakes his head. "You are so eager, baby." He walks toward me and yanks me against his body, spanking my ass. "Now get on that bench and spread those legs wide. I'm going to fuck you so damn hard."

I shudder and nod. "Yes, sir." I walk toward the

bench, giving him a look over my shoulder. "I can't wait to have both my holes stuffed."

"That's because you are my dirty little slut, baby girl."

I nod. "Always."

He groans as I position myself on the bench, thighs wide apart. "I love it when you are so eager for a good fucking." He walks toward me and fastens the restraints around my wrists, spanking my ass as he walks around the back to do the same for my ankles. He places the blindfold over my eyes and fastens it at the back of my head, robbing me of my sight.

And then I feel his tongue between my already slick lips, thrusting inside of me as if he's ravenous. "You taste like fucking heaven, and I'll never get enough of you." He spanks my ass, and the pleasure builds in an instance as his breath teases against my lips, driving me higher.

I groan as he feasts on me the way he promised he would. His teeth, tongue and fingers driving me higher and higher as he pushes me toward the edge with an expertise that always astounds me, even after being with him for over a year. He never ceases to amaze me.

"Killian," I moan, my thighs shaking as he sucks on my clit and thrusts two fingers deep inside of me.

He spanks my ass. "Come, baby girl."

I cry out; the waves breaking inside of me with such force that I can hardly think straight.

"Good girl," he purrs, his fingers still meeting their

mark as he pushes me through it. "We need to get this pussy nice and wet if it's going to fit two dildos, don't we?"

"Yes, sir," I moan, arching my back at the thought.

He spits on my pussy, which makes me moan more. "How many times do I need to make you come before you are ready?"

"Make me come on your cock and then I'll be ready, sir."

He grabs hold of my hips painfully. "That is so greedy, Mia. Are you telling me that you want me to fuck that tight little cunt first and get it nice and wet for the fuck machine, and then you want my cock in your ass?"

I groan, the need becoming almost too much to bear. "Yes, please, fuck my pussy and make me come."

He growls softly, but I hear him unzipping his pants and then I feel the thick head of his cock as he drags it through my soaking wet lips. "Such a dirty girl, and all mine," he murmurs, almost to himself. And then he thrusts every inch inside of me, burying himself to the balls in my pussy.

He's so deep I feel him all the way inside as he begins to move with brutal thrusts, fucking me hard and deep the way we both love. The wet sounds coming from my pussy are both perverse and arousing, as he fucks me with such speed.

"Such a wet, tight little cunt gripping my cock so well," he murmurs, his hands gripping my hips with more force. "I think it's already ready for two cocks." He grabs a fistful of my hair, making me arch my back in an unnatural way. "Whose dirty slut are you, Mia?"

I swallow hard, trying to organize the thoughts in my mind. "Yours, sir."

"Good girl," he purrs into my ear, getting at an angle that drives his cock even deeper inside of me. "Take every fucking inch and moan for me."

I moan, as I can't resist following this man's orders in bed. And then he spanks my ass hard, the pain adding another dimension to the pleasure. I attempt to buck my hips, driving myself toward the edge again.

Killian holds me still and reaches around to grab my throat, starving me of oxygen. "Don't move, baby girl. I'm in control."

"Fuck," I gasp, as stars burst behind the blindfold.

"That's it, come on my cock," he orders, squeezing my throat even harder. "Come while I choke your throat and fuck your cunt just like that."

I scream as I tip over the edge for the second time and squirt around his cock, making it even wetter between my thighs.

Killian grunts, but doesn't come apart. Instead, he pulls out of me, making me whimper at the sudden empty sensation. I hear him padding toward the edge of the room, my hearing amplified by the fact I can't see. And I know he's going to fetch the machine and set it up behind me, which makes me tingle all over. I wriggle on the bench, trying to find some friction against my throbbing clit, but it's impossible because of the design of the bench.

"Now it's time for you to be fucked be two cocks," he murmurs, spanking my aching sex.

I yelp, moving forward at the sudden pain in such an intimate place.

It takes him a few minutes to set it up, but once he's done, he doesn't even warn me. Suddenly, two dildos spear into my dripping wet pussy and stretch it. I groan, the speed on slow as they thrust in and out of me in a steady rhythm.

And then I feel him squirting lube on my tight asshole, and the cold sensation makes me shudder. The stinging pain is increased because my stuffed pussy squeezes the channel tighter than ever before, as his thick head pops through the tight ring of muscles.

I moan loudly, unable to believe how good it feels to be so full. He slides as deep as is possible as the two dildos continue to piston in and out of my soaking wet pussy. I groan at feeling so full and know that within seconds I'll come apart again.

"Killian," I gasp his name as he stops pushing and rests balls deep inside of me.

"Fuck," he groans, his hands parting my ass cheeks. "This is one beautiful fucking sight, baby girl. I don't think I'll ever get tired of watching you get fucked by three cocks."

I moan at how dirty it is, imagining the image in my own mind. "I'll never tire of being stretched like this."

He lets go of my ass cheeks and then I feel him lean forward and grab something. And then I feel that excruciatingly good pain as he slowly drips hot candle wax over my back, sending shivers through every nerve ending in my body.

"Fuck," I cry, knowing that despite the fact Killian hasn't even moved inside me yet, I'm already on the edge. "I'm going to come."

"Good. Come for me like the dirty little slut you are, Mia."

The pain of the wax and the sting of being stretched so much, mingles with the pleasure and drives me off the cliff edge. Add that to his intoxicating degradation, and every inch of my body tingles with desire as I come apart, shaking violently on the bench as he holds his thick cock still inside my ass.

"I haven't even started fucking your ass, and you're already coming shamelessly, aren't you?"

I can't speak, my mind won't allow it.

"Now, it's time for the real fun to begin." He tightens his grasp on my hips and moves his hips backward, withdrawing his cock almost entirely from my ass. Only to slam back in which such force it makes me scream.

I whimper as he fucks me brutally, his cock thrusting in and out of my stretched, lubed hole. My nipples harden to peaks of stone as he fucks me with such intensity, driving me right toward another climax. Or perhaps he's just heightening the last. I can't tell anymore when one orgasm ends and another starts. Everything just merges into one as I'm fucked in both holes.

It feels like I'm no longer present in my body and all I can do is take the pleasure as it hits me in waves. My teeth sink into my bottom lip as the pain of the hot wax on my back eases, but the pressure of being stretched out increases the pleasure.

"Tell me how much you love being stuffed with so many cocks, baby girl."

My stomach flutters as I feel myself heading toward the cliff edge for the third time. "I love being stuffed with three cocks, sir. Fuck my ass harder."

The rumble from his chest is more animalistic than human as he thrusts into me harder and faster. "Good girl," he purrs. "Such a good girl."

His praise is just as arousing as his degradation, and I know I'll never get enough of it. "Please," I moan, knowing if I don't come again, I'll die from the torture of it.

"Please what, Mia?" he asks, a teasing tone in his voice.

"Make me come," I say.

He chuckles, the sound rich and deep. "My greedy little slut. You want to come for the fourth time, do you?"

"Yes," I moan, trembling as my climax is so close, but just out of reach.

Suddenly, the tempo of the fuck machine increases as it matches Killian's thrusts into my ass.

"Oh God," I cry, my body so close to exploding it feels like I might die any moment.

"You are such a good girl. Come with my cock lodged in your ass and milk my cum. Make me breed that tight asshole."

That's all it takes as I scream at the top of my lungs, my body shuddering so much it feels like something is wrong. Killian fucks me erratically, grunting and groaning as he comes apart right with me, filling my ass with his cum. He sinks his teeth into my shoulder, heightening every sensation coursing through me.

I groan as the fuck machine continues to fuck me and Killian remains lodged in my ass, breathing against my neck for a few minutes. Finally, he puts me out of my torture and slides out of my sensitive ass, turning off the machine and then moving around to stand in front of me. He pulls off the blindfold and then releases me from the restraints. Once all four are removed, he lifts me off the bench and carries me over to the bed, laying me down softly.

He grabs a soft towel and a bottle of water. "Turn over, baby girl."

I do as I'm told and carefully he uses the water and towel to wipe away the wax which has dried on my skin, and it stings a little. Once it's all removed, he grabs a bottle of aloe vera from the night stand and starts to massage it into my back. "How does it feel?" he asks.

I shrug. "A little sore, but it was worth it."

"That was so fucking hot, baby girl," he murmurs, his hands working the sore skin tenderly. Once he's finished, he turns me over so I'm lying on my back and he lies down next to me, staring at me with such love in his eyes.

"I hope you are ready for round two."

I shut my eyes and groan. "No way. I'm completely and utterly fucked out."

He laughs at that and kisses me softly. "I bet you'll change your mind soon enough." He pulls me closer to him so my head is resting on his hard, muscular chest. I trace the lines of the tattoo on his chest.

"What are you thinking?" he asks.

I smile and look up at him. "How happy I am."

He shakes his head. "Why? Because I fucked you so good?"

I shake my head. "No, although it doesn't harm." I search his eyes. "Because I love you so much and I'm so glad I'm building a life and family with you." I sink my teeth into my bottom lip. "In fact, I have some rather crazy news."

His brow arches. "What news, baby girl?"

"I'm pregnant," I say.

His eyes widen. "Again?"

I nod. "Yeah, it's a little soon, but I'm excited."

He smiles. "If you are happy, then so am I." His brow furrows. "How many kids do you want? We've never talked about it."

I shrug. "At least four. I loved growing up with lots of siblings."

He nods. "Aye, me too." He nods. "Four sounds good. Maybe five if we match your family."

"Maybe," I say, sighing as I rest my head down. "I love you," I murmur.

He smiles, and it warms my insides in a way nothing else can, other than our son. "I love you too, more than you will ever know."

We fall into contented silence together, holding each other as we contemplate a bright future together, as we build a family. The Callaghan Clan and Morrone family finally getting over old grievances and becoming one.

---

THANK you for reading Dirty Secret, the sixth book in the Chicago Mafia Dons series. I hope you enjoyed following Killian and Mia's journey. The seventh and final book of the series is Dark Crown, and it will release on the 31st of August. It can be pre-ordered here, or it will be available on Kindle Unlimited and Paperback from that date.

## DARK CROWN: A Dark Arranged Marriage Mafia Romance

**I'm shackled to a monster, and the only way out is death.**

My arranged marriage to Adrik Volkov soon turns into a nightmare. Two months before our wedding date, he forces me down the aisle. Then, drags me to a club where he shoots my father dead in front of my eyes. The man I'm married to is a beast who will stop at nothing to get what he wants.

And he wants the crown that rightfully belongs to my brother. I'm his claim, since we're married, it gives him the right to lead the Estrada Cartel. If all of that isn't bad enough, he wants to torture me, too. Our wedding night is when he tears away my innocence without a care.

If only his cruelty ended there. When I look into

those hazel eyes, I know this man is dead inside. A man who has no compassion for others. He intends to break me, ruin me, and then revel in my destruction.

And he expects me to enjoy it. The sickest part of it all is he wants me to call him *daddy*. A man so cruel, so dark, and depraved. The nickname doesn't fit the man, and yet when he demands it, I melt.

He's found my biggest weakness, and he's going to use it against me. Adrik takes everything my family has built, but it's not enough. He won't rest until he's claimed every part of me, including my heart. I fear he'll have to carve it from my chest if he wants it that badly.

There's no way I could love a monster like him... is there?

ALSO BY BIANCA COLE

**The Syndicate Academy**

Corrupt Educator: A Dark Forbidden Mafia Academy
Romance

Cruel Bully: A Dark Mafia Academy Romance

**Chicago Mafia Dons**

Merciless Defender: A Dark Forbidden Mafia Romance

Violent Leader: A Dark Enemies to Lovers Captive Mafia
Romance

Evil Prince: A Dark Arranged Marriage Romance

Brutal Daddy: A Dark Captive Mafia Romance

Cruel Vows: A Dark Forced Marriage Mafia Romance

Dirty Secret: A Dark Enemies to Loves Mafia Romance

Dark Crown: A Dark Arranged Marriage Romance

**Boston Mafia Dons Series**

Cruel Daddy: A Dark Mafia Arranged Marriage Romance

Savage Daddy: A Dark Captive Mafia Roamnce

Ruthless Daddy: A Dark Forbidden Mafia Romance

Vicious Daddy: A Dark Brother's Best Friend Mafia
Romance

Wicked Daddy: A Dark Captive Mafia Romance

**New York Mafia Doms Series**

Her Irish Daddy: A Dark Mafia Romance

Her Russian Daddy: A Dark Mafia Romance

Her Italian Daddy: A Dark Mafia Romance

Her Cartel Daddy: A Dark Mafia Romance

## Romano Mafia Brother's Series

Her Mafia Daddy: A Dark Daddy Romance

Her Mafia Boss: A Dark Romance

Her Mafia King: A Dark Romance

## Bratva Brotherhood Series

Bought by the Bratva: A Dark Mafia Romance

Captured by the Bratva: A Dark Mafia Romance

Claimed by the Bratva: A Dark Mafia Romance

Bound by the Bratva: A Dark Mafia Romance

Taken by the Bratva: A Dark Mafia Romance

## Wynton Series

Filthy Boss: A Forbidden Office Romance

Filthy Professor: A First Time Professor And Student Romance

Filthy Lawyer: A Forbidden Hate to Love Romance

Filthy Doctor: A Fordbidden Romance

## Royally Mated Series

Her Faerie King: A Faerie Royalty Paranormal Romance

Her Alpha King: A Royal Wolf Shifter Paranormal Romance

Her Dragon King: A Dragon Shifter Paranormal Romance

Her Vampire King: A Dark Vampire Romance

# ABOUT THE AUTHOR

I love to write stories about over the top alpha bad boys who have heart beneath it all, fiery heroines, and happily-ever-after endings with heart and heat. My stories have twists and turns that will keep you flipping the pages and heat to set your kindle on fire.

For as long as I can remember, I've been a sucker for a good romance story. I've always loved to read. Suddenly, I realized why not combine my love of two things, books and romance?

My love of writing has grown over the past four years and I now publish on Amazon exclusively, weaving stories about dirty mafia bad boys and the women they fall head over heels in love with.

If you enjoyed this book please follow me on Amazon, Bookbub or any of the below social media platforms for alerts when more books are released.

Printed in Great Britain
by Amazon